Letters from Grace

THE STORY OF AN AMERICAN FAMILY

A NOVEL

Priscilla Audette

PAGE PUBLISHING, INC.
Conneaut Lake, PA

First originally published by Page Publishing 2020

ISBN 978-1-64701-923-5 (pbk)
ISBN 978-1-64701-924-2 (digital)

Printed in the United States of America

The family is the first essential cell of human society.

—Pope John XXIII

To the Hawk
a messenger who soars above the earth
and whose shrill cry asks us to
seek the truth.

PART I

Returning Home

May your cottage roof be well thatched and those inside be well matched.

—Irish Blessing

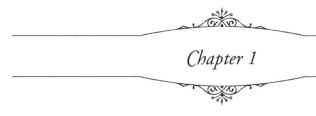

Chapter 1

Savannah pulled open a dresser drawer and stood back with her hands on her hips.

"What are we going to do with all these T-shirts?"

Dakota reached in, snatched one up, and snapped it open. Laughing, she said, "Good grief, her goofy T-shirts."

Austin obliged by reading the one Dakota held. "Dear Math: I am not a therapist. Solve your own problems."

"See, they are so ridiculous."

"But so representative of Mom's sense of humor."

Dakota started to say something then leaned in and sniffed the shirt; her face crumpled as she promptly burst into tears. "Oh my god, it smells like her." She buried her face in the soft cloth, breathing deeply while drying her streaming eyes with it at the same time. "It's been three months"—her voice was muffled—"and it still smells like her."

Savannah's eyes grew wet in response to Dakota's emotions. "Why do you think I've been sleeping in her room instead of my old room? Because the pillows still smell like Mom." She gently lifted a T-shirt out of the drawer, brought it to her face, and took a deep breath then shook her head. "This one just smells like Tide." Shaking it open, she held it up and read, "You can't scare me. I have two daughters."

The girls smiled teary smiles at each other, while Austin rolled his eyes. "Yeah, poor me, surrounded by women all my life. I mean, except for Dad."

"Who died when I was five," Dakota added. "So yeah, between Mom, us, your wife, and your two daughters, you are surrounded by women."

He reached for the T-shirt Savannah still held. "Which makes me the obvious recipient of this one." He waggled his fingers, waiting for her to hand it to him.

A typical sisterly reaction, she resisted for just a moment before tossing it in his direction. "She always bought large because she liked them roomy. See if it fits."

Peeling off the one he wore and dropping it on the bed, Austin pulled his mother's T-shirt over his head. Standing in front of the dresser mirror, flanked by his sisters, they all looked at their reflection in appraisal. The T-shirt was snug against Austin's muscular arms but didn't look too tight, and the two-tone shades of blue in the shirt made his sapphire eyes pop. He had a healthy-looking tan, and the sun had bleached his auburn hair so it was slightly streaked. He looked more like a surfer than the forty-something business executive that he was. To his left stood his big sister, Savannah; she'd put on a little middle-age spread when she crested forty a few years back, but as she had been skinny as a rail all her life, it only made her look normal now. She had a few smile lines around her blue eyes, and thanks to the highlights in her hair, no one knew how many gray strands were in there too. Dakota, the baby of the family, who was still a year shy of thirty, was almost a carbon copy of her sister, except for the smile lines and eyes that were closer to a greenish hazel than blue. She was as slim as Savannah used to be, and they both had the same laugh and sense of humor. All three of them looked like the blend of their English-Irish-Scottish heritage.

"Damn, we Quinns are good-looking people."

Savannah nudged her brother with her elbow. "Egotist."

"Genetics," Dakota explained. "Our parents were a good-looking couple, so they couldn't help but have good-looking kids."

"Well, let's hope we didn't inherit Mom's pancreatic cancer." And on that sobering note, they went back to the chore of cleaning out their mother's dresser: keeping this, packing that for Goodwill, and tossing the other in the trash pile.

*   *   *   *   *

The disease had spread like wildfire, and from diagnosis to the realization that her children would have to be told was a matter of a very few months. What bothered Grace the most was the fact that she'd never live to see her grandkids grown and off into their own lives. But at least she had gotten her kids off to a good start in life, and they all were doing well. Savannah was a second-term congress-woman, Austin was an executive in a top-ranking corporation in Silicon Valley, and Dakota had opted to follow in her father's foot-steps and become a college professor. Other than major holidays, they rarely saw one another unless there was some big family event, like a wedding or a birth or a funeral. That thought had made Grace sigh. Weddings, births, deaths, they were the milestone events that brought family members back together when they drifted apart to live their separate lives.

It had been nearly twenty-five years since her husband, Barrett, had died. She'd never remarried. He'd been the one and only for her. The love of her life. She'd mourned his passing and lived her life. And now, sick and dying, she needed to break it to her children. Except for Savannah, who lived almost next door in Denver, they lived so far away, scattershot across the country from Maine to California. And it would be a chore for them to have to disrupt their lives to come back to their childhood home in Laramie, Wyoming. But that was what family did. Her family, they were her all!

Savannah had graduated summa cum laude with a degree in political science and gone on to law school after college, passing the bar on her first try. When she decided to run for public office, Grace wasn't surprised. And the fact that she had won her first election by a landslide, with votes from both major political parties, well, that didn't surprise her either. Savannah had learned about bipartisanship at the dining room table, as her father was a dyed-in-the-wool Republican and she, as her husband always said, was a bleeding-heart Democrat. Still she worried about her daughter's choice as she knew that politics was an environment that encouraged hatred. But she kept her worries to herself, mostly, and supported her daughter in every way possible.

Savannah doted on her nieces but didn't get to see them as often as she liked. She had never married, and at forty-four, Grace didn't think she ever would. Savannah loved what she was doing with her life, dated occasionally, rarely had long-term relationships, and laughed about the fact that a century before she'd have been dubbed an old maid. On one occasion Grace had, once again, come right out and queried her daughter about her single status. Just as candidly, Savannah had told her mother, "Men are intimidated by my ambition."

"What about compromise?" Grace had asked.

"I'm fully willing to compromise, but I'm not willing to settle." That had ended the discussion. Oh yes, she worried about her eldest, but she was also as proud of her as a parent could be.

Austin, in the prime of his life at forty-one, lived in California with his wife and two young daughters. He had drifted the farthest away from Grace, not geographically, but emotionally. Grace often told herself the jingle, "Your son's your son 'till he takes a wife. Your daughter's your daughter for the rest of your life." It saddened her that she and Austin were no longer close. Thank God for daughters, she'd think to herself, because a son could break your heart and not even know it. Yet she'd never forgotten what a fun little boy he had been. They had been close then, so close that at one point she'd feared he'd grow into a mama's boy. But then he discovered golf, a sport her husband had no interest in whatsoever. Austin spent most of his preteen and teenage years on the golf course with some very fine male mentors. And before she knew it, he was his own man, off to college, and soon after jumping into married life.

And then there was the baby, twenty-nine-year-old Dakota, who lived in Maine, taught Composition at an academy, and who was newly engaged to be married to one of her fellow teachers. She and Dakota had such a special bond. She thought of Dakota as a gift because if not for her, she'd have rattled around all alone in this big old house after the two oldest headed off to college. The past eleven years of living alone after Dakota too had flown out of the nest had made all those years alone with Dakota a sweet, sweet memory. What a precious, unexpected baby she had been.

Dakota had been bitten by the same travel bug as Grace and spent her summers exploring exotic realms. Luckily her fiancé, Daniel, also loved to travel, and that made them very well suited to one another. That she wouldn't live to dance at their wedding briefly had Grace reconsidering the chemo she'd rejected. But in the scheme of things, she believed more in quality of life than quantity of life, so she determined to die quietly, peacefully, and gracefully, doing it her way. "Go with the flow" had been Grace's motto all her adult life. Over the course of that life, she'd learned to accept whatever the future held. And if dying from pancreatic cancer was what the future held for her, well, she wanted to die as she lived—just going with the flow. And she knew her children well enough to know what to tell them and when.

So Grace had kept her cancer a secret from her children. They only discovered it toward the final days and were outraged that she hadn't fought harder against the disease that ultimately took its toll. She had simply let nature take its course, refusing radiation or chemotherapy. After all, "No one got out of this spaceship alive"— according to one of her T-shirt slogans.

Grace had been a traveler. In the early years, she wrote primarily for travel magazines. Later she also wrote for magazines about the western part of the country as well as the occasional newspaper Op-Ed piece. When the periodicals she submitted her work to went under after the technological explosion, she wrote for online magazines. As far as her travel pieces, she wasn't one of those armchair writers who just researched a place then wrote about it. She physically traveled to the locale and lived in it for a while, rubbing shoulders with the locals in pubs, talking to moms in parks while watching toddlers play, and scoping out the tourist haunts too.

Grace had married in her early twenties. She met her husband on a trip to Wyoming. Barrett was a Humanities professor at the university there. She had been wandering around the campus and noticed him talking to a few students on the quad. There was something about the way he tilted his head when talking, the way he gestured, the way he smiled then laughed at something one student said. She heard the words "What an attractive man" and realized she had said them out loud. She looked around embarrassed, but no one was nearby to hear. When the students dispersed, leaving the man alone, she watched as he walked over to a concrete bench, sat, turned his face to the sun to bask for a moment, and then opened a book and started reading. Grace approached, asked if she could sit, introduced herself as a writer doing a piece on Laramie, and the rest, as they say, was history. Regardless of the fact that he was twenty-plus years her senior, they fell in love, had a whirlwind courtship, married, and set up housekeeping. Barrett was set in his ways and a creature of habit, but that suited Grace to a tee. It gave her a sense of security and comfort knowing exactly what to expect.

Shortly after their marriage they, like all couples, had to weather their first fight. Well, it wasn't exactly a fight, but it came close. Grace's editor was sending her on assignment; she was to write a travel piece on the Black Hills and Devil's Tower. When she told Barrett she'd be gone a few days, he simply told her, "No." One word, simple and to the point, let her know that he wouldn't tolerate her gallivanting off somewhere. Grace had been shocked into silence. She lay in bed that night staring into the darkness. At first her thoughts were scattered, but as the night deepened, she became more focused. Her grandmother had often said, "Begin the way you mean to go on." And that was exactly what she intended to do. At some point she had finally drifted off to sleep but awoke quickly when she heard Barrett get up. He was always an early riser.

She waited until he had his coffee made before she entered the kitchen. She sat at the kitchen table across from him, her hands folded on the table in front of her. "You may be old enough to be my father, Barrett, but you are not my father. You are my husband. And in this day and age, husbands no longer dictate to their wives. When my editor asks me to go on assignment, that's what I am going to do. You're simply going to have to accept it."

Barrett's glasses had slid down his nose a bit, so he was looking over them, completely focused on Grace and her words.

Grace concluded, "I'll only be gone a few days."

When she stood up to go pack, Barrett stood too. He took her hand to hold her in place. "I see" was all he said at first. Grace could all but hear his thought processes and knew he'd have more to add to that in a moment. He gave a slight nod when he was ready to speak. "I have spent most of my life alone, so I was completely astonished when I realized how important you've become to me in such a very short space of time. I guess like Henry Higgins, 'I've grown accustomed to your face.' You are the best thing that has ever happened to me, Grace. Please don't be gone too long."

She walked into his embrace, and they held each other in the cozy kitchen. In that moment, she knew they were equals in this marriage. She had begun the way she meant to go on. She had sailed over that first hurdle and knew that while there would be others, she'd be equal to them too. Yes, life was good.

So on occasion she continued to travel to write, that is, until the babies started coming. Then she traveled less often, but often enough to keep her job. Sometimes she traveled with the family, sometimes alone. One way or the other, she got her job done. And probably not ironic at all, she ended up naming her children after places she had visited and loved.

Savannah was her sophisticated eldest. Grace had only been to Savannah, Georgia, once in her youth, right out of college, and in fact it was the first travel piece she'd written that was published. No, she'd never been back, but she had never forgotten the place either. It was a city that lent itself to walking, and that was just what she did. She walked all over the city, nearly twisting her ankle on one of the cobblestone streets, thanks to the strappy-heeled sandals she'd worn that day. She immediately bought some sensible walking shoes, and the rest of the visit to Savannah went smoothly. The paddlewheel riverboat cruise, the horse-and-carriage tour, the restaurants, what wasn't to love about Savannah?

When in college, Grace had taken art history classes and some architecture classes too, so she always scoped out the buildings when visiting a new place. The architecture in Savannah was, in a word, majestic—the city was an elegant regal lady. It was also the oldest city in the United States, and when she had her first child, who would be the eldest of several if she had her way, she named her Savannah. The oldest city, the oldest child, she liked the symmetry of that.

The one thing Grace remembered most about Austin, Texas, was the perpetual sunshine. So with a name like Austin, how could her son help but have a sunny disposition? Restaurants galore and as food was one of her favorite things, Grace was in seventh heaven during her visit to Austin. And if you loved music and culture, it was a must-see city, but it wasn't only the city that beckoned. A quick getaway into the hill country was one of Grace's fondest memories of that trip.

She'd lost two babies before Dakota came along. Brighton, named after the English town with the beautiful beaches—where he'd been conceived—died the same hour he was born. Catalina, his twin sister, lived two hours longer. The doctor gave her a convoluted explanation that boiled down to underdeveloped lungs. Grace never knew if it was something she had done or something she hadn't done that caused the babies' lung problems. Every year on the day of their birth and death, she put flowers on their graves, nearly forty years' worth of flowers. She never missed a year.

And then there was Dakota. Well, the kids sure had loved that trip to the Black Hills and the Badlands in South Dakota, not to mention the endless wheat fields and sunflower fields in North Dakota, so when the baby had been born, Savannah insisted that she be named Dakota.

Chapter 2

Settled in a comfortable chair out on the deck, Dakota placed the crust of her sandwich on the nearby paper plate and continued daydreaming. She had been thinking about her mother's T-shirts and remembered playing in her mom's office one time when she was very young, sitting on the soft Oriental rug that blanketed the hard wood floor, putting puzzles together while her mother was writing an article. It was always so cozy in there with a winter storm raging outside and being so warm and safe inside. So there was Mom, banging away at the computer keyboard when Dakota had noticed the T-shirt she was wearing. The word on it was *Jenius*. "That's spelled wrong," Dakota had pointed out.

"What's spelled wrong, honey?"

"*Genius* on your shirt is spelled wrong."

Grace sat back from the keyboard and chuckled. "That's the whole point, Dee. Most people who think they are geniuses really aren't."

Dakota had never forgotten that.

Bickering broke into her reverie. Lunch was over, and it looked like Austin and Savannah were at it again.

Savannah was saying, "In the early years, I saw the internet as a tool. But things have changed. For example, the younger generation especially seems to view it as a place—a universe. Beyond that, as far as I'm concerned, the internet has evolved into a wasteland populated with offensive people and inconsequential trivial ideas, not to mention the ever-present porn. And then there is the Snowden thing. His revelations exposed the alarming surveillance—"

Austin butted in with, "He shouldn't have done it."

"Why? Because he aired your dirty laundry? Because he let out your dirty little secrets?"

"Me? I'm not NSA."

"No, but you guys in Silicon Valley are in bed with them. They'd never be able to do the level of surveillance they do if you didn't enable them."

Dakota heaved a sisterly sigh and ran interference. "Oh no, are you two getting started on Snowden again?"

Ignoring her, Savannah glared at her brother. "I'm sorry, but the Fourth Amendment is the Fourth Amendment. Today it comes down to privacy controls."

"It's a brave new world, Savvy. It's all about security."

She shook her head. "Buy into that and we create a culture of fear. We have to stop trading our liberties for security."

"Save it for your speeches, Savannah. I know what I know."

"So tell me, what *do* you know?" When all he did was level a look at her, she continued. "Oh, so it's one of those need-to-know things, and I, a US congresswoman, don't need to know?"

"All you need to know is that information is power, and those of us in charge of the information are the ones who wield the power."

"But—"

"And you can't do anything about it."

"So then what? You think the entire Congress is impotent?"

Austin raised an eyebrow. "Rhetorical question?"

"The difference between us, Austin, is that I have faith in the American people and you don't."

"After the last election?" When she opened her mouth to respond, he plowed on. "What I have faith in is technology. You're not even capable of understanding this technology."

"I understand it enough to know that I don't trust it.

"All right you two!" Dakota had had enough. "You guys beat that same dying horse every time you end up in the same space. Can we change the subject?" Savannah's response was to stand, gather up the paper plates from their lunch, and head inside. "Why do you guys always fight like that?"

"It's invigorating. We like to."

"*You* like to. I don't think Savannah likes it."

"Sure she does. She usually starts it. Besides, it keeps her sharp. At the top of her game."

"So you just say what you say to get a rise out of her?"

Austin shook his head. "No. I believe what I say."

Ending the conversation with a "Whatever," Dakota rose and stood by the railing on the back deck and watched a hawk make lazy circles in the sky, just like in the song from that musical. The sky was as blue as the T-shirt Austin had on, and there was only one wispy cloud far off to the right.

As it was late afternoon, the sun had moved on to the other side of the house, leaving the deck shaded and if not quite cool, at least cooler than it would have been if the sun had been overhead. Austin leaned on the same railing, back to upending a long-necked bottle of beer and holding his phone to his ear, while the ever-efficient Savannah had returned to the deck and finished clearing the table of their lunch remnants.

Conversation over, Austin polished off his beer. Dakota asked, "What was that all about?"

"Just work. Come on, Dee, enough of this, time to get back at it. The house isn't going to empty itself."

As she moved away from the railing, the hawk gave a shrill cry and flew off over the house and toward the sun. "What room is next on the list?"

"Office. Come on." Austin slid the door open, and they both went back into the house.

Chapter 3

Grace was not only a writer by vocation, she was a writer by avocation as well. In recent years, in addition to the magazine articles she wrote, she had also written many letters to the editor of various newspapers and magazines. She was a woman of strong opinion, and letters to the editor were a place where she could express those opinions and not have people's (particularly her children's) eyes flutter shut in a here-we-go-again response when she got up on her infamous soapbox. So Grace wrote letters and, a product of the pretechnological generation, kept copies of them in one drawer of an old metal filing cabinet. And dealing with her articles and letters was what her children were facing now.

Austin assembled yet one more cardboard banker's box, tossed it in the pile with the others, and then flopped down on the couch in his mom's office off the living room. Savannah sat behind the desk, looking through drawers, and Dakota was going through the filing cabinet. "Good grief, it looks like she kept copies, *hard* copies of everything she ever wrote, even those ubiquitous letters to the editor. Sheesh! That adds up to a lot of stuff here."

"Not to mention carbon copies of the letters she wrote to us at over the years." Savannah dumped a handful of something from one of the desk drawers into the trash basket under the desk.

"I never even bothered to read the ones she sent. I mean, she just went on and on, the letters were so dang long." When both his sisters just looked at him with eyes widened, Austin amended in self-defense, "Well, I skimmed them." After a moment he added, "And what the heck are we doing with all these boxes? We're not going to fill them all, are we? What we need to do is to haul all the paper in that file cabinet to the firepit and light a match."

Dakota's response was to pull a file folder with his name on it out of the drawer. "Look here, copies of letters she sent you. You can read them now. Or later. But I suggest you read them sometime." Austin looked horrified. Dakota was flipping through the folder. "Oh, hey, this also includes the letters you sent her."

"I never sent a letter."

"Au contraire." Scanning the letter she'd pulled from the folder, she cleared her throat. "This one doesn't have a signature, but Mom wrote 'From Austin, July 1991' on it. Here goes: '*Dear Mom and Dad, How are you doing? I am doing fine. We had a grill at Aunt Susi's house. We had tri tip and hot dogs, and for dessert we had homemade brownies. On the plane I only had one glass of pop. Aunt Susi is making a list of magnets she needs of the western states. The twins and Emma are doing fine. Dave is talking weird. Set for cool and bunk out for go to bed.*'"

"I remember that trip. My first one away from all you guys by myself. You were just a baby, or maybe not even born yet? At any rate, I don't remember writing that letter."

"Aunt Susi probably made you."

"Probably."

"But"—she held up another piece of paper—"she didn't make you write this one."

"I wrote another letter?"

"Not that trip. This one is dated July 27, 1997. '*Dear Family, I apologize for not writing or calling. I have been very busy. I have made good friends with most of the British employees. It is ironic because when I first met them, I thought they were the rudest bunch of people I had ever encountered. Well, that is all I have to say for now. I will call soon. Love, Austin.*'"

"I remember that summer too. I worked at that Summer Camp in Maine. That was the year or two after Dad died."

"And wrote a letter home."

"Yeah, I don't remember that part."

"That's weird." Dakota kept skimming the file.

"What?"

"She has copies of letters she's written to both you and Jill, but nothing at all to Jill for the past couple of years. Why?"

"Who knows."

Savannah stopped cleaning out the desk drawer and looked up. "That was a statement, not a question. Ergo, it means you *do* know. So spill. Why did Mom stop writing to Jill? She never said anything about a falling out."

Austin looked both embarrassed and exasperated. "Because I told Mom to stop writing to Jill, that's why."

"Because?"

"Because every time we got into a fight, Jill would bash me over the head with 'Your mother said blah, blah, blah.' Or 'Your mother told me blah, blah, blah.' Or 'Your mother just won't blah, blah, blah.' I got so sick of it I told Mom to cut it out, to stop giving Jill ammunition to use to shoot me down. Not that Mom realized that was what she was doing. But it turned out that way."

"That must have hurt her feelings."

"Yeah? Well, there are times when you just have to do something to protect yourself."

The sisters, well aware of their volatile sister-in-law's propensity to temper tantrums, exchanged a glance like there was a lot to say that would remain unsaid, at least in front of their brother. Savannah settled for, "I'm sorry."

"No, you're not."

"Are you an abused spouse, bro?" She said it jokingly, but with a serious undertone.

"Just cause we fight doesn't mean she's abusive. I mean, I can be a jerk too."

"Well, I'll agree with you on that." Savannah winked at Dakota.

"Yeah, I thought you would."

Dakota added, "Well, it must have hurt Mom when you told her to stop writing. I mean, that was her thing, you know."

To move the subject away from him, Austin said, "So, Dee, what are you going to do with that file cabinet full of stuff?" He then looked pointedly at the trash basket that Savannah was filling up in record time.

Dakota looked at Savannah. Savannah looked over toward the file cabinet. Sometimes without speaking, they often had the same thought. Dakota pulled out a folder with Savannah's name on it. "Here." Then she handed Austin the one with his name on it. And finally she pulled out the file with her name on it. "As far as the rest, we divvy them up. Every now and then we read a letter, either a copy of one she wrote to us or one of the letters to the editor, or one of the letters she wrote to someone else that she saved, and that gives us a little piece of Mom. It will be like hearing her voice from afar helping us through life's twists and turns."

Austin was frowning. "Like I've got time for that."

"We're all busy, but Dee has a good idea." Savannah wore a considering expression on her face. "I mean, while I did read the letters she wrote to me, I know I rarely ever read her letters to the editor. Or even the articles she wrote. It might be interesting to see what she had to say."

Austin watched as Dakota started pulling out file folders and putting them in three equal stacks. He picked up one folder and flipped through it then dropped it back on the pile that was forming in front of him. "Good grief."

Dakota stood back and looked at the three piles to make sure they were equal in size.

"It's going to take months to get through all that!" Austin's resistance was palpable. "And all this is only from one drawer!"

"It's only the one drawer. One drawer is bills and other household stuff, and one is her articles, and one is just junk. See, already it's not as much as you thought it was going to be."

Putting out her hand, Savannah wiggled her fingers. "Hand me some of those folders with her articles in them. I think we should read those too."

Austin's groan was audible. "Please, you're killing me here."

Dakota just started handing out a few more folders. "Look, bro, children don't really know their parents just as parents don't really know their grown children. So if we do this thing, read Mom's letters and articles, they might give us some insight into who she really was."

"And we need this insight because…?"

"Yes, *because*." Dakota snapped the word out, and Austin knew it was time to stop poking at her.

He plucked a folder from his pile and noticed it said *Subbing*. "Here." He handed that one toward Dakota. "You're the teacher, and this looks like things Mom wrote about when she was substitute teaching."

Dakota took the folder and skimmed the contents. "Oh yeah, I'd forgotten she ever did that."

"Well, it was before you were born. She started to do it part-time after Savvy and I started school. She did it for maybe ten years, then you came along."

Putting the folder in her stack, she withdrew one and handed it to Austin. "Then you take this one on Wyoming."

"Why not?" He was resigning himself to all the reading that was being heaped upon him.

"So," Savannah was already planning, "next year, on the anniversary of Mom's passing, we get together again and talk about what we learned about her over the year."

"That only gives us nine months, and that's a lot of file folders Dakota just stacked in front of me."

"What about her birthday then?" Savannah paused in recollection. "Remember how she wanted us all to come home for her birthday last year, but we all had other commitments, so it didn't happen. I told her she was only going to be sixty-eight and that wasn't a big birthday. I promised I'd browbeat both of you to make it to her seventieth and we'd do it up right. Damn, I wish we would have come."

Dakota sighed and said, "She never made it to her sixty-ninth. Yeah, we really should have made the effort the year before."

Austin shook his head, saying, "There was no way we could have known. It's all water over the dam and under the bridge. Woulda, coulda, shoulda."

"Anyway," Savannah got back on track, "let's meet next year on her birthday, which would have been her seventieth."

"That still gives us less than a year to get through all of this."

Glaring at her uncooperative brother, Savannah said, "Okay then, we decide at some later date when to get together."

"Where will we meet? This house will be sold by then, hopefully. And we all live in different directions."

"We don't have to make that decision today either." Savannah tossed her brother a banker's box and started placing her file folders in a box of her own. After she snugged a lid on it, she added, "We'll figure it all out later."

Chapter 4

Too exhausted to fix dinner, they had ordered a couple of pizzas and cracked open some beers. The pizza boxes, now empty but for a few uneaten crusts, sat on the coffee table in the living room. The girls slumped on the couch, and Austin reclined in their father's old La-Z-Boy. At one point, Savannah pulled out the little notebook she always carried with her and started jotting something down. Her siblings, accustomed to her habits, left her alone.

"Set a date yet?" Austin broke the after-dinner quiet that had descended.

"Next summer. Probably around this time of year."

Austin couldn't help sing-songing a jingle from their childhood. "First comes love, then comes marriage, then come a baby in a baby carriage."

"Ha ha," was all Dakota could come up with as a response.

"You do realize you are marrying a man-child?" That got her attention. Dakota looked over at her brother who was wearing his serious big brother expression.

She considered several different responses then said, "You only met Daniel once when he flew out here for the funeral. What makes you say that?"

"He's a practical joker, Dee Dee. A real goofball."

She just shook her head at Austin. "No. He's not a practical joker. He's made a study of practical jokes. That's a different thing entirely. Not that he's beyond pulling a prank or two," she conceded. "He's fun and funny. He makes me laugh, and we have a good time.

I like the whimsy. But he isn't always that way. He has his serious side too."

"If you say so."

"I do."

"So you guys ever talk about having kids?" Austin tipped back his bottle and swallowed the last of the beer.

"We talk about *not* having kids."

"Really? Why not?"

"Why not indeed!"

"That's not an answer."

So Dakota regaled him with her reasons. "Does overpopulation sound like a good reason? How are we going to feed and house all the billions already here on Earth? Fossil fuels are depleted and will soon be gone. There is only so much arable land to grow food. Some of that will have to be given over to growing crops that can be made into biofuel instead of food when fossil fuels run out. Add to that that the polar icecaps are melting, causing the oceans to rise, resulting in less land to grow the necessary food and fuel. I just cannot with good conscience bring children into a world that is in its death throes."

"Good grief, you're beginning to sound like the congress-woman." Savannah surfaced from her notebook while he gave her a brotherly smirk. "But seriously, Dee, doom and gloom notwith-standing, I have to tell you from personal experience, you would be missing out on a lot. Having kids has been the hardest job I've ever undertaken, but also the most rewarding. You might not want to miss out on all that."

"It's not that I don't have the mothering instinct. It's just I'm not a glass-is-half-full kind of person on this particular topic. Maybe I'll want to adopt someday. There are plenty of kids out there who need a good home."

"You're right about that."

Savannah slipped her notebook into her hip pocket and reached for her beer just as Dakota's phone dinged with a text. She looked at it then the put the phone down again.

"So, Savvy, when are you going to come into the real world and get a smartphone like Dee?"

She snorted. "Probably never. I like my flip phone. And the fact that only family has the number, I like even better." To change the subject, she turned to Dee. "So you and Daniel are heading to Iceland this summer?"

"We decided to do some glacier hiking before there are no more glaciers. With global warming, that might be sooner as opposed to later. So…"

"Mom never did make it to Iceland, did she?"

"No. But I bet she would have loved it."

While Dakota had been speaking, Savannah had gotten up and was rummaging through the storage bench that sat under the hooks for coats and jackets near the front door. "Ah-ha! I knew it was here." She tossed the item to Dakota.

"Mom's knit hat?"

"It's crocheted actually, don't you remember when she was on that crocheting kick?"

"What do you want me to do with this?"

"Bring it to Iceland and wear it when you do the glacier hike. That way, Mom will be there in spirit."

"Oh, Savvy, what a good idea!"

Austin just rolled his eyes. "It's ugly."

Dakota stood, put it on, and struck a pose. "But warm. That's what matters. It served its purpose during the winter months." She tried to stifle a yawn but failed. "And on that note." Dakota stretched. "Time for bed, guys. We have a lot to finish up tomorrow." She wasn't even halfway up the stairs when she heard her siblings start squabbling about something. "Now, children," she said over her shoulder, "no fighting."

Dakota shut her bedroom door, tucked the hat in her suitcase, flopped down on the bed, and called her fiancé. "Hey, honey, I'm taking the red-eye out of Denver tomorrow night so will be home the following morning. You going to pick me up?"

"Of course."

* * * * *

Austin was saying, "Money buys access to politicians. As a politician, you know that, Savvy."

"But it's never been my modus operandi and you know that."

"That moral high ground must be a lonely place. We all thought that your idea that you could run for office without soliciting money from special interest groups was a surefire way not to get elected."

"Yeah, well, it's working so far."

"Barely. It may have been working great when you were on the state level, but now that you're federal, this past election, you barely skimmed by making it into office."

"Granted, that was a rough one. Nonetheless, I'm working on a bill advocating that we eliminate taking private money for public elections."

"Yeah, right. That's never going to pass."

"It will at least open up the dialogue, and it has been working for me, I might add."

"Once again, barely, and you are still rubbing shoulders with all those greedy, money-grubbing politicians. Some of it's bound to rub off on you eventually."

"You should talk, Mr. Silicon Valley millionaire, or is it billionaire by now?"

"Apples and oranges, Savvy. Besides, it's all really moot."

"Why do you say that?"

"You know as well as I do that Congress is nothing more than just a symbolic institution anymore. The self-lobotomizing of Congress has left the entire country in a real fix."

She opened her mouth then shut it. "I don't even know how to respond to that, so I won't." She stood, stretched, and said, "Dee was right, we do have a busy day tomorrow, so I guess I'll go up." Pointing at the pizza boxes, she asked, "You'll clean this up, won't you?" When he nodded, she waggled her fingers in farewell as she headed out of the room. "Night-night."

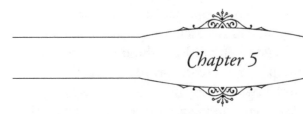

Chapter 5

It had been a long few days of packing up the house, but it was mostly done with just a few odds and ends to attend to the next day. The girls had both gone up to bed, but Austin wasn't the least bit tired. He'd migrated out onto the deck with a nearly empty bottle of beer and the moon to keep him company. The beer had gone warm, and the moon kept slipping behind a cloud. Every now and then, he slapped at a pesky mosquito that wanted to feast on his arm, and his thoughts turned back to his childhood.

Sitting around the dinner table at mealtime, which was an aberration for most families anymore, had been the status quo for the Quinns. Friday night was spaghetti night, and after indulging in seconds one long-ago Friday, Austin decided once again to try to convince his mom to agree to getting him a computer. As usual she was having none of it. But once Austin had gotten a hold of an idea, he didn't let it go. "Everyone has one."

"Oh, I don't think everyone has one. They're probably just a fad anyway."

"Mom, they're not a fad. We use them at school all the time."

"What do seventh graders need with computers? I mean, I know they are using them in the high school now, they have a computer lab and all, but seventh grade?"

Austin rolled his eyes. "I just want to know when we're going to get a computer."

When Grace, once again, shook her head, his father said, "Son, maybe the better question would be to ask is why, as in, why is Mom so resistant to getting a computer?"

"Yeah, that!" Austin was starting to glower.

Grace considered her resistance. "I suppose it's because I don't trust the internet. I mean, if we had a computer and we could get out there on the internet, that means someone on the internet could get in. It would be like leaving the door open for a stranger to enter. I don't like that. I think if we had a computer, I'd feel exposed, unprotected, like there was no way to lock the door and be safe."

Austin was frowning but didn't know how to respond to that. That's when his dad went to bat for him. "You know, honey, we can get a computer and just not hook it up to the internet. Use it for word processing and games and such. The kids could write their school papers on it. And you could use it for your articles. Once you learn the program, it could save you time. It's really not such a bad idea."

"It would be stupid not to hook it up to the internet." Savannah had to get her two cents worth in.

"Why?" Grace was all ears.

"Because we could do email."

"Oh, good grief!" Grace stood and started clearing the table. "Why would we ever want to do that?" It seemed the subject was closed.

"Daaaad." Austin knew he was whining, but he couldn't help it.

"No worries, son. Computers are here to stay, and we'll end up with one sooner or later."

The next morning Austin had gotten up early and biked over to the golf course. He got his clubs out of his locker and headed out to play. He loved the course in the early mornings before hardly anyone was around. He was still enough of a kid that he liked the way his footprints appeared on the dew-covered grass as he cut across to the back nine, but at the same time, grown up enough to remember the rules of etiquette when on the course.

He drew an iron out of his golf bag and teed up at a par three hole. As young as he was, he had a powerful swing, and a wood would have been too much. He moved into a comfortable stance, dropping one shoulder, and took a practice swing before swinging in earnest. As he hit the ball, he heard the *thwack* and knew he'd hit the sweet spot, and his follow-through was perfect. He stood frozen for a second or two, club high behind him, arms cocked at the exact perfect angles, and his eye still on the tee, and he knew without looking that it was a great shot. Raising his eyes, he saw the ball arching straight for the pin, then something strange had happened. It was as if time suddenly stood still for just that one instant. And in that nanosecond, clarity bloomed. He knew what he intended to do with his life. Last night, his mom had said about the internet, "If I can get out, somebody can get in," or words to that effect. There was a future in that, a career, even a calling, and in that moment, he realized he intended to answer that call. When the ball dropped neatly into the hole, he wasn't the least surprised. It was his first hole-in-one, and there wouldn't be another one for four years, but he hadn't known that then. What he did know was that he had a lot to learn to become that guy who could *get in*. Yes, a lot to learn.

He walked up to the hole and, looking down, smiled at the ball nestled next to the pin in the cup. Then he glanced around the course. Of course nobody had been around to witness it. And that had become a theme of his life—doing things that nobody noticed. Not being noticed was the key.

*   *   *   *   *

Austin glanced at his watch. Not many wore watches in this day and age. But it had been his dad's, and it seemed like such a part of him he felt naked if it wasn't on his wrist. He intended to call Jill, but with the time difference, he knew she'd be putting the kids to bed then watching *NCIS*, so he figured he'd wait and call her when that was over. After a few moments of pure solitude, something that drove him absolutely crazy, he made his way into the office and started shuffling through the box of folders he'd packed for himself. It was slated to be sent home via UPS tomorrow. And he'd promised himself he'd have his assistant scan the works so he wouldn't have to deal with all these hard copies. But for now, he pulled out a couple of folders and retreated back to the deck. The first folder contained some of this mother's articles; the article that found its way into his hands was titled, "In the Heart of the Wild, Wild West." It was the first of a three-part series of articles his mother had written after settling down in Laramie. He made himself comfortable and started to read.

> *Wyoming's cultural heritage lies buried deep in the psycho-historical vision of the Wild, Wild West. The West became a crucible reducing everything and everyone to its basic core. Westerners lived in the now, and that, coupled with an authentic morality, provided an immediacy to life as evidenced by the implementation of swift frontier justice. Examples of this behavior have been depicted in literature time and time again. For example, Owen Wister's Virginian, in the book by the same name, found himself in the unenviable position of having to take the law into his own hands by lynching a one-time friend for cattle rustling. This incident, based on an actual occurrence, provided a sense of gritty realism to this early Western novel. Such behavior as the lynching of horse thieves or cattle rustlers by vigilantes was deemed necessary because the freedom of the West lent itself easily to lawlessness.*
>
> *Even those Western men who weren't criminals at heart worked hard and drank heavily. On Saturday nights in frontier saloons, rough-and-ready bravado often disintegrated into drunk and disorderly free-for-alls. On top of that, these Westerners were well armed, the six-shooter, of course, being the weapon of choice. More than a century ago, when Butch Cassidy was released from the Territorial Penitentiary in Laramie, Wyoming, he exercised his constitutional right to bear arms and purchased a .45 caliber Colt single-action army*

revolver. Needless to point out, he wasn't the only man in the West carrying a sidearm.

The six-shooter, it turned out, was not enough. The white man, an intruder in Indian Territory, felt it necessary to protect his claim on the West by building forts and stocking them with soldiers. Fort Laramie, on the eastern edge of Wyoming, was considered by members of long-ago wagon trains to be the last outpost of civilization: beyond that lay the frontier. The magical, mystical implications of the frontier filled the breasts of those unhappy factory workers in the East who yearned for something new and better. For some, the thought of the West had Rousseauian overtones. However, the noble savage and the bucolic back-to-nature idea and ideal were only a part of it. Throwing off the shackles of urban servitude and fleeing to the West provided hope and fed dreams. And so the mystique of the West was born. The West became an environment where fresh starts and new beginnings were possible. It was a robust utopia where one could run away and become…a cowboy.

Naturally cowboys weren't the only inhabitants of the frontier. There were Indians too, and the conflicts between red men and white are legion. History, of course, bears witness to the fact that each of these races had already perfected its own version of man's inhumanity to man against its own kind before they ever came face-to-face. Once they did come face-to-face, however, it was inevitable that the two different cultures would clash. For the nomadic Indians respected the land, believing it was owned by all, to be shared by all, while the white man believed not only in owning the land itself, but he was also guilty of abusing the land by stripping it of its natural resources, such as minerals and timber, or by allowing his livestock to destroy it from long-term overgrazing. In addition, the white man also drove away or killed off the game that sustained the Indians, particularly the buffalo. Sheer strength of numbers and weaponry eventually tipped the scales in favor of the white man as wave after wave of them migrated westward.

And the Indian? Well, the United States government and the US Army had some ideas about what to do with them. They were herded onto reservations and, as has been documented again and again, occasionally given blankets infected with smallpox or measles. Another thing the United States government did, in its infinite wisdom—or perhaps with an ulterior motive in mind—was to put both the Arapaho and the Shoshone, two blood-enemy tribes, on the same Wind River Reservation in Wyoming. Could it be that they were hoping each would take care of the other if such things as the measles and smallpox didn't do the trick?

In retrospect, however, the outcome of this diabolical manipulation had positive ramifications. By learning to tolerate each other and to cooperate with one another, these two tribes have righteously thumbed their noses at the government who wished them ill. By making the best out of a situation that was far from optimum, these two tribes have given us a gift by teaching us that tolerance works. And today, if only it would, the rest of the warring world could learn lessons of diplomacy and getting along from the Arapaho and the Shoshone, who, by their successful continuation, provide us with an example of a cultural evolution of survival—and survival is what life is all about.

Clearly, actually surviving in the Wild West was a very different breed of cattle from just imag-

ining it from an armchair in the East. If human beings expected to harness the wilderness, and indeed that is what the white settlers had in mind, their survival could not be equated to some idyllic pastoral poem.

The sparse population in this isolated male environment, with the showdown-at-sundown mentality, allowed testosterone to run amok unchecked by the civilizing social structures of law, education, and religion found in the East. This wild, unruly, lawless, primal, uncivilized aspect of western violence is reflected in this often bloody litany of stagecoach robberies, train robberies, gunfights, fistfights, shoot-outs, cattle rustling, vigilantism, lynchings, ad infinitum.

To be Continued…Next Month

Okay, the hallmark of a good piece of writing was if one wanted to keep reading. Austin had to admit he was intrigued enough with part one that he wanted to see how it was followed up in part two. But not tonight. He'd save it for another day, when he was at home and maybe feeling nostalgic for Laramie, something that actually didn't happen all that often.

Reflecting on what he'd read, he did think to himself that the times they are a-changing. He knew his mother had written that article several years ago and that today using the word *Indian* would be a big no-no. Political correctness had become the norm, and to fly in the face of it would be professional suicide for a writer. Still cowboys and Indians worked. Cowboys and Native Americans didn't have quite the same ring to it.

Tapping his knee with the rolled-up article, he realized that reading it had evoked a lot of memories about Laramie. The town still had that rough-and-ready roughhewn flavor. When he had been in high school, drinking and brawling was still a favorite pastime. And he wasn't sure things had changed that much even twenty-plus years later. Although he knew the drinking laws had changed since then, gotten a lot more severe. He and his friends had gotten away with a lot when they were kids. Glancing at his watch, he shook his head as it was still too early to call home; slipping the article back in the folder, he pulled a letter out of another folder and read it too. Hearing some rattling around out by the trash can in the alley, he slid the letter he'd just finished into his back pocket and went to investigate, approaching cautiously because if it was a skunk, he didn't want to be baptized. It turned out to be a dog, which he chased away with a few harsh words of warning. Once again glancing at his watch, he saw it was now safe to call Jill without interrupting her show.

"Hi, Sweetie. How's everything going in California?"

"When are you coming home? The girls are just such a handful without you here."

The moon scudded behind another cloud while he bit back the first retort that came to mind, which was "You *know* when I am coming home." Instead he said, "I'm flying out late tomorrow afternoon, sweetie. I'll be there to help tuck the girls in tomorrow night."

The rest of the conversation was in much the same vein. When he clicked off, he pocketed his phone and reminisced about growing up in Laramie.

One thing he recalled was how desperate he'd been to get out of Laramie when he'd been in high school. He had been so envious of Savannah back then, off to college in Denver. And then his dad died during his senior year. Talk about a rough patch for the whole family. He'd been planning to go away to college just as Savannah had but told his mom that he'd go to UW so he could stay at home and help her with Dakota, who had just started elementary school. But his mom wouldn't hear of him changing his plans, not even for that summer when he and a couple of golf buddies were going to travel to several golf resorts and play the courses.

And even Savannah, who had blasted through her undergraduate work in record time and was graduating from college after three years, told her mom she'd move back home to take care of Dakota.

"Why on earth would you do that?" Grace had said. "Dakota and I are just fine. You are all signed up with Habitat for Humanity, to build houses this summer with Jimmy Carter, so go do your thing and don't worry about us. Dakota and I will take a road trip when school is out and come watch you pound nails."

Austin was so amazed at his mother's strength during that horrible time.

Realizing it was late and that they had a lot to do before heading to the airport tomorrow afternoon, Austin let himself back in the house, locked the door behind him, and headed up to bed.

Chapter 6

Savannah rolled over in bed and stared out the window. She'd left the blinds open on purpose. A thin sliver of moon and the shadow of tree branches undulating just slightly from a puff of breeze were all she could see. The night before, in an effort to fall asleep quickly, she had closed the blinds to keep out any ambient light. The room had been as dark and quiet with only the occasional Fourth of July fire cracker breaking the silence. She was lying on her side, just ready to drift off, when she felt the weight of someone sitting down on the far corner of the bed. And that had given her more than pause!

She had closed the bedroom door; she knew she had. She was alone in the room. She hadn't heard the door open. No one was in the room but her. And yet on some deep subatomic cellular level, she sensed something. She could feel the weight of someone sitting at the foot of the bed waiting patiently for her to…to what? Slowly Savannah rolled over and looked. No one, nothing was there. Well, of course nothing was there! But from that point on, sleep eluded her. Time stopped. She stared at the corner of the bed until her eyes felt dry. Had she even blinked? She didn't think so.

In the wee small hours before dawn, off in the distance, she heard the lonely whistle of a train as it passed through town. She loved that far-off sound. It had always been like a lullaby to her when she was a kid, hearing a train in the distance. They lived just far enough away from the tracks that they weren't bothered by constant noise. It was just in the still of the night when sound carried that the occasional train could be heard ever-so-faintly. The familiar sound soothed her, and she finally started to relax. The sun was just slipping over the horizon, heralding dawn, when her heavy, tired eyes finally won the battle, and she fell into sleep. A short time later, she had been brutally awakened by Austin pounding on the door telling her to get her rear in gear as they had a lot to do that day. Upon reflection, she decided to keep the spooky incident of the night before to herself rather than take any grief from Austin or Dakota.

Tonight she'd left the blinds open, and still she couldn't sleep. She kept tossing and turning and looking at the corner at the foot of the bed. "You're being an idiot," she told herself as she rolled over and shut her eyes. They popped open again. "Maybe I can't sleep because tonight is my last night here. Yes, that's it—childhood home about to be sold to strangers and all that. And I'm talking to myself." She glanced at the foot of the bed again. Last night's…hallucination was probably just the result of too much wine, an overactive imagination, and the fact that she was sleeping in her mother's room, full of her mother's things, and her smell, and…oh drat! It was all just so unfair!

Giving up on sleep, Savannah threw the sheet back and got out of bed. She stood in the window and, resting her forehead on the glass, thought about her mother. Her mother had lived in this house for nearly half a century. She had slept in this room and looked out this very window. Planted that tree and those shrubs. With a little shiver, the nude Savannah pulled on her blue jeans and one of her mother's T-shirts.

The weight of that person on the corner of the bed the night before had felt so real. And yet nobody had been there. Had it been her mother trying to communicate with her? Then another thought tiptoed into her mind: *Maybe it wasn't Mom.* Savannah looked around the bedroom. Her mother had died downstairs in her office where hospice had set up the hospital bed, but her father had died in this very room. Savannah remembered something she had successfully blocked out of her mind for years. She remembered how, the day of her father's funeral, her mother told her that when she'd walked into the bedroom that morning to grab a jacket before heading to the church, she'd seen him standing right by the bed. She'd said he looked so confused, like he hadn't a clue what had happened to him; then he just faded out of sight. The pragmatic Savannah, home from college for the funeral, had chalked that experience up to her mom's overactive imagination coupled with her grief.

Then, about ten years ago, when she had come home for a short visit, she'd had a *woo-woo* experience of her own. She thought back to that time when she had been alone in the house one night. Her mother had undergone a colonoscopy and should have come home that same day. But she'd had an allergic reaction to the drug they had used to relax and sedate her during the procedure, so they kept her overnight at the hospital for observation. Savannah had been watching television with the sound way down and the lights out. She had always loved watching her shows in the dark. Suddenly she heard footsteps crossing the floor upstairs. She sat bolt upright, knowing she was alone in the house yet also knowing what she had heard. Then she questioned herself. Were they footsteps? Old houses were notorious for settling and creaking and moaning on occasion. She relaxed. That's all it was. Then she heard them again. She looked up and realized her mother's bedroom was right above the living room. Her rational brain told her to go up and investigate. The lizard part of her brain cautioned against such rashness. So she stayed where she was, thinking and remembering that her mother had seen her father up there on the day of his funeral. When her show was over, instead of going up to her old room to go to bed, Savannah spent the night on the couch in the living room with a crocheted afghan thrown over her to keep off the chill. She hadn't closed her eyes that night either, she recalled.

Later the following afternoon when she and Grace sipped cups of tea in the kitchen, Savannah broached the subject. "Remember that time, the day of Dad's funeral, when you saw Dad in the bedroom?"

Grace nodded. "I'll never forget it."

"Did you ever see him again?"

Grace shook her head. "Noooo, not saaaaw." She drew the words out with meaning.

Savannah sat back in the chair and put her fingers up to her bottom lip. Then she whispered with a hint of suspicion in her voice, "What does that mean, 'not saw'?"

"I know he's still around. I feel him. That's all." Grace spoke matter-of-factly.

Savannah shook her head. "Look, Mom, I know you believe in a hidden reality and all that. But I don't believe in ghosts, and you know that."

"You don't have to believe in something. Doesn't mean it isn't there."

"Mom…"

"We are made up of energy, Savannah. Where does that energy go when we die? I believe your father's energy is still around here with me. That's all. No ghost, just his essence."

"Does it scare you?"

That was when Grace laughed. "Now why on Earth would your father still being around scare me? We loved each other. There's nothing frightening about him watching over me. It's like he's just waiting patiently for me to come to him."

"Really, Mom?"

"Really."

Recalling that conversation made Savannah smile. It wasn't that she didn't buy into her Mom's philosophies of life and, well, life beyond life; it was just that she really didn't have an opinion on that subject at all. She supposed that was why she so easily put those woo-woo things way to the back of her mind and didn't remember them until they slapped her upside the head. She looked around the bedroom, focusing her eyes once again on the corner of the bed. Whether she had sensed her father or her mother sitting there the other night, there was nothing to be frightened about. Still, she felt goose bumps rising up on her arms in response to her thoughts, so she was pretty sure she wasn't ready to try to sleep.

Spying the framed picture of her parents that was on the dresser, she picked it up after snapping on the light. The picture had sat in that very spot for as long as she could remember. It must have been taken soon after they were married. There was a sense of that first flush of love simmering between them palpable even from the faded photograph. Her dad's glasses had slid down his nose so he was looking over them, as she recalled he so often had. And one of his arms was behind Grace, resting his hand, Savannah surmised, on her mother's bum. She shook her head and whispered, "What the heck, Mom? Why didn't you bite the bullet and just get the chemo. Dad had been gone for almost twenty-five years. He could have waited for you a couple more." She well knew her mother's feelings about such things as chemotherapy. But she also felt her mother was a little naive. Because her mother had no faith in the medical system in this country, she turned her back on it when she needed it the most. If her mother had just tried the chemotherapy, she might still be alive...if...if...if. She started to put the picture back on the dresser then changed her mind and placed it in her suitcase. It was late. She knew she should go back to bed and get some shut-eye. She tried to yawn, but it was an unsuccessful parody of a real yawn. Savannah stood rooted in the middle of the room evaluating the degree of her tiredness. No, definitely not ready to sleep.

Feeling a bit like a naughty little girl, she went to her Mom's closet and cracked open the door. Looking up, she spied the box right where she knew it would be, on the top shelf in the corner.

Sitting on the bed, she opened it up and started looking through the items. It was full of baby clothing that Grace had saved from each of her children: little bonnets and booties and such. Her first pair of tiny little pink socks and the shiny white patent leather shoes caught her eye. So cute. She picked up the sock. Had her foot ever really been that small? She ran her finger over the embroidery of a cowboy and his horse on one of Austin's little shirts with western-style snaps. Then she picked up the little white dress that had been Dakota's and held it to her cheek. Putting everything back where she found it, she closed the closet door and looked, once again, at the uninviting bed.

When she was a little girl and couldn't sleep, her mother would come into her room and give her a back rub and tell her poems until she drifted off. Well, Mom wasn't around to tell her poems, but her letters and articles were here. Savannah tugged the top off the banker's box and at random dipped her fingers into one of the file folders entitled Letters to Editor of the Laramie Daily Boomerang and extracted a letter.

She read it and burst out laughing.

Dear High School Seniors:

Do you know that when Mary Shelley was your age, she had already written Frankenstein? *She was not only intelligent but well read. Does that make you wonder?*

Are you aware that your school system has failed you by not holding you to higher standards? When the No Child Left Behind Act was passed, it turned out to be a disservice to all. Instead of encouraging students to excel, it held them back until the slowest among you caught up—which, by the way, never happened. So No Child Left Behind became Every Single Child Left Behind. But what's your excuse? You have a brain. Why didn't you use it to teach yourself? You heard about Abraham Lincoln reading books by the light of a fire to educate himself. And of Frederick Douglass teaching himself to read and write. Oh, wait a minute, you were never taught about those things, so you don't know. Hmmmmm? But you do have a brain just like those men did. Why didn't you figure out that you needed to educate yourself if your school wasn't doing the job? Why put yourself on cruise control and just coast through life taking the path of least resistance? Why not challenge yourself?

Yeah, yeah, I know, you can lead a horse to water, but you can't make him drink. So it's up to you to drink the water or not. It's not too late. Pick up a book and read it, digest it, ponder it, and then do something with your lives. Don't become one of the multitudes of children who were left behind because the public school system failed you. Don't fail yourself! Do something!

In High Hopes,
Grace Quinn

After her heartfelt chuckle, Savannah said, "Oh, Mama, that's a little simplistic, don't you think?" All her mother was seeing was the tip of the iceberg with the public school disaster. But that was her mom, seeing a problem and alerting everyone to it. She was like the lookout in the crow's nest of the ship, seeing the iceberg and warning those who actually steered the ship (of state) to move in another direction before a disaster of titanic proportions occurred. She wondered if the letter had ever actually been published in the local paper.

When footsteps tracked down the hallway and then the third stair squeaked under someone's weight, Savannah guessed it was most likely Austin heading down to the kitchen. She had heard him come upstairs about a half hour before, so she guessed he was experiencing sleeplessness as she was. And as there were two pieces of apple pie left in the fridge, it didn't take a rocket scientist to know where he was headed. Dropping the letter she had just read on the bed, she was after him in a shot.

Chapter 7

Austin, holding the pie plate in one hand as he rested the small of his back against the kitchen counter, had a forkful of pie pointed toward his open mouth when Savannah burst into the kitchen. "You can't have both those pieces. Give me one."

He took his bite. "You'll get fat." He spoke with his mouth full.

"Shut up." She pulled a fork from the drawer, budged him over, and the two of them stood hip to hip, eating pie from the pie pan and savoring every bite.

"There are only two more pies in the freezer." Austin rinsed the pie pan in the sink. "And when they are gone, no more of Mom's pies. Ever. And that's a sin."

"No kidding. I never order pie in a restaurant because I know the crust will only disappoint. No one could make a crust like her. Mom was a genius in the kitchen." Savannah went over to the stove and turned on the oven.

"What are you doing?"

"Preheating the oven. I'm going to bake those two pies so we can eat pie tomorrow, and when we all leave here in the afternoon, we'll divvy up what wasn't eaten for lunch and take pie home with us."

"You're right. No point in leaving it for the people who buy the house." He sat down at the kitchen table, while she pulled the two pies out of the freezer.

Glancing at him, she asked, "You're not going up?"

He shook his head. "No, not tired."

"Me either."

He watched Savannah bustle around getting the pies into the oven, wiping down the counter and the appliances, and just making herself useful. "You got something on your mind?"

"Why do you ask?"

"Just looks like you are trying to keep busy to, you know, distract yourself from something."

Wiping her hands on a dishtowel, she sat opposite her brother. "Do you believe in ghosts?"

"You seeing things, Savvy?"

"Yes, no, not seeing things. Feeling things."

"And?"

"Do you remember when Daddy died?"

"It was a Sunday morning. You were at college. I was on the golf course, and Dakota had a sleepover at one of her friend's house." After a pause he added, "I wish I'd stayed home that day."

"Because then you'd have been here to help Mom when it happened?"

"Because then it wouldn't have happened!"

"What are you getting at?"

"He died while they were having sex. If one of us kids was home, they wouldn't have been having sex on a Sunday morning."

Savannah sat back, looking closely at her brother. "Have you been blaming yourself all these years for Daddy's death? It wasn't your fault. You do know that, don't you?"

He simply shook his head. "Intellectually, yes, I know it wasn't my fault and that I couldn't have done anything to save him. But emotionally, no. If I'd been home, they wouldn't have been behaving like teenagers who had the house to themselves."

"The way he ate, he was a massive coronary just waiting to happen. His heart would have blown sooner or later." She walked over to him, and pressing her face close to his, she whispered, "It wasn't your fault." Then she kissed him on the forehead and sat back down opposite him. "Mom always said she could feel Daddy around. I was just wondering if you ever felt him…around?"

He shifted his eyes away from her and looked out the window into the dark.

"Ah-ha! You have!"

When he looked back at her, his eyes had a faraway look. "He always smoked that pipe, remember? When we were at the cemetery when Mom was interred, I thought I smelled his pipe tobacco. I mean, people don't smoke pipes anymore. It was just so weird to smell it. It brought back so many memories."

"You never mentioned that."

"And sound like a dork? I don't think so." They were silent a moment, then he suggested, "Hey, why don't we change the subject."

"So how are the kids?"

"Well, Chelsea just got her yellow belt in Tae Kwon Do." He gave a little chuckle. You should see her all dolled up for class and missing those two front teeth. My baby, losing her baby teeth, she's growing up way too fast."

Savannah tapped her cheek behind which resided a pesky molar. "Speaking of teeth, I had to have another root canal. Having tooth issues just keeps reminding me that I'm getting older. I wish evolution had caught up with the fact that humans don't die at forty anymore and provided us with a third new set of teeth then. 'Cause trying to live with the same set of choppers from seven to ninety-seven sure isn't fun."

"Maybe you could legislate something."

"Ha ha. But back to Chelsea and her Tae Kwon Do. Good for her."

"Yes, it is good for her, but good grief, seven years old and she's breaking boards with her hands and feet."

"More power to her. Sadly, little girls need to be taught to defend themselves, to fight to the death if necessary if some pervert tries to snatch them. The world is just not a safe place. It's not like when we were kids. We had the perfect little universe in this house. It was like living in a black-and-white 1950s sitcom. You were Bud, Dakota was Kitten, and I was…whoever that character was played by Eleanor Donahue. Hey, it just hit me, I wonder if she was related to Troy Donahue?"

"Who's Troy Donahue?"

"Good-looking actor before our time. Blonde. Looked kinda like you."

"I'm not blonde."

"With those highlights in your hair, you coulda fooled me."

"At least *mine* are from the sun."

She flipped him the bird as she had done a hundred times before over the course of their lives.

"If your constituents could only see you now." Which caused them to crack up.

"Hey, there's people trying to sleep up here." Dakota's muffled voice came from above.

"Oops." Savannah put a finger to her lips and spoke in a stage whisper, "Dee's miffed at us. Guess we'd better tone it down."

"I guess."

"What were we talking about anyway?"

"We were the perfect little sitcom family, which was an aberration to begin with because in my estimation, every family is a dysfunctional family."

"Talking from experience, bro?"

His sigh came from way down deep. "Not really. But back to the craziness in the world we were talking about. I just read one of Mom's letters to the editor earlier tonight and"—he put his hand up like a stop sign—"and don't say whatever it is that just jumped to your lips. I am only trying to make a point. She kind of pointed out the same thing we were just talking about in a bizzaro kind of way." He pulled the letter out of his hip pocket and showed it to Savannah.

> *Dear Citizens of Earth:*
> *I read an article the other day about what happens when there are too many rats in a cage. If you have just a certain number of rats in a cage, they all get along fine. They form a society with rules and families, and they all get along just dandy. But then they start to multiply. At a certain point there are way too many rats in the cage, and anarchy sets*

in: murder, cannibalism, chaos. Their society completely breaks down.

That is what is happening to us here on Earth. Earth is the cage, and the people are the rats, and we now have too many rats in the cage. All you have to do is look around to see what is happening. Society is breaking down.

Overpopulation is killing Mother Earth. People aren't going to stop having babies. Medical science has arranged it so elderly people live way past their expiration dates. There are too many rats in this cage! And it makes one wonder if all the efforts to save the Earth, to prevent disaster, are futile. Is it too late? It just might be.

With a Sad Heart,
Grace Quinn

Savannah handed the letter back to her brother. "She sure is good at spotting problems. It's on fixing the problem that we as a people need to focus."

"But she also hits the nail on the head in her own way. Because here we were talking about how I am preparing my daughters to live in a world that isn't a black-and-white 1950s sitcom because we have way too many rats in the cage, society is breaking down, and people are running amok. Kids are taking guns into school and killing at random." He shook his head sadly. "I do worry so about my girls."

"They are good and smart girls. Not like some kids today who don't have the sense of a billy goat. And not like the kids of parents I work with every day trying to…well, I won't start on that. You're a good daddy to prepare them for the uncertain future."

"Well, having kids sure does make a person think about the future. But speaking of being a parent, Savvy, why didn't you ever have kids?"

"What?"

"You know, marriage, kids, the whole enchilada. Why didn't you go that route?"

"I don't know, bro, I guess I'm just not mommy material."

"Bull! When Shannon was born, you were right there, helping out. Jill was useless, scared of the baby, until you pep-talked her into even holding her, showing her that the baby wouldn't break. Ditto when Chelsea came along, you were right there. Of course Jill was no longer scared of handling a newborn by then, but with the toddler underfoot, you were such a big help those first few days. And way back when Dee was born, I remember hearing you getting up in the middle of the night to change diapers and feed her so Mom and Dad could get some sleep. You were so good with her. A natural all the way around."

Nostalgia captured her. "Yeah." She sighed. "I remember getting up with her at night, but I didn't realize you were aware, snot-nosed kid that you were."

Austin looked intently at his sister. "Yeah, I was just a kid, but I remember a lot. I wasn't as obtuse or as self-involved as you guys thought I was."

They made eye contact, and Savannah didn't know if there was a challenge in Austin's eyes or not. "What does that mean?"

"Nothing. I was just making the point that you were so good with Shannon and Chelsea and Dakota when each of them was born. You love kids, why not have some?"

"I have a full and busy life. I've got no time for a family."

"I guess you are the best judge of that." Savannah had been gently sliding her fingers over the tabletop as they conversed. "Whatcha doing there, Savvy? Caressing the table?"

"I just love this old kitchen table. What's going to happen to all the furniture when the house sells?"

"We'll probably sell it too. Have a big ole yard sale or take it to a used furniture store."

Her sigh was heartfelt. "Well, I'm glad the Realtor talked us into leaving the house furnished while it's listed. It would look so forlorn left empty."

"Yeah, I know what you mean." With that, Austin stood up and stretched. Bidding his sister good night, he went up to bed. Savannah snapped off the kitchen light and sat in the dark until the timer went off. After setting the pies on racks to cool, she too made her way up to bed, hopefully to sleep.

Chapter 8

Austin took the lid off the toilet tank and jiggled something. "I thought you sisters of mine were all about equality, so how come it's the guy who has to fix the toilet that won't stop running?"

"'Cause he's the only one who knows how." Dakota patted him on the shoulder as he bent over the tank looking at what was to Dakota mysterious inner workings. "But that jiggling didn't work. It's still running."

"Really?"

"So what are you going to do now?"

"Fix it. Just go away and do what you guys were going to do before this happened."

"Okay. We'll be back shortly. Need anything while we're out?"

"I'll text and let you know if I do."

Savannah was stacking the bags of clothes for the Salvation Army on top of the boxes for UPS that Austin had already placed on the back seat of her car.

Dakota squeezed another item into the trunk that was full of other boxes that were also destined for the Salvation Army and slammed it shut. "Let's go get all this unloaded so there's room for our luggage."

Sliding behind the wheel, Savannah said, "Wave to Mrs. Rutherford."

"Noisy old busybody," Dakota mumbled as she waved and slid into the car.

The donations had been dropped off, and the two of them now toted boxes into a building and put them on the UPS desk. The woman at the counter smiled at Dakota. "Weren't you in here a few days ago?"

"Yep."

"Might have been cheaper to rent a U-Haul."

"Well, can't put a price tag on childhood memories, I guess." She swiped her credit card, paying the freight for the boxes heading to both Maine and California.

"Anywhere you need to go before we head back home?" Savannah turned the car key, bringing the engine to life.

"No, not really."

"No desire to drive past any favorite childhood haunts before we blow this town?"

"No, not really."

"Okay, then. Don't say I never offered." She pulled out of the parking lot while switching on the radio that was perpetually tuned into a news station.

"Oh, I did just think of something. Not now, but before we head to Denver, let's stop by to the cemetery."

"Sure. Good idea."

Dakota looked at her phone. "Bro just sent a text, he needs something at the store." Calling Austin, she asked, "What do you need?" He started explaining, and she cut him off. "Stop right there. Just take a picture of the part and zap it to my phone, okay?" To Savannah she said, "Guess we'd better head on out to Walmart."

Flicking on her clicker, Savannah said, "I'm not driving all the way out there." Turning at the appropriate corner, she headed for Ace Hardware.

Item purchased, they were back in the car listening to some commentary about the welfare state.

"Oh, that reminds me, I meant to tell you, before I flew out here, I was listening to CNN one night and heard part of that speech you gave on children who are living in single-parent households. The one where you quote all those statistics about a certain percentage of suicides are from single-parent families."

"That would be 63 percent."

"And whatever percent are chemical dependent—"

"Yeah, a whopping 75 percent."

"And like half of them are incarcerated."

"And?"

"And…did it ever dawn on you that I was pretty much raised in a single-parent household?"

For a moment, Savannah looked poleaxed. Then her eyes flew to Dakota's. "That…it…I wasn't…"

Dakota started laughing at her discomfort. "Hey, I'm just jerking your chain. Lighten up. I believe your statistics. It's just that there are single-family households and single-family households, if you get my drift. I was so little when Daddy died. And Austin was getting ready to follow you out the door and off to college. I was basically raised by one parent. That's all I was pointing out."

"I'm sorry, Dee." She reached over and rested her hand on Dakota's knee.

"Hey, don't get me wrong. It's nothing to be sorry about. It wasn't your fault or Austin's or anyone's, for that matter. The way things turned out, I think I got the best of Mom. I mean, I got *all* her attention. With you guys being raised together and with Dad, Mom had to spread herself thinner. I think I got the best of her."

"Well, you're probably right about that." She patted the knee where her hand rested then put it back on the wheel.

"Anyway, that night, after I heard your speech, I thought about all the negativity in those statistics. So I started thinking about some positive things that I think that those of us raised with only one parent have in common."

"For example?"

"Well, we are a very independent, self-reliant group of people. If our one parent was busy, we learned to do things on our own. Ergo, we are used to doing things by ourselves because we often had only ourselves to depend upon. And it wasn't my case, but in a lot of single-parent households, the parent works two or even three jobs. So I think that would instill a work ethic in the kids who witness that. It might not be a bad idea to put out some positive press when you talk about things like that. Get the kids in single-parent households who are listening to realize it doesn't have to be seen as all bad."

"You know, you're right."

"And here's something else I'm right about, when we get back to Colorado this afternoon, I don't think you would want the people who voted for you to read that slogan on your T-shirt. They might misinterpret it."

Savannah glanced down to remind herself what it said: "Cleverly disguised as a responsible adult."

"See, they might wonder if you aren't a responsible adult, then what are you, and why did they vote for you?"

"Once again, you're right." After a pause she said, "So how about you take this one and give it to Daniel."

Dakota digested those words and then got her back up. "Excuse me? Why don't you guys like my fiancé?"

"Hey, Dee Dee, I do like him." She pulled into the driveway and turned off the car. "He's just…the biggest little kid I've ever met. That's all I meant."

"Humph."

"I wasn't trying to be insulting. I think he'd get a kick out of this shirt. Really."

"Maybe."

"Aw, come on." Savannah gave her a nudge. Then more seriously she said, "I know you really love him. I've never been in love. Tell me, how did you know he was the one? I mean, you said yes when he proposed, so how did you know?"

"I remember asking Mom the same question once. I asked her, how did she know Dad was the one for her? She quoted Oscar Wilde and said, 'Never love anybody who treats you like you're ordinary.' Isn't that a great yardstick? Daniel has always treated me as if I was so very special. That was a good start. Compatibility certainly helped. Then there was the spark. All those things mixed together and we couldn't help but fall in love."

"You're lucky, you know that?"

"I do. Now, let's get the suitcases in the car and get this show on the road."

Chapter 9

Austin, standing next to the For Sale sign that had been pushed into the lawn, was giving last-minute instructions to the Realtor. "You've got all our respective phone numbers, so if one of us isn't available, you can connect with another one of us. And if for any reason you need to shoot us an email, copy it to all of us."

"It's not my first rodeo, Austin. We got you covered. I don't expect it will be too long before we get an offer."

"Okay, then." He shook the Realtor's hand. "Thanks." When the Realtor got into his car and drove off, Austin strolled across the street and knocked on Mrs. Rutherford's door. As it was answered in record time, it was obvious she had been hovering. "Hi, Mrs. R. How's it going?"

"Just fine, Austin. What can I do for you?"

"Well, we're all ready to take off in a few minutes, and I was wondering if you would just keep an eye on things for us. You know, as you have been the past few months."

"Of course I will, dear, you know that."

"It won't be for too much longer. The Realtor assures me the house should sell fairly quickly."

"I just hope the new neighbors will be nice. Your mother was so loved by all of us."

"Us too. Thanks, Mrs. R." He gave her a little hug and headed back across the street just as the girls came out of the house pulling the door shut behind them. Dee saw Mrs. Rutherford waving at her, and she waved back while making a beeline for the car.

"Hey, Dee, you don't have to sit in the back again. You were stuck there on the way here."

"No, that's okay. You're legs are longer than mine. You'll be more comfortable up front." All settled in, she asked, "How come you asked her to watch the house? You know she's going to anyway."

"Because it gives her permission so she doesn't have to feel sneaky about it."

"Humph, maybe you should have been the politician."

On the way to the cemetery, Austin torqued around and looked at Dakota. "Did you get a chance to read any of Mom's letters or articles last night?"

"No, but I put a couple of file folders in my carry-on. Did you guys get started on the reading?"

"I read an article on Wyoming in the old days. It was pretty interesting."

"And I read a letter that you'd get a kick out of, Dee." Savannah looked at her sister in the rearview mirror. "Mom was pretty much going off on the public school system and how the whole thing sucks."

"Well, it does suck, that's for sure. Daniel and I have discussed many times that the kids in our college classes aren't the least bit prepared for college. Some of them can't even write a complete sentence. It's ridiculous. And sad. But the irony is that those same students who don't know the difference between *too*, *to*, and *two* have this really high self-esteem. They got out of school being told they were all winners, and they believe that! For example, if a group of kids was running a race, they all got trophies. Now how's that for *not* giving them a sense of the real world. I mean, if you came in dead last in a race, you know you lost the race and that you don't deserve a trophy. But they get the trophy anyway. So even when they fail their core competencies, they don't think it's a big deal. They just think they are all winners. College is a real eye-opener for them. When they get an F on a paper, in their eyes, it's my fault because I don't let them do it over for a better grade."

"How do they handle that?"

"I explain that I have already marked everything wrong on the paper, and if they did it over and made all the corrections that I pointed out for them, then whose A is it? Is it *my* A or *their* A?"

"Do they get it?"

"No. So I go on to tell them there are no do-overs in the real world. But they don't believe that either."

Savannah was nodding. "Yeah, that *everybody's a winner* attitude is just one more example of the whole educational infrastructure of this country falling apart. It's almost like the powers that be don't want the masses to have educated children. It seems almost deliberate."

"Working on another speech, Congresswoman?"

She nodded at her brother. "Always."

Dakota said, "What's weird is that you got that letter on education. Didn't I get *that* folder?"

"Well, I guess Mom's filing system wasn't all that accurate. She might have meant to slip it in one folder and it ended up in another one."

"Hey, Savvy," Dakota piped up, "don't forget to stop at the store so I can run in and get some flowers."

*   *   *   *   *

Turning into the cemetery, Savannah parked the car. "Come on, let's go see the family."

Their mom was tucked neatly between her husband on one side and the two babies who'd died on the other side. Dakota placed flowers on all the graves then stood back. No one shed tears as they had three months before at the interment.

"Did you guys ever see the babies before they died?"

Savannah shook her head. "No, we were too little to really know what was what back then. Later on Mom told me about how Dad had been invited to do a series of lectures at, I don't remember, maybe Cambridge? They both went, and Aunt Susi came and stayed with us. It was like a second honeymoon for them. They'd take little day trips or weekend trips to different places like Bath or Cornwall or Brighton. She'd write her travel pieces. It was all in all a lovely little holiday for her and a working vacation for him. When they got home and she discovered she was pregnant, she figured out it was during their weekend in Brighton that it had happened. Hence"—she gestured to the baby's gravestone—"Brighton."

"And Catalina. What a pretty name for a little girl."

"Next time you come to California to visit, why don't we plan a little side trip to Catalina? See if you like the island as much as you like the name."

"That sounds like fun. Maybe for Thanksgiving break?"

"Okay."

"You in, Savvy?"

"Sure. I should be able to swing that."

They stood quietly for a few moments.

"Okay, you guys, it's time to say goodbye."

The three of them stood in a row holding hands and looking down at the graves.

The mound on their mother's grave still looked fresh even after three months. Austin cleared his throat. "How do you say goodbye when you don't know when you'll be back again? I mean, after the funeral, we knew we'd be back here to clear out the house, but now, who knows when we'll be back. So how do we tell her goodbye?"

Savannah squeezed her brother's hand and said, "Maybe we just thank her for some of what she taught us over the years."

"Well, Mom," Dakota decided to go first, "one of the things you taught me was that transcendence reveals itself to us in the events of everyday life. You said once a beam of sunlight illuminating dust motes might be revealing universes to us that we are just too blind to see. I've never forgotten that. You taught me that the things that we thought limited us were actually challenges to encourage us to greater effort. When I was really little, you taught me how to skip stones on the water out at the lake. And you told me the ripples you see when one of the stones drops into the water are like our actions in life. Those ripples show us that our actions reach out beyond themselves and have impacts that one might not realize. That was a valuable lesson to me in thinking about how my choices reach far beyond me. And most importantly, you were always there when I needed you. I miss you, Mom."

Savannah cleared her throat. "That was really beautiful, Dee." She paused, gathered her thoughts, then began, "Mom, you taught me more than I can ever remember. But one important lesson I do remember was that each person is created for the fulfillment of a unique purpose. You told me that we discover this purpose by becoming aware of those things which stir our soul. And when I made missteps and stumbled, you held me up and helped me to become the person I was meant to be so I could fulfill my unique purpose. I love you, Mom. Give Daddy a kiss and a hug from me." Her eyes had filmed a little, and she gave a little sniff to regain her equilibrium.

"You two make this look easy." Austin took a breath then remained silent.

"It's not hard, bro." Dakota winked at her brother. "Just start talking extemporaneously and see what comes out."

"So," Austin began, "I remember the time in high school when you were proofreading a paper I had to turn in to English class. You told me it was a good draft but it needed to be revised. That it lacked *development*. I told you, no, I was turning it in as it was written. So you tore it in half and handed it back to me." He started laughing then went on. "So I went to the computer and printed out another copy and turned it in just as it was: no revisions. A few days later when I came home from school, I showed you the paper. It had an A on it. You said to me, 'That was not an A paper.' And I told you, 'I know that, and you know that, but the teacher didn't know that.' That was when you said to me, 'That was no excuse for not doing your best.' I've thought about that more than once. And later, whenever I was tempted to do just the bare minimum to get by, I'd hear your voice in my head saying, 'That was no excuse for not doing your best.' That was a good lesson, Mom. Thanks."

On the way back to Savannah's car, Dakota spied a penny on the sidewalk. "A penny from heaven." She picked it up and looked at the date. "Whoa, it's the year Daddy died. It must be him saying hello."

"Woo-woo." Savannah unlocked the car and got in. She had the engine roaring by the time the others had slammed their doors. Pulling away from the dead, the three of them headed toward Denver.

The drive was long, and somehow the conversation came around to Austin's relationship with their mother. Dakota was saying, "I know there were a few years there when things seemed a bit rocky between you."

"Yeah, well, I made the mistake about taking my troubles with Jill to Mom. And then she'd try and give advice that I didn't really want, and then I'd end up snapping at her. It was just a vicious circle. I should have kept all my relationship bull to myself."

"So what all happened?"

"I'd yell, well, not really yell at Mom, but criticize her and scold her. Making it out that my troubles were because of her. They weren't, but...I almost brought her to tears a couple of times, but she was pretty stoic. She'd never actually cry, but I could tell she wanted to sometimes...she probably cried when I wasn't there."

"So now you're feeling bad about being an ass all those years ago?"

"When people are being asses, they know they are being asses. But they don't always know why."

"So now you know why?"

"When everything turns upside down in your life, you need to blame someone. So it's easiest to blame the person who brought you into this life."

"Do I dare ask how things are now with you and Jill?"

"I'd rather you didn't."

Chapter 10

Savannah dropped Austin and Dakota off in front of the Denver airport. Hug, hug, kiss, kiss and they were on their way. She'd be home by the time they finally got through security. Savannah lived in the southern part of Denver near the Cherry Creek Mall. It was a quiet neighborhood with very nice older homes. For a woman who mostly lived modestly, that beautiful big house was her one indulgence. It had four bedrooms and three bathrooms. It also boasted a family room that she liked to call a parlor, a den, and a library—each with a fireplace. She also had a fireplace in the master bedroom. When she bought the house, she had all the fireplaces converted to gas so the cost of heating the house in the winter wouldn't disappear up all those chimneys. With the help of a housekeeper and a gardener who each came in once a week, the place always looked well groomed.

Savannah spent as much time in Washington as she did in Denver, so she'd had a top-of-the line security system installed. Leaving the car in the driveway, as she'd have to unload it sooner or later, she got out of the car and stretched. She just wanted to go into the house and unwind. "Home at last, home at last, thank God Almighty, I'm home at last," she paraphrased Martin Luther King Jr. as she put her key in the lock. Entering the house, she tapped her code into the keypad attached to the wall in the vestibule then headed to the fridge and poured herself a glass of chilled white wine.

She'd noticed a pile of mail on the credenza that her housekeeper had stacked neatly for her, and when she detoured into her office, she saw the flashing light on her phone indicating messages. She chose to ignore both for the time being. Tomorrow she could begin the business of being a congresswoman again; today was a day to wind down after a whirlwind week of cleaning out her mother's house with the sibs. Yes, downtime was definitely foremost on her mind, but first, she'd better bring the stuff in from the car.

*   *   *   *   *

Running a nice, hot bath in her old-fashioned claw-foot tub, she began thinking about that penny Dakota had found in the cemetery, which had her thinking about her father, when it dawned on her that they hadn't even thought to thank their father for what he'd taught them. However, as she dipped her hand into the tub to test the water, she realized he probably hadn't really taught them as much as Mom had. He had been a professor at the university and spent most of his life with his nose in a book or lecturing to students. She remembered over-hearing her mother saying to her dad once, "Philosophy is one thing, but lived experience is another." Were they having a fight? She didn't think so; it had sounded more like it was just a conversation. The reality was they had been content with their lives, her father wrapped up in his lofty thoughts and her mom being a mom and a writer. One thing was true though, she had been Daddy's little girl. He could always get her to crack a smile if she was pouting about something. "Hey, thun-dercloud, turn that frown upside down," he'd tell her. Then he'd tickle her ribs until she giggled. Daddy was the one who took her out for ice cream, who would tell her bedtime stories, and who always stopped what he was doing to listen to her. But as far as making decisions, he was also famous for saying, "You'll have to check with your mother on that." Daddy was the soft touch showing love, patience, teamwork, and respect. Mom was the iron fist in the velvet glove. Between them both, she had to admit, they had been good parents.

The yawn almost cracked her jaw. After two sleepless nights, Savannah was looking forward to crashing early in her own bed. But if she went to bed too early, she'd be awake long before the birds. So a bath would relax her and help pass the time until she could go to bed. There! The water was perfect. Now she needed something to read. That was how she relaxed at the end of a long day: a hot bath, a glass of wine, and something to read while she soaked in the tub.

A little while ago, she'd put the banker's box of folders in her office. She found herself fingering through them wondering which one to choose. At first she pulled out the folder of letters with her name on it then immediately rethought that. Usually her mother's letters to her had been chatty and light-hearted, but sometimes she brought up things that Savannah just didn't want to hear. She would challenge her daughter's choice to live the chaste life. "Barren of the messiness of relationships" was one phrase she remembered her mother leveling at her. Another was "Does anything live in isolation, Savannah? I think not." And then there was the "Are you punishing yourself, Savannah? Life is punishing enough. There's no need to continually, perpetually punish yourself." Sometimes Mom just tweaked a nerve that she preferred be left alone.

After one of those letters admonishing her about living her life alone, she had immediately shot a letter back to her mom. "Right back at you, Mom," she had said. It was after Dakota graduated from graduate school and had just gotten a job back East. "You're one to talk. Daddy's been gone for years. Maybe it's time for *you* to find some companionship." After that, Grace stopped her campaign to encourage Savannah to find a significant other.

No, tonight Savannah was too tired to reread letters that were sometimes hard enough to get through the first time. So she put that folder back in the box and found a folder that said "Matthew Shepard" and was subsequently tossed back a couple of decades. She remembered her mom had written something about him after his murder and the trial. That ought to be interesting reading.

Settling into the bath, Savannah picked up the rather lengthy letter to the editor and read:

> *Dear Citizens of Laramie:*
> *Wyoming prides itself on being the equality state. I wonder how many of you realize that initially this was an advertising gimmick endeavoring*

to convince women to come out west to this land of dirt, dust, wind, snow, and little civilization. What, the men asked themselves with a wily glint in their eyes, could or would induce respectable women to move out here and marry them? The carrot on the stick proved to be the offer of the vote and equality. The women came, and the men knew better than to renege on the bargain. The men of Wyoming had gambled and won. Women were drawn to the equality state by the hundreds. And Laramie basked in the glory of being in the news as the vanguard of the future.

Nearly one hundred and thirty years later, the eyes of the world are once again on Laramie. This time it is not because we are celebrating equality; it is because we are guilty of bigotry. A young man, named Matthew Shepard, was beaten to death here because he was gay. Much has been said in the media about this incident. The hows of the murder are known; the whys still elude us. The era in which we live contributes to the catastrophe that occurred here in our town one cold October night, and an exhortation is being made to all of us. Whether we pay heed or not remains to be seen. However, the death of a loved one can serve as a catalyst that transforms our lives, and the death of Matthew Shepard will surely do that.

Metaphor, symbol, and archetype are things that need to be addressed here. For example, the last names of two people who were murdered in close proximity to each other might at first seem to be a mere coincidence, interesting and nothing more, but one wonders. One name was Lamb and the other Shepard. The poor little Lamb was an eight-year-old girl who was abducted, raped, and killed by her playmate's stepfather. The other who followed the little Lamb was a Shepard who was crucified. Simply by mentioning this particular coincidence to several friends and acquaintances, their reactions have indicated to me that there might be more than just coincidence at work here. Their arms popped up with gooseflesh, their eyes widened, their respiration became visible, and they took steps backward. Each and every one of them felt hit by something, something difficult to explain. Perhaps it was an elusive archetype slithering through the unconscious depths of their psyches. We may be too rational to recognize symbols consciously, but our bodies recognize them and react to them for us.

Taking a closer look at Matthew Shepard, it becomes apparent that his name and his crucifixion on a wooden fence post are both suspiciously familiar. At the risk of being accused of blasphemy here, I plead innocent. I am not equating Matthew Shepard with Jesus Christ, the Lord as Shepard, per se. Christ, accepted by many to be the omniscient son of an omniscient father, lived and died the way he did out of choice. He chose to get his message across archetypically because that was the way it would touch the greatest numbers of people in his generation and beyond.

Matthew Shepard, unlike the deliberate Christ, unfortunately just happened to get caught up in an archetypally recurring pattern. A pattern, I might add, that he relived almost to the letter. Witness his last supper with his like-minded friends; his lonely vigil at the bar, perhaps silently beseeching his God, "Why me?", and finally being taken away by today's Roman guards, the men who resented and didn't understand his lifestyle, the men who represented the shallow-minded masses. There are those who become symbols for others intentionally, such as

Martin Luther King Jr., and those who end up as symbols unintentionally, such as Matthew Shepard. The end results are if not the same, at least similar.

Throughout the country, and even the world, the human psyche became collectively electrified when it learned that Matthew Shepard had been beaten to death because of his sexual preference. The people were shocked not just because it was a hate crime but because intuitively, on a deeply unconscious level, they recognized the archetype. The entire nation focused its accusing eyes on Laramie, Wyoming, less than a day after Shepard's nearly lifeless body was discovered. And when he died from the vicious beating that he'd received days before, the archetype had come full circle.

Now that Shepard is gone, the issue of homosexuality has been brought fully to the fore. Hate-crime legislation is being enacted, and light is being focused on what had formally been a hidden practice. What is revealed under that splash of light is simply wonderful. Gays and lesbians, this group of people numbering to the millions the world over, are offering the rest of humankind the greatest gift of all: the gift of love. Love is love whether experienced by a man and a woman or by members of the same sex. Love is love.

Shepard's untimely death throws a bright and illuminating light on a once dark subject resulting in a revelation. The calamity does indeed lead to a new vision of life. And so something good can grow out of something evil.

With a broken yet healing heart,
Grace Quinn

The water had gone stone-cold. Savannah dropped the letter on the floor and got out of the tub. After drying off, she draped the towel over the shower rod, retrieved the letter, and padded out of the bathroom. She remembered that her mother had been very upset about all that had been going on in the aftermath of Matthew Shepard's murder, but she hadn't realized the depth of her mother's passion. Her old-fashioned flip cell phone was on the dresser, and she saw that she had a couple of texts. Dakota's flight was slightly delayed, and she was waiting it out patiently. Austin had been bumped from his flight, and he wouldn't be flying out until the next day. He was staying at the Ramada Inn as it was convenient and the airline was paying. So much for life's little surprises when traveling. She slipped between the sheets with the letter in hand, wanting to reread it before she went to sleep.

If anything, the second time through left more of an impact. It gave a person much food for thought. But Savannah decided she'd think about it tomorrow. There was a time for thinking deep thoughts, and it wasn't when one was exhausted. She let the letter slip from her hand and managed to click off the light before she fell into sleep like a stone falling from a cliff.

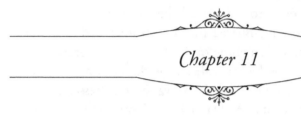

Chapter 11

Dakota sat cross-legged in the roomy chair in the airport. Her plane had been delayed, and as an experienced traveler, she didn't sweat the small stuff. According to the departure board, she had a good forty-five minutes before they'd board, so she'd wandered away to an area not overcrowded with milling passengers waiting to get on her flight. She always had a book with her, and her first instinct was to pull it out of her pack and pass the time until they could board. But she recalled she'd slipped a couple folders of her mom's letters and articles in the side zipper of her laptop case and decided on second thought to read a couple of them to while away the time.

One folder was labeled Miscellaneous so she figured the letters would be an eclectic hodgepodge of this and that. The letter she held in her hand was folded in half. On the outside was written, "To Christine after her mother's death." Before she opened the letter to read it, Dakota looked off toward the middle-distance, reliving the past with unfocused eyes.

Christine had been one of her high school girlfriends. Someone she hadn't thought about in years. Christine's mother, a single parent who spent as much time in the bars as she did at home, had died when they were seniors. It was late November. Christine's mother had gone to the bar one night and, according to witnesses, drank herself into a near coma, which wasn't unusual. Apparently, she was picked up by someone (nobody witnessed that part) and was driven to the edge of town. There was speculation if this was one of those sexual favors in exchange for money kind of deals. What happened was that the nude body of the woman was discovered early the next morning dumped along the side of the highway like yesterday's garbage. Christine's mother had died of hypothermia. Christine had enough credits in school to graduate early, and in January, she moved away from Laramie. Dakota had never heard from her again.

Dakota ran her fingers over the letter her mother had written to Christine. She had tears in her eyes when she finally unfolded it and read:

> *Dear, Dear Christine,*
>
> *I was so sorry to hear of your mother's passing. It's never easy, and yet it is one of those experiences that after it happens, sometimes you start to see the woman who gave you birth in a whole new light. This doesn't happen right away, but over time. I know her drinking was a burden and an embarrassment to you. You told me that yourself. I know you have spent your high school years angry with her for not being the mother you wanted her to be. It's an interesting thing how we hold our parents to a different standard than we do our friends or ourselves. I know that more than once Dakota has brought you home with her after a party, and I have heard you in the bathroom being sick after a night of drinking. Your mother taught you much, didn't she? But was that the lesson you need to take away from this horrible experience? I have more to say about that, but first let me tell you about my own mother.*
>
> *I remember my mother's funeral. I was completely floored by the number of people who showed up. The church pews were filled to capacity, and people spilled out the door. So many people? People who mourned my mother's passing, who loved her, who amazingly even liked her? Clearly their experience of this woman was a far different one than mine.*

My mother wasn't a lovable, or even likable, woman from my perspective. She was a harsh disciplinarian and one of the most unhappy individuals I had ever met. She clearly was miserable being married to my dad and raising us girls. She clearly didn't want to be boxed into that life. But she was.

She shunned my father, putting him down to us girls. And we could never do anything right in her eyes. And when we hit those turbulent teen years, well, I'll skip over that part.

In later years, looking back with perspective, she appeared to me to be a woman who had to settle. And why does a woman have to settle? Probably because she has no choice? She and Daddy were married in January, and their firstborn arrived in November, a respectable eleven months later. If they had been a happy couple, there wouldn't have been a mystery. But because they weren't a happily married couple, I often pondered their enslavement to one another.

They had lived in Washington, DC, and when they decided to marry, they eloped to Maryland. A place that didn't require a marriage license procured several days before a marriage. The first question in the mystery was why the rush, why did they elope, apparently on the spur of the moment? Then comes another part to the mystery. Her wedding dress wasn't a wedding dress at all. It was a nice dress, but more an afternoon tea kind of dress, not a wedding dress. That in itself wasn't the surprising part as a woman eloping wouldn't be wearing a real wedding dress. But I digress. It was a simple off-white dress with little teacup sleeves just barely over the shoulder. It was that unattractive length that women wore back in the forties, meaning it came to midcalf. I believe she only wore the dress that once, but she kept it hanging in her bedroom closet for the remaining years of her life. It wasn't until years later that it dawned on me that it was clearly a springtime dress, not a winter dress, and that's where the plot thickens. That springtime dress for a January wedding led me to speculate and draw some conclusions. Perhaps they were erroneous conclusions, but as no one was around to enlighten me about my parents' wedding/marriage, I reinvented a potential and feasible backstory as to why they were so unhappy. So yes, my conclusions are based on circumstantial evidence, but they are my conclusions nevertheless.

My eldest sibling didn't look at all like the rest of us kids. And yet that child was our mother's favorite. My younger sister and I, well, we were the outcasts, the ones who got spankings for any little thing; we were the ones who trembled in fear of this larger-than-life, volatile woman who could fly into a rage at the smallest thing. Had our mother, like so many women over the centuries, found herself in a fix and married in the nick of time to avoid scandal? Married someone who wasn't the one who was the father of her baby? Had they just told people they had married in January to hide an indiscretion? Did my father know that she was expecting? Did he suspect he wasn't the baby's father? And if he did know, why did he go along with the charade? Is that what happened? Is that why she had the appearance of a woman who had settled? Is that why she was so boxed in and unhappy? Is that why she wasn't really fond of the children she had with her husband but truly loved the one child who came first?

I never did solve the mystery, and I expect I never will, but my experience growing up in an unhappy family did make an impression on me. It taught me a lesson. It taught me I didn't want to perpetuate that set of circumstances. I have learned to sympathize with whatever it was that made her so unhappy. At the same time, I work so very hard not to be like her in the way I raise my children. She was harsh. No was the only word she knew, and she took great pleasure in denying us things we wanted. "No, you can't do that." "No, you can't have this." And the prolonged spankings we endured at her hand were not something any child should have had to experience. So I guess I went in completely the opposite direction when raising my kids. I was probably way too lenient and spoiled them way too much. But I had learned by experience how not to raise children.

Likewise, you can learn what not to do from your mother's behavior. Do you understand what I am saying? She gave you a valuable lesson in how not to behave, how not to ruin your own life. And now some hard truths. For the past year or so, you have been emulating her behaviors because that is what you saw, what you know, what you learned. It's time now to take another lesson away from her example. She was showing you how not to be. By ignoring that and by following her example, you are being led into a lifetime of unhappiness. You have your whole life ahead of you. Please stop, think, and then take that lesson from her example of how not to be away with you. I think that's what your mother would want.

All my love,
Your Surrogate Mom,
Grace

Well! That was a walk down memory lane she hadn't expected to take. Poor Christine. And poor Mom. She'd really had no idea her mother had such an unhappy childhood. *We really are the center of our own universe,* Dakota thought. We so often wore blinders when it came to others and their lives. Her mother's story of her childhood pulled at her heartstrings. And what Christine had been through pulled at them too. Whatever happened to her? Dakota pulled out her phone and skimmed through different search engines trying to find Christine. It was almost impossible not to be on the internet somewhere these days. Nothing. The woman was completely off the grid.

She remembered how Christine would drink herself almost into oblivion at parties, and Dakota, usually the designated driver, would see that Christine got home safely. Or when going home wasn't an option for her, she'd bring her home to her house. That she'd been headed down a very bad path was clear even back then to Dakota. She wondered if the letter Grace had written to her after her mother died was too little too late.

Dakota had been such a lucky person because she had family who cared enough to keep her from making mistakes. Her mother had given her a few serious talkings-to when she was in high school. She'd say things like, "Dakota, certain experiences mark you. Your life will never be the same from that point on, so look before you leap into things that you might regret." Yes, her mom and both her sister and her brother had kept her from falling into peer pressure to drink or take drugs. Too bad Christine hadn't had a mom and a big sister and brother like she did.

She and her siblings had always had an easy bond. They'd kept her on the straight and narrow when she'd been living in Laramie, and she had managed to graduate from high school without suffering any teenage traumas. Yes, too bad Christine hadn't had any siblings to help her.

Glancing at her phone for the time, she gathered up her laptop and her carry-on and headed for the gate. She boarded her flight and spent a few minutes wondering about her long-lost friend. Then, after a glass of wine, and realizing the flight was long and she wasn't about to be able to sleep, she decided to give herself something else to think about and pulled a rather lengthy article out of one folder and settled in to read.

Chapter 12

Dakota got off the plane in Bangor, pulling her wheeled carry-on behind her. As she passed through the gated area into the airport proper, she instantly spotted Daniel and had to laugh. He stood there wearing a chauffeur's cap and holding a sign that said, "Dakota. Don't know if it's North or South?"

"Ha ha." She gave him a kiss that he returned with enthusiasm.

Stepping back to look at her, he read the caption on her T-shirt, chuckled, and then asked, "What is that all about?"

She shrugged, a bit embarrassed. "It's one of Mom's T-shirts."

"You always made fun of her T-shirts."

"I know. It just makes me feel close to her, wearing it."

He read it again and laughed again. There was a picture of a bejeweled crown. Above the picture it said, "My dentist said I needed a crown." Below the crown, it said, "I was like, 'I know, RIGHT!?'"

Picking up her carry-on by the handle, he slipped his other arm about her waist and started heading toward the exit. "Come on, let's go home."

"This way." She steered him toward the luggage carousel. "I have a checked bag too."

"You didn't leave with more than this one."

"There were things I wanted."

"I already figured that out. The UPS guy dropped off a bunch of boxes earlier today."

"There will be more."

"Do we need to move to a bigger house?"

Daniel paid the attendant and pulled out of the airport parking lot. There was a fine mist in the air, but it wasn't really raining, so the wipers were on delayed wipe. Every few moments, they cleared the windshield and rested.

"So how was the flight?"

"Long, exhausting. I can never sleep on a plane."

"You can always take a nap when we get home."

"Good idea."

"Maybe I'll take a nap with you."

She smiled. "Even better idea. Particularly on a rainy day." She yawned hugely. "And a night without sleep has just caught up with me."

Daniel pulled into their driveway and parked close to the stairs on their split-level house.

"Come on, let's get you upstairs and into bed for your—"

"Nap?"

"I was thinking welcome homecoming." Daniel carried the suitcase then stopped and stood at the foot of the stairs that led to the kitchen door.

Dakota started up the steps ahead of him. She figured he always waited for her to go first because he liked looking at her butt. Halfway up, she suddenly stopped dead in her tracks. At the top of the steps sat a skunk. She looked at the animal, looked over her shoulder at Daniel, then could immediately tell something was up by his expression. Looking closer at the animal, she realized it was a stuffed toy.

"Gotcha!" He laughed. Brushing past her as he ascended the steps, he picked up the toy, handed it to her, and held open the door, ushering his fiancée over the threshold and into their home.

The house was a lovely split-level home set way back from the road on about five acres of land, most of it wooded. There were neighbors, but not so close as to crowd them. A few doors down, one of the neighbors had chickens and a rooster who would crow not only when the sun rose but at other odd times as well. On occasion they would see a few deer munching on the grass in the backyard who, if startled, would turn and bound back into the woods, their white tails waving goodbye. And one time a bear cub ran across the yard and into the woods. Dakota's thought was, *If there's a cub, there's a mama.* And that gave her pause for the few days and weeks after that sighting. She didn't want to be in the yard alone if a bear was going to come lumbering out of the woods. But when they never saw the bear cub again, she relaxed.

Dakota finished brushing her teeth and was just slipping the brush into the holder when Daniel gave a holler, "Hey, sweetie, do I have to say some magic words to get you to come to bed?"

Teeth all brushed, Dakota padded into the bedroom. "No magic words, just show me how much you missed me." She slid between the sheets and rolled into his waiting arms.

Chapter 13

Austin hugged his wife. "Here, I thought you'd get a kick out of having one of Mom's T-shirts."

She unfolded it, read it, and frowned at him. "What's this supposed to mean?" It read, "To save some time, let's just assume I'm always right."

Well, he thought she'd like it because she had reiterated to him more than once over the years: "You know I'm always right." But he guessed that her saying it and having him say it, even with a T-shirt, were two different things. "You know, you're right. What was I thinking? It worked for Mom because of her sense of humor, but it's completely wrong for you." He took it back and tossed it in the direction of the kitchen trash can. Grabbing his suitcase, he hauled it upstairs to the bedroom and started unpacking.

Austin was in no mood! He'd been bumped off his flight the day before, spent the night in a Ramada Inn near the airport, and then nearly missed his wake-up call. It had subsequently been a long day with a touch-and-go layover in Salt Lake City. First it looked like he was going to miss his tight connection, then when he finally got to the gate, that flight had been cancelled, and he was eventually put on another one six hours out. But instead of landing in San Jose, it only got him as far as San Francisco. After he finally made it to Frisco, he rented a car and had to drive to the San Jose airport to retrieve his own car. Then there was bumper-to-bumper traffic creeping its way along until he figured he'd never get home. And now, after all that, was he greeted like a conquering hero home from the wars? No, all he got was attitude.

He peeked in the girls' room discovering both were sound asleep. When they had been really little and he got home from work, they'd rush to him squealing "Daddy's home!" and give his legs hugs and reach up for him to lift them up for big wet, sloppy kisses. When he'd go into their room to read them bedtime stories, they would jump up and down on the bed in their little girl nighties, so happy they couldn't contain themselves. Shannon at ten had outgrown her little girlishness and was insisting that she needed her own room now as she was too big to be sharing with a little sister. He looked at their sleeping forms. Such amazing little people. He didn't want to wake them up so blew them both a kiss and retreated back to his room.

Austin filled up the hamper with dirty laundry from his suitcase then flopped down on the bed and stared up at the ceiling. Apparently, the girls had been long tucked into bed, and if the sound from downstairs was any indication, Jill had just started the dishwasher.

Marriage! It sure was a chore!

Right now he was too tired to do anything about it, to try to come up with an answer to the question of "What does Jill want?" He knew what he wanted. Right now he wanted a beer, but he wasn't about to go down and get one.

The night before when Dakota was boarding her red-eye flight to Bangor, Austin had been in a bar in Denver doing just that, enjoying a beer. When he'd been bumped from the flight and told he couldn't catch another one until the next day, he had briefly thought of calling Savannah and asking her to backtrack to the airport and get him so he could spend the night at her place. But they had been too much in each other's faces this past week, so the Ramada Inn it was. He took a shuttle there and then went and found sustenance.

By the time he was on his second beer, he figured he was relaxed enough to call home and give Jill the news, that he wouldn't be arriving until the next day. He moved away from the bar and sat at a table in the back where he'd have a little privacy. He punched in speed dial and then took a deep breath. After the phone call, it took another beer for him to get back to that relaxed place. Wanting to take his mind off his miseries, he thought about part two of his mother's article that earlier he'd tucked into his jacket pocket. Pulling it out, he took a swig of beer and started reading.

Austin thought of that article while staring up at the ceiling of his bedroom. Part two of the trilogy had been about the weather, and after reading that article, he had been reminded why he really didn't miss Wyoming at all. Between the constant wind and the occasional blizzards, it sure could get nasty at times. He remembered being safe and sound at home during a Wyoming storm. A person's home should be their port in a storm. But what if the storm raged inside the home? Then where did one go to find safety?

He remembered his mom telling him once after he and Jill had a blowout fight that sometimes just putting one foot in front of the other was all one could manage to do to get from day to day. "I think that's where you are now," she had told him. "Just getting by from day to day. Sometimes our lives are shrouded in opaqueness and we can't see any way out, over, under, or through the mess except to just keep on keeping on. One foot in front of the other."

Later in that conversation, his mom had gone on to say, "There wasn't a month during our marriage that your father didn't tell me I was the best thing that ever happened to him."

"Sounds like bullshit to me, Mom."

"That type of bullshit is the fertilizer that keeps a marriage blooming. And if you can't tell your wife that she was the best thing that ever happened to you, if in fact she isn't the best thing that ever happened to you, maybe that says a lot about your marriage."

Jill came into the room, stood next to the bed, then said. "Look, honey, I guess we got off on the wrong foot, let's try again. How was the flight?"

He looked over at her and saw that she was actually trying. "Stressful." Then he noticed she was wearing the T-shirt. He raised an eyebrow in question.

Smoothing it down, she said, "Well, it works as I am always right." She smiled at him, and they both gave a half-hearted laugh. "Did you have anything to eat before the long drive home, or do you want me to fix you something?"

"I'm good." God! It sounded like they were polite strangers. He put his arm out and motioned her toward him. "Come here." When she did, he pulled her down beside him and just held her for a moment. When she relaxed and he felt her breath on his neck, it felt almost like old times. He recalled something he'd read once upon a time: genuine dialogue can be either spoken or silent. Maybe they were sharing a dialogue now.

PART II

Traveling Afar

All journeys have secret destinations of which the
traveler is unaware.

—Martin Buber

Chapter 14

By the time Grace had married Barrett, twenty-plus years her senior, he had already paid off the house he owned. He'd always been smart when it came to finances. And in this particular instance, refusing to let the bank strong-arm him into a ridiculous thirty-year loan had been the right decision. He'd bought the house when he was a still-wet-behind-the-ears twenty-seven-year-old assistant professor, and fifteen years later, by the time he was barely into his forties and a tenured full professor, the house was his. Wrapped up in his career, he hadn't had time for the nonsense of dating. Oh, he'd had a careless liaison with a student in the early years that could have cost him his job. He didn't have to touch a hot stove twice to learn that it burned, and he thanked his lucky stars that the indiscretion hadn't imploded all he had been working toward at the university. After that, he met an occasional woman here or there when the need arose, but as he was a much more cerebral than physical man, libido wasn't the driving force of his life. At forty-six years of age, he met Grace, and for the first time, he thought about settling down into the family life. For him, one of the most attractive things about Grace was her intelligence. The fact that she was as pretty as a springtime bouquet of flowers was only an added bonus.

Without the expense of a mortgage payment during the years their kids were growing up, they had been able to add generously to their savings each month. The upshot was that when Barrett died, he had left Grace fairly well off. Money had never been a worry, and Grace had never needed a full-time job outside the home. As a widow with the life insurance added to what they already had, she was set for the rest of her life. She still traveled both to write her travel pieces and just for fun. One year, after Dakota had left the nest, Grace flew to California, where she had been born and raised, and she and her sister, Susi, took a train up to wine country, spending several days touring the various wineries. They discovered that they were very compatible travel companions, and as they'd had so much fun on that trip, they got the idea to do Tuscany. The next year they spent two weeks basking in the Tuscan sun and enjoying those wines. After that, they decided to explore their Irish roots and spent a couple of weeks in Ireland. The next year, they decided to explore their Scottish roots. There was always an adventure around the next corner, and life was good. Over the years, they enjoyed many trips together.

When she wasn't traveling or writing about it, Grace had much to keep her occupied at home. In the years when she'd been a substitute teacher, she had bonded with three other subs, and over the years they had invented a birthday club. On each of their respective birthdays, they'd meet in a nice restaurant and celebrate with a luncheon. The person whose birthday it was didn't have to pay that day. And of course the wine flowed freely. Sandy had been a February baby, Grace was an April baby, Cora was a July baby, and Kathy was an October baby. They always had so much fun catching up on each other's lives.

In addition to the birthday club, she'd belonged to a book club for almost as many years as she had lived in Laramie. It wasn't that the club members were sexist; it just happened that all nine of the members were women. And as they met only nine months of the year, it was perfect. They took December off for obvious reasons, and they took July and August off for summer. Every June they came up with nine books to be read the following year that commenced in September, just like a school year. Each member led the discussion of the book chosen for the month assigned to her. One month they would read a novel; the next month it would be a nonfiction book. They read everything from modern best-sellers to classics. Grace had particularly enjoyed the month they had read *The Tao of Physics*. She had been assigned to be group leader that month, and not only had the reading been fascinating, the discussion was more animated than usual that evening. One passage from the preface of the twenty-fifth anniversary edition of the book had always stuck with Grace: "Mind is the process of life, the process of cognition. The brain (and indeed the entire body) is the structure through which the process manifests itself." Yes, that book certainly had precipitated a lively discussion.

Many years before that, when the kids were still in school, the book club read Gabriel Garcia Marquez's *The General in His Labyrinth*. At the dinner table one evening, she was sharing a bit of what she'd been reading. "The book said that over the course of his life, Bolivar had written over ten thousand letters! Imagine! Some were written by him and some he dictated to others."

"Well, of course," Austin had piped up, "'cause he was a *dictator*. Get it? *Dictator*?" And then he had cracked up at his pun.

Grace had to admit to herself that she was mighty impressed with her son, who, still only in ninth grade, could not only make a connection like that, but even know who Bolivar was in the first place. That was amazing. She knew the curriculum at the school didn't include South American history, so she wondered where her young son had learned about Bolivar. She was pretty sure that she wouldn't have known who Bolivar was when she was in ninth grade. Be that as it may, the book was fascinating. There was one line from that book that she'd remember always: "The supreme command of the patriots had been eliminated by the simple formula of hanging every man who could read and write." Perhaps this country's abysmal public school system was kept the way it was for a similar reason. If the majority of citizens couldn't read and write…no, the powers that be couldn't be that deliberately diabolical, could they?

Writers are notoriously avid readers. So not only did Grace read the books assigned by the book club, but she read many other books as well. She read to broaden her mind, but she also read to escape. One of her favorite escape authors for years had been Nora Roberts. Grace would devour her novels as soon as they came out, buying them because she knew she would want to read them more than once. Over the years she'd ended up with shelves and shelves of Nora's books. It was soon after she had become a widow that she noticed that when she read Nora's books, she would find herself skipping over all the lovemaking scenes. She used to devour those scenes, and now she didn't. The plain and simple fact was that those scenes were arousing. Barrett had always been the lucky recipient of Grace's arousal after reading those pages and pages and pages of steamy sexual content. Now that her husband was gone, well, reading those passages just got her hot and bothered with no outlet. So when reading, she'd just lick the tip of her index finger and quickly turn pages and pages and pages, usually ten or twelve at the very least, until the sex part was over, and she'd get on with the story. Of course, as any good psychologist will tell you, suppress an urge and see what happens!

After about five years of suppressing her sexuality, temptation stepped in. The garbage disposal had broken down, and Grace called a plumber. He'd fixed the appliance and handed her the bill. She wrote him a check, and that was that. She closed the door behind him and, after he left, gave a little sigh at the fact that just being in the same room with him had left her feeling a little tingly. Pushing those thoughts aside, she headed toward her office. Getting ready to proofread an article before sending it off, she heard a knock on the door. The plumber had returned.

He queried, "Was it just me, or did we have a vibe going?"

Grace opened her mouth to say something, but nothing came out.

The plumber glanced down toward her breasts that weren't trapped in a bra, and the February cold with the door open had the girls nice and perky. "Love the T-shirt." He smiled with a gleam in his eyes.

Not even remembering what T-shirt she'd pulled on that day, she glanced down and read "Got Milk?"

When he left the house for the second time that day, Grace was glad she had paid him in advance for fixing the garbage disposal as she sure would have felt awkward handing him a check after, well, after. That he'd left her sated was no doubt, but that it would not happen again was also of no doubt. It had been wonderful, but it had also been wanton, and she did not like seeing herself as a wanton woman. As the afternoon wore on, she started feeling an unfamiliar sensation in her stomach and in time realized that it was shame creeping in, probably because he had been wearing a wedding band.

No, there would be no more trysts of this nature. But what to do when bodily needs arose?

It just so happened that the birthday club was meeting the next day. When they'd all had a few sips of wine, Grace broached the subject of men. "Cora, you've been divorced about as long as I've been widowed…what…how, I mean, don't you miss sex?"

Cora chuckled at Grace's discomfort with the topic. "There's a new thing out there called dating. Maybe you should try it."

Grace was shaking her head. "Forget I mentioned anything. I'm really not interested in a…full-time man in my life. I mean with Dakota and all."

"Dakota isn't going to get all possessive if you get a boyfriend."

"No, I really don't want to have to make room for a boyfriend in my life."

Kathy pointed out, "Dating doesn't necessarily mean boyfriend. There are such things as one-night stands. And did you just start blushing?"

Grace put her hands to her cheeks, which were indeed hot. She hadn't blushed since she was thirteen years old. "I've spent years grieving and not even thinking about missing sex, but suddenly, well, I guess my body hasn't forgotten how to get aroused. I just discovered that recently, and hence why I brought up the subject."

Sandy, always the pragmatist, said, "So you're hot to trot but don't want to date. Why not just dig out the sex toys you had when you were married and fly solo?"

"Excuse me?" Grace was literally scratching her head. "Barrett and I never, I mean, we didn't need tools."

"Toys, Grace, toys, not tools." Laughter all around.

"Guess he managed to hit all the right spots without them, huh, Grace?" Kathy saluted her with her wineglass.

"I wouldn't know a sex toy if I saw one." Looking around the table from one friend to another had her realizing they knew more than she did. "I guess that makes me pretty naive."

"Well, if you never needed them, so much the better. But I know my vibrator sure comes in handy with Charlie's diabetes and high blood pressure medication and all."

"So?" Kathy wasn't about to let the subject go. "Tell us about this one-night stand."

Grace groaned. "Well, you know my type is Barrett, tall, lanky, smart, quiet."

"Yeah, we know, Jimmy Stewart. So…spill."

"This guy was Tony Soprano."

"You go, girlfriend!" Cora gave her a high-five. "Good for you."

Two months later when the club met again for Grace's birthday, not only did they pick up the tab for her lunch, but they gave her a present as well. It was the first vibrator she had ever seen, and she didn't really have an idea about how to go about using it, but it made for a nice gag gift, and it also turned out to serve a purpose.

By the time Dakota was fully on her own, Grace found she needed to find something to fill some empty days. There were two times a year that the university offered noncredit classes for the community. They were evening classes that met once or twice a week and that lasted from one to ten weeks depending on what the class was. After taking a couple of those classes just for fun, Grace looked in to teaching a writing class. She talked to the administrator, and between the two of them, they thought offering a memoir writing class might be a fine addition to the curriculum. So twice a year, once in the fall and once in the spring, Grace taught a class that met one evening a week for six weeks.

Between her clubs, teaching her writing classes, taking short trips, and writing her articles, she was busy. And in time she met a man who made a nice companion for dinners out and such, so her days and nights were full, and she was content.

Chapter 15

Ever since the recent presidential election, Grace had felt a sour feeling in the pit of her stomach. At first she thought it was the result of just being unable to digest the political turn of events in Washington. But when the sour feeling turned into actual bona fide pain that just wouldn't go away, she broke down and went to the doctor. The evening of the day Grace received her diagnosis, she sat out on her deck looking at a night sky that was nearly barren of stars. There had been an unseasonable January thaw melting all the snow, so the deck was clear. As the patio furniture had been stored away in the garage for the duration of the winter, she had hauled a dining room chair outside and was just sitting out in the cold. Cold, it turned out, was a relative thing. Being so cold on the inside since receiving the calamitous news, she barely noticed how cold it was on the outside.

The diagnosis had been a surprise, but as death is unavoidable, she couldn't claim to have been completely blindsided. She knew that as people aged their bodies broke down. It was just a matter of time before something would manifest. Still she found that she was more annoyed than afraid. Oh, the fear of the unknown was just around the corner, she was pretty sure of that. But for right now, in this moment, she wasn't afraid. What did she feel if not fear? Resignation? Relief? She wasn't sure.

The doctor had given her many options but rather than choose one, she told him she needed time before deciding what to do. She went home and had spent a couple of hours on the internet researching pancreatic cancer. She discovered that by the time this type of cancer was diagnosed, it would have already spread beyond the point of no return, making any cure unlikely. She learned that while chemotherapy and radiation might slow the growth, the end result would be the same. If it had been early enough in the discovery of the disease for surgery, the website said that in half of those cases, by the time the surgeon operates, it has already spread beyond an operable stage anyway. To say that prognosis was poor would be to understate the obvious dramatically. It was now just a matter of time. She knew a smattering of Latin. The term *memento mori* came to mind—remember that you must die. Yes, everyone must die.

So this was the last leg of her journey here on Earth. The journey's end. Was there anywhere she wanted to travel, anything she wanted to see that she hadn't yet seen? For a woman who had been a lifelong traveler, her answer surprised her. "No," she said aloud to the night, "I don't want to go anywhere. This is a good place to die."

Right then she felt detached. Yes, that was the word. Detached. She was curious, though. She thought of the quote from *The Tao of Physics* that was one of her favorites: "Mind is the process of life, the process of cognition. The brain (and indeed the entire body) is the structure through which the process manifests itself." To her, mind was consciousness or even the soul. And she began to wonder what happened to consciousness/soul when a person died? The vehicle through which consciousness passes, the body, ages and dies, but not the consciousness. Surely that didn't die. She began to wonder why she had been so drawn to that sentence in the first place, so drawn to it that she'd memorized it and thought of it often. Peeling away layers of potential reasons, she had, well, not an epiphany, she'd call it an *ah-ha* moment. In a roundabout way, that sentence reminded her of Rene Descartes precept, *I think therefore I am*. He didn't say, "I am therefore I think." *I think*, being the mind, came first. The *I am* part, the vehicle through which the thought, the consciousness passed, came second. Mulling that over brought other things to mind. She focused on a vanishing point at the very back of the endless night as she tried to unravel the mysteries of time, aging, and death.

The vast silence of the night seemed to suck her into it, and she experienced a waking dream about the infinite number of things we know nothing about. She recalled thinking the same thoughts on many a dark winter's night when the power had gone out because of a storm and the room danced in the light of a single candle. Nights like that were times for deep thoughts.

As she contemplated the void, it suddenly seemed as if she were floating above herself in the inky darkness. Hovering there, she began to retrace the path of her life. Interestingly, all the memories, both happy and sad, made her melancholy. She wanted to lay them at the side of the road as Christian did with his pack in the *Pilgrim's Progress*, but there was no road where she was floating, and there was no pack. By the time she came back to herself sitting outside on her deck in her dining room chair, she was chilled to the bone. Getting up and dragging the chair back into the house, she headed toward the bathroom for a long hot shower.

The next morning she pulled a T-shirt on over her head in defiance. It said, "Seriously?"

"I mean really!" she said to herself, "Is this *seriously* happening?" She wore that shirt every day for a week before getting out her sewing sheers and cutting the shirt into strips and throwing it in the garbage. Over the course of the next few days, the word "Preposterous!" exploded from her lips a few times.

Weight fell off her frame as if she were an ice cube melting in the sun. And she found herself brushing her teeth several times a day. It was the smell of decay that she couldn't get rid of, the odor of putridity that drove the point home to her. She was dying. She was deep in the belly of the beast now.

Pain became her constant companion, and she had no appetite to speak of, but her friends weren't about to forsake her. They took turns dropping by and bringing her comfort food: a creamy macaroni and cheese, lasagna, soft ice cream sundaes, even the classic cure-all chicken soup. She'd nibble when they were present, but when they left, the food was tossed out.

As Grace grew weaker, her determination grew stronger. She wasn't going to be a burden to her children or anyone until there was no longer a choice. When she got on the scale one morning and realized she weighed all of ninety pounds, she flew into a fury at her body's betrayal. It was wasting away without her permission! The next morning, she awoke to discover the pillowcase was wet. Had she been crying in her sleep? She had spent years grieving for her husband, her dead babies, and now it seemed the process of grieving for herself had begun. Necessary work, she supposed. The next day when she realized that going upstairs to the bedroom was proving to be too much of a chore for her, she decided to sleep on the sofa in her office. She lay there on her side staring out the bank of windows on the opposite wall. The moon was just past being full. Something told her she'd never see another full moon again. And the following morning, when she arose and did what she did every morning, got on the scale, she could no longer deny the gravity of her condition. She was down to eighty-seven pounds and as weak as a newborn kitten; it was time to ask for help.

Chapter 16

Savannah was in Denver when she got a phone call from her Aunt Susi; she canceled an appearance, dropped everything else, and breaking all speed limits, fled to her mother's side. By the time she got to Laramie, a mere few hours after the phone call, the light was fading. The horizon was the color of a fresh bruise. She pulled into the driveway parking next to another car that she didn't recognize. She assumed her aunt was using her mother's car, which would be in the garage, so evidently someone else was here already, yet it was too soon to be Austin or Dakota.

Susi was in the kitchen baking brownies. Savannah hugged her. "Why didn't you call me sooner, Aunt Susi? Never mind. I'll go up and see her now."

Her aunt took her hand and just held on to it. "The hospice nurse just got here, so give them a few minutes."

"Hospice!" Savannah tried to tug her hand out of her aunt's to get to her mother, but Susi held on.

"We need to talk." She drew Savannah over to the table, and they both sat, still holding hands. "You'll be shocked at what you see. Your mother's lost a lot of weight. She really can't even eat anymore."

Savannah, having a hard time processing, asked the first thing that came into her mind. "Then why are you baking brownies if you know she can't eat them?"

"She likes the smell of things. Yesterday she had me make spaghetti sauce because she loves the smell of the onion and garlic sautéing in the pan. She can't eat, but she can still smell the smells."

"Yesterday? How long have you been here?"

"Just a few days. When I got here, she had gotten so weak she could no longer go up and down the stairs to her room. I could see the handwriting on the wall, so I got a hold of hospice, and they got a hold of a hospital bed. We put it in her office, as that is her favorite room in the house. The bed is next to the bank of windows so she can look out to the backyard."

"Hospice?" Savannah was really having a hard time processing. "But that doesn't happen until the end. Surely she doesn't need hospice? Surely there are treatment options. What *are* the treatment options?"

"You are asking the same questions I did when I got here, but at this point, there are no options."

"At this point! Why didn't she call us sooner?"

"I don't know, Savvy. People make their choices, and it's up to us to respect those choices. Right now the only option we have is to make her comfortable, and that's what hospice is doing. She is on a morphine drip for the pain. That's where we are now."

Savannah just shook her head knowing that she would run screaming into the falling night if she didn't do something to pull herself back in control. For a moment her mind was completely blank. Then, giving herself a shake like a wet dog, she pulled herself back to the present and said, "I need to see my mother. Now."

She stood in the doorway of her mother's office listening to the hospice nurse talk to her mother in soft, soothing tones. "Would you like some music?"

"No, thank you." Grace's voice was barely above a whisper.

Unable to hold back a sob because her mother was nothing more than a sack of bones lying in a bed, Savannah entered the room and bent down to hug the woman who had given her life.

When Dakota arrived the next day, she was as shocked as Savannah had been. "But why is she so thin?" She stood in the kitchen with her aunt and her sister literally wringing her hands.

"Thin? I'd call that emaciated." Savannah shook her head.

"But how?" was all Dakota could think to ask.

"I think, as the cancer and the pain got beyond the point of bearable, she just couldn't eat anymore."

"We have to do something." Dakota was adamant.

"We have to honor the choice she's made." Susi was just as adamant.

When Austin arrived and he saw the condition his mother was in, he sided with his aunt. "How much time?" he wondered aloud.

Susi just shook her head.

Each one of the kids spent time alone with their mother. Grace wasn't in a mood to talk, so they finally accepted that simply holding her hand or reading aloud to her from one of her books was enough.

Grace lay on her side looking out the window. She could feel Austin's hand resting gently on her forearm. He was more patient and less demanding with her than the girls. They kept wanting to connect; he just let her be. She focused on sunbeams dancing on the windowsill. She then looked beyond them toward the sky. There it was again, a hawk that made the occasional appearance. It swooped down, making a figure eight before disappearing out of sight around the corner of the house. She was glad it hadn't been around that morning when she had seen that little rabbit bound across the lawn. Surely that would have been the end of the rabbit.

After supper on the second night there, they all sat in the living room holding vigil over a woman who was soon to die. Dakota was wiping tears off her cheeks. "She's so weak that she can't even swallow anymore. All that saliva just makes noise in her throat whenever she takes a breath."

"That's what they call the death rattle." Her aunt squeezed her hand. "She's been that way for the past couple of days. It won't be long now. Maybe another day at the most."

"She doesn't even want to talk to us. She will just smile when we go in there and then turn and look out the window."

"Don't take it personally, sweetie, she's just removing herself from this life and getting ready to move on to the afterlife. That's all."

Savannah, who had been staring out the window into the dusk that was fast becoming dark, turned toward her aunt and asked, "Do you want me to spend the night on the couch in the office tonight? You must be tired of sleeping in there."

"No, Savvy, she asked me to be the one to sleep there. She still has her pride. Doesn't want her kids to have to clean up after her, if you get my drift, it's a matter of respecting her dignity."

Savannah wondered aloud, "We were all here at Thanksgiving. Why didn't we notice anything wrong then?"

"Maybe if we'd come back for Christmas, we would have noticed something." Austin was thinking back. "But we were slated to go to Jill's parents for the holidays."

"And Daniel wanted me to meet his dad."

"I should have come, but the flu had laid me low, and as you guys weren't going to be here, I just skipped it." Savannah's voice held regret.

Grace heard low murmurs coming from the living room. Sad sounds in the twilight. Slowly she managed to pull herself into a sitting position. It took a Herculean effort, but she managed to do it. Just as slowly, she managed to stand beside the bed. She hadn't been out of it in days. She held on to the foot rail with one hand and her morphine drip pole with the other and managed to walk the few steps to her desk. She sat down in the chair at her desk just as the spots in front of her eyes were pooling into blackness. Dropping her head onto her arms which rested on the desk, she managed to push away the edges of faintness. The chair felt so familiar as to be almost an actual part of her body. With all the writing she'd done at this desk, if you added up all the hours she'd sat in this chair, the sum must literally be years. After a few breaths, she was able to lift her head and sit back in her chair.

Austin was saying, "I guess you'll be doing the eulogy, Savvy, being the oldest and used to speaking in public forums and all."

She was shaking her head before he'd even finished speaking. "People see me speaking and they think political platform. I don't want that at Mom's funeral. As the only son, you should do it."

"Not going to let you get away with that sexism. Besides, I'm not that great of a public speaker. I only do it when I can't get out of it."

"Which might be for your mother's eulogy."

"Hey, you two," Aunt Susi got their attention. "I think Dakota should do it."

"Me?"

"Yes, you. You were the one who really knew her best. You and she lived alone for years and formed a special bond. You guys"—she pointed to the other siblings—"have been gone forever."

"Well, it's not like I haven't been gone for years too."

"Still, I vote for you. What do you say, should we make it unanimous?"

Grace could feel the presence of her books on the shelves directly behind her. All her beloved books. Her desk was an L-shaped unit, her computer was to her right on the short end of the L. Turning toward it, she focused on her bulletin board on the wall above the computer. It was covered with snapshots, postcards, notes, flyers, all the minutia that represented the things and people she loved. Her eyes found a quote by Pablo Picasso that held the place of honor on the board. It said, "Inspiration exists, but it must find you working." She had certainly found that to be true. She would begin writing her articles and before she knew it, she had entered that special zone, that stream of consciousness place. When there, her fingers would just fly over the keyboard, and later when she reread what she had written, she often couldn't believe how good it was. Had all that come from her? Or had it more likely just come through her? Yes, inspiration must find you working for it to manifest.

Then there was a picture that Austin drew when he was in maybe fourth grade. The word *bang* was in bold block letters in the center of the page. Radiating out from it were pen and ink lines indicating an explosion, i.e., obviously the Big Bang. And in the far left bottom corner of the picture, a little spaceship skedaddled away from the event like a guilty child running away from the broken cookie jar on the kitchen floor. What an imagination her boy had!

The photograph of Barrett in his easy chair with Savannah on his lap and Austin sitting cross-legged on the floor in front of the chair always made her smile. Barrett was reading to them, a chapter from Scott O'Dell's *The Island of the Blue Dolphins*. Austin's expression was rapt, while Savannah was so cozy to the point of bliss in her father's lap.

And there was Shannon and Chelsea all dressed up for Easter, Austin holding their hands and striking a pose for the photo. Such adorable little girls. She remembered an Easter when she and Susi were all dolled up wearing scratchy dresses made of a dotted Swiss fabric. Hers had been lavender, and her sister's had been pink. She didn't have a picture of it, but she could recall it in her mind's eye. They'd had on little scalloped ankle socks and patent leather shoes. And white gloves too. And petticoats! She had forgotten petticoats, which had gone out of style so very long ago. Her eyes traveled over the bulletin board, and she found a picture of the two of them as adults, smiling from ear to ear sitting in a booth at Joselito's with Cadillac margaritas in front of them. She could never remember a time in her life when Susi wasn't a part of it.

Finally she focused on a photo of her two girls. It must have been taken at Dakota's graduation, but which one? College maybe? She couldn't remember. Dakota was sitting in a chair at the dining table cutting a celebratory cake, and Savannah was standing behind her, bending down and hugging Dakota. They were cheek to cheek and so lovely; two peas in a pod in coloring and both all smiles. Her girls. She turned toward her filing cabinet, and thanking her lucky stars that her chair was on casters, she slowly walk/rolled toward the cabinet. Finger walking through the file folders in one drawer, she found the one she was looking for and, rummaging through it, pulled out a letter.

Susi stood stock still in the doorway when she'd entered the room to see if Grace was all settled in for the night or if she needed water. The bed was empty, and Grace was sitting in her office chair next to her filing cabinet. The drawer was open, and Grace held a letter in her hand. Closing the door behind her, Susi queried in a low voice, "What on *God's green earth* are you doing?" She flew to her sister's side.

Grace slowly folded the letter she'd been reading. Pointing to the stack of envelopes that were on one of the shelves beside her, she asked, "Would you?" The words were barely a whisper.

Susi handed her an envelope. "Do you want me to mail another letter for you?"

Grace shook her head as she tried to slip the letter into the envelope but failed. Holding both out to Susi, she asked, "Would you?"

Susi tucked the letter into the envelope and handed it back to Grace, who slowly fingered the file folders until she found the one she wanted. Tucking the letter deep into the file, she gave the drawer a push to close it. Again she failed.

"Let me." Susi closed the drawer and then helped Grace back to bed. "There. By the way, that letter you had me mail to Savannah after I got here probably didn't arrive until after she left to come here."

"Oh well," Grace barely mouthed the words.

"Do you want the kids to come in and say good night?" Grace just gave her head a small shake. "They wanted me to ask. I told them you were probably already asleep."

"Thank you." Her lips moved, but no sound emerged. Then she closed her eyes and turned her head away.

Well, Susi thought to herself, *that is a pretty clear statement.* She kissed her sister's forehead and, opening the office door, slipped out of the room.

When the kids had all gone up to their respective bedrooms, Susi changed into her nightie in the bathroom, brushed her teeth, and pulled on her robe. She wandered around downstairs in the darkened house. Grace had loved this older home. It was the perfect place to raise her kids, and she could never say enough good things about it. Barrett had bought it because it reminded him of his childhood home in New Hampshire. In fact, his older sister had still lived in that home until her death, which had come many years after Barrett's death. Barrett had been gone for such a long time, and now Grace was following suit. The kids were going to be orphaned, as happens to everyone sooner or later. Thank goodness they were adults.

Susi tiptoed into the office and lay down on the sofa, pulling a blanket up as the night was chilly. Lying on her side, she watched her sister inhale and exhale in her sleep, the rattle still apparent as it had been the past couple of days.

What?

Something got her attention. She must have drifted off but was now fully awake, staring into the dark. It was then that she heard it clear as a bell tone, the almost harsh sound of the last breath. It was a whoosh as if something was forcefully passing out of the body and into the night. Grace's soul? Susi got up and felt for a pulse. Nothing. No pulse, no more breaths. It was over. She spent a few moments alone with her sister then went up to awaken the kids and let them know.

It had happened before any of them was ready for it; their mother had passed on to a new journey, and they arranged for her funeral.

Dakota gave the eulogy. Standing at the pulpit in front of the church they rarely attended, Dakota looked out at their friends and family. She found Daniel sitting in the first row. He had arrived the day before. Giving her a small smile and a nod of his head for encouragement, Dakota began: "One of my mother's favorite symbols was the yin-yang circle that is representative of a dynamic system. The symbol is half black and half white with an S-shaped line separating the two halves. The black symbolizes the feminine and the shadow, the white masculine and light. But within each is a splash of the other. So the black side contains a small circle of white in it and vice versa. That is because they are interrelated. Neither can exist without the other. These forces are complementary, not opposing. My mother told me she was particularly drawn to that symbol because it drove home the point that we are all a blend of light and shadow. No one is just one or the other, no one is perfect, and knowing that, she taught her children that it's easier to forgive someone his or her missteps. A valuable lesson to learn.

"Authenticity is a word that describes my mother because with Grace, what you saw was what you got. There was never any pretense. Abdication of responsibility was a big no-no for Grace. She was both a pacifist and a warrior, both funny and profound, rarely ever stern, and always energetic. Mom was all of that. Grace had a talent for living in the moment, and while once in a while she could zing out a bitingly sarcastic comment, usually she was a straight shooter telling you like it was. She lived in harmony with her surroundings and courted quietude.

"When I was a teenager and out for the evening, my mother always left a light burning for me. That symbol of a light in the window welcoming weary travelers was so representative of my mother. She was like that, a light, a welcoming beacon. I learned a lot about travel at my mother's knee. For Grace, travel had a mystique about it. Expanding one's horizons with travel was more than an education for her, she believed it enriched a person. It gave definition to a life. And simultaneously, it expanded one's psyche as well. She always believed that travel was the best teacher. My mother was one of those rare happy, content people. She enjoyed each day as it came. I don't know how long it took her to learn how to do that. For many of us, life isn't as easy as she made it look. But she was a fine example of living life the way one ought to. Grace taught us how to be ourselves. One thing she taught me in particular was not to be passive, not to let life happen to me." She looked first at Savannah and then Austin before continuing. "All of her children became doers. We went out there and did things. And she was proud of all of us.

"I'll end with a little children's verse that exemplifies my mother's life in a nutshell: 'Row, row, row your boat gently down the stream. Merrily, merrily, merrily, merrily life is but a dream.' If life is the dream, Grace is now awake. And I find myself speculating what wonders she's awakened to. And I also hope someone left the light on for her to welcome her home. Happy travels, Grace Quinn, your new journey has begun."

Chapter 17

Savannah finished reading a letter her mother had written not so very many months ago. She tossed her reading glasses across the broad expanse of her desk and sighed. She and her mom hadn't always seen eye to eye when it came to politics, but on this particular topic, they really did. Savannah did her best thinking when looking out her window, and right now she was doing just that. A fat little robin perched on the lattice archway in the garden snagged her attention. The bird too was looking off into the middle distance, and Savannah wondered what he was thinking. Do robins think? She had read somewhere that crows will grieve when their mate dies. So if birds could feel, surely they could think too. So maybe the robin was thinking about something lofty? Well, where had all those thoughts come from?

She'd be flying to DC tonight on the red-eye as they still had three weeks to go before the August recess. And when she got there, she would be, as usual, hitting the ground running. In fact, Savannah always hit the ground running. When she was in Denver, by 5:30 a.m. she was out the door, power walking; by 6:30 a.m., she was back home fixing her oatmeal for breakfast; at 7:00 a.m. she was in her office awaiting the call from her chief of staff based in Washington, who would have preferred to Face Time, but as Savannah didn't, they used the phone. The landline phone. Not so very long ago her chief of staff, once again, had chided her. "Why are you so stubborn about getting a smartphone? Not only would I have twenty-four-seven access to you, but you'd have access to the world in the palm of your hand and wouldn't have to rely on me as much."

Savannah didn't want to go into all that she had gleaned over the years from Austin regarding how easy it was to access a person's information via their smartphones or computers. He regaled her once about this password-cracking software that was so proficient it could make over a billion guesses per second. And she knew he was speaking as the voice of experience. That's why she did so much by hand, the old-fashioned way. But in answer to her staffer's question, she simply queried, "Is your job becoming too much for you, Beatrice? Do I need to find a new chief of staff?" That had stopped the questions regarding her choices.

But it wasn't just her chief of staff that gave her grief on that subject. It drove Dakota crazy that Savannah wasn't big on social media. Dakota told her, "The benefit of social media is that it gets the information out there in record time. You need to take advantage of that."

"But you only get the information if you are hooked into social media. What of all the people who aren't? They don't get the information."

"That group is fewer and fewer each year," Dakota pointed out.

Certainly that may be true, and maybe someday she'd have to connect herself into the social media outlets, but for now Savannah just felt more comfortable not being sucked in to all that. And that they had a president that Twittered, well, how ridiculous was that?

And just thinking about the current president and the crazy times in which they lived had a sentence dropping out of the sky and into her head. She jotted it down quickly. "There are times in history when the potential for heroic measures abound. This is one of those times." Reading what she'd just written, she nodded. Not bad. It might be the kernel of a speech to come.

Each morning while waiting for the call from her chief of staff, she'd write her daily to-do list. *Prioritize* was her watchword. She'd write it at the top of her piece of paper each day and let the list evolve from there. This morning before she'd started her list, and because she'd noticed the banker's box of her mom's letters and articles in her office, she had decided to read a letter or an article each morning before she moved on with the rest of her day. That the one she read this morning had to do with politics set just the right tone for her upcoming day. Who knew when she'd moved away from home to go to college that she'd end up a politician!

Savannah had barely gotten her feet wet as a junior congresswoman when Gabrielle Giffords was shot in an assassination attempt. Six people died that day, and another thirteen were wounded during the attack. Savannah had been shaken to the core after Gabby, as her friends called her, had been shot. But she knew if she let fear in, it would cripple her. She needed to keep on keeping on or all would be lost. After the attack, Grace wrote to her daughter:

> *It's such a worry...you, a rising young politician, and on top of that, Dakota has decided to become a teacher, certainly influenced by memories of your father, adds to that worry. Both of you girls in professions where psychos might use you for target practice. I realize your goal is to make the country, the world, a better place. You look people in the eye, you really, really listen to them; for you it is a high calling, and you don't take the responsibility lightly. But with that beautiful young congresswoman being shot, I'm beginning to think the country is broken beyond repair. I see you working so hard to make a difference, and I am reminded of that little Dutch Boy with his finger in the dike.*

Well, Savannah wasn't the only one with her finger in the dike. There were many, many who, to mix a metaphor, worked hard to keep this ship afloat. She intended to keep working hard. It was all she knew. It was all she'd ever done.

She recalled writing back to her mother:

> *Yes, the attack on Gabby certainly sent a bolt of fear through those who know her. But if you let it, fear can be paralyzing. If people live their life in fear, nothing gets done. It's my job to rub shoulders with*

the voters, to listen to them. I can't be afraid to do my job or it won't get done.

That message became the heart of a message in a speech she delivered at a commencement ceremony. That speech went on to say, "Partisan bickering undermines all of us. We need to buckle down and do our jobs and work at providing a better life then the generation before and offer it with both hands to the generation that follows, hoping they will do the same. Leaving the world a better place than we found it is a tall order, but it is something we must strive to achieve." Oh yes, she took her job seriously.

When the press described Savannah, they used words like *eloquent, enthusiastic, idealist, charismatic, poised.*

She'd plotted her course long before she ran for office. All that volunteer work had been the foundation. When she was in college, she volunteered for Planned Parenthood. Her empathy and compassion made her a good candidate for working with the young women who came to the center, often after it was too late to prevent conception. "Your life is not over," she had counseled more than one distraught woman. "You just need to look at your options. And there is more than one option." She'd made a real difference in those years, not just counseling, but raising money. Donations were the life blood that kept Planned Parenthood going, and she discovered she had a talent for raising money.

This past year Savannah had fought so hard against the cuts the Senate had recently passed. The defunding of Planned Parenthood centers across the nation would be the worst blow to women's health legislation in decades. Losing access to health care would be devastating for these disenfranchised women. The extremists in Congress working to gut health care, Wendy Greene in particular, made her blood boil. Wendy, her nemesis, was a beefy woman, and while it made her feel just a little bit catty that she'd even noticed that, it was still a fact: she was beefy. It seemed if Savannah was for a bill, Wendy worked hard against it. And conversely, if she was against passing certain legislation, Wendy went to bat for it. Savannah knew it was just that their political ideologies were polar opposites, yet it seemed that Wendy was always out to undermine anything she fought for—above all, quality health care for women. Yes, being a civic volunteer at a local Planned Parenthood center focusing on women's health had been the beginning for her and it continued to remain one of her major focuses. But volunteering there hadn't been the only thing that set her on the path to Washington.

After law school, she volunteered in a different capacity as a legal aid. She fully believed in free legal services for low-income people, and for a couple of years she thought she'd found her niche in life. She helped battered wives obtain a divorce. She helped families avoid property tax foreclosures. She prevented nursing home evictions, and that was when Savannah really broadened her concerns from the young women at Planned Parenthood to the growing senior population. One elderly woman in particular, who was still living at home on a fixed income, came to her with a notice from the electric company. "They are getting ready to shut off my 'lectricity service." The woman's hand shook as she proffered the notice, whether from nervousness or age, Savannah hadn't been sure. The end result of that consultation was that Savannah became a pro at preventing utility shutoff for the elderly. Seniors were the largest growing group of people. There were now more people over sixty-five years of age then there were people under the age of five. That the country needed to take responsibility for this group of citizens was also a major focus for her.

And during her volunteer years, when the point was driven home to her again and again that a lot of these people at both Planned Parenthood and in her legal aid office were illiterate, well, she began a literacy program that over the years had evolved into a foundation. Reading comprehension was key to being a success in life. Savannah would sit with the people she was trying to help, listening to their lack of fluency when they haltingly made their way through the page of a children's book. Reading haltingly limited comprehension, and so it was necessary to become fluent. But how to do that? Limited was the operative word. Limited vocabulary and limited background knowledge were stumbling blocks that needed to be removed to aid in literacy. That even today more than 25 percent of third graders fail to meet state reading standards, well, she still had her work cut out in this literacy area.

Years ago, when Savannah had decided she was ready to run for the state legislature, she wore her knuckles raw knocking on all those doors. She was pretty sure she had knocked on every door in her district. And what an eye-opening shock that had been for her. She'd peeked into doorways that often revealed brief glimpses of loss, pain, despair, and anguish. Her heart went out to her people, and she was determined to do what she could to help make their lives better. And to do that, she needed to win the election. She knew the way to win was to get the people to know who she was and that she was running for office. She knew she had to talk to the people and to let them talk to her. She would speak to any group that would ask her to speak. And then the leap from state to federal, her drive and ambition provided the momentum, and she just kept moving forward. She had certainly traveled far since those early days. And her commute to Washington and back certainly had her feeling as if she were always on the go.

The fact that she'd just barely won the last election was a bit of a sore spot with her. The current president's campaign hadn't helped her campaign at all. Her former supporters began jumping ship, and it had been a battle down to the last minute on election day. That she had just barely squeaked by to win was bad enough, but when the losing candidate had demanded a recount of the vote, well, what a few stressful days that had been.

The ringing phone brought her back to the present. She had a pencil in her hand and a legal yellow pad in front of her. "Go," she told her chief of staff, and her day evolved from there.

*   *   *   *   *

It wasn't so very late in the day when Savannah got home, but she was as exhausted as if she had just run a marathon. She stepped out of her shoes and left them in the entryway. The bra came off next;

she unhooked it and pulled it off through one of her sleeves. Entering the kitchen, she tossed the bra toward a closed door, which was the adjoining laundry room, then poured herself a glass of wine. From there she padded into the living room and sank into the welcoming cushions of her favorite chair. She took her first sip and closed her eyes with a contented sigh.

Those Girl Scouts had been as sharp as a box full of little tacks. When she'd been asked to come and talk to the local troop, she readily agreed. And that they were all third and fourth graders was a bonus. She loved seeing fresh, interested faces looking up at her like little flowers opening up to the sun. Thinking back, she figured they must have been coached as they asked really good question. Or maybe it wasn't that they were coached but that their scout leader had actually taught them about the government in preparation for her visit.

One little girl started it all off by asking her, "What does a congresswoman do?"

Savannah was prepared for that one as it was the first question she got no matter what the venue. "Imagine if we were a country without laws," she told the girls. "What might happen if we didn't have any laws?"

They had certainly nailed the answer. Robberies, murders, violence was at the top of their list. But some kids realized that even if we didn't have traffic laws, things could get pretty chaotic on the roads too. The ensuing conversation with the kids was quite entertaining. When they had run out of steam on that subject, she told them, "That's what it might be like here if we didn't have Congress and congressmen and women like me."

"But what is your actual job?" That same first little girl was not to be deterred.

"To represent my constituents. That's you. My duty is to represent the people who elected me. That would be you, or actually your parents. I must keep *your* interests up front when I vote to accept or deny passing a law."

"And you make laws we want?" another little girl asked.

"Yes. When we congresswomen and men meet in Washington, DC, many different bills are offered to us to discuss before they become law. Not all of them will become law."

"How do you decide?"

"Well, we study the bills carefully. To do that, we form committees. Each committee looks at bills on one topic, such as farming or environment. If the committee is pleased with the bill, they present it to all the other congresswomen and men. If all of the representatives like it, it passes and goes on to the president to be signed into law."

It had been a fun albeit exhausting afternoon. Oh boy, was she glad it was over!

When she caught herself nodding off, Savannah stood up instead and stretched. It was time to pack her carry-on and head on out to catch the red-eye heading east. Her commute between Denver and Washington, and Washington and Denver, then Denver and Washington again, there must be a rut in the sky between the two places she traveled that route so often. And when she resided at that point between departure and destination—in the air flying—she imagined it akin to being in a womb. It was sometimes a place where she could sleep, but not always. When she couldn't sleep, it was a place to think outside the parameters of there or there. It was simply here and now, a suspension that she could only enjoy to the fullest if the person sitting next to her respected her desire not to visit. She sure hoped she didn't end up with a chatterbox beside her tonight.

Chapter 18

Dakota plopped the suitcase on the bed and opened it up. The empty suitcase made her smile. She strove to live her life according to one precept of the Dalai Lama's. He said, "Once a year go someplace you've never been before." Seeking out new experiences, traveling to new places, it was in her DNA, thanks to her mother.

Dakota laid out piles of jeans, tops, underwear, and other items on the bed next to the suitcase. Remembering her mom's winter hat, she tossed that on the pile too. A seasoned traveler, Dakota was a wiz at packing light. Usually. But the hiking boots, the rain pants to pull on over regular jeans, and her heavy hooded jacket for the colder weather they were sure to encounter in Iceland had her rethinking and repacking twice. How the heck was she going to squeeze everything that she needed into one suitcase?

Standing back and realizing that the suitcase was definitely going to bulge when it was zipped up had Dakota reconsidering. Did she really need to take three pairs of jeans? Wouldn't two be enough? Or even one? That would give her a little more room. As it was, there was no room for her cosmetics bag, which had her rethinking taking any cosmetics at all. They were going to be hiking on a glacier. She didn't need to put on foundation, blush, and mascara for that. Okay, no makeup. That decided, she put moisturizer and sunscreen in a zip lock baggie, tossed that in the suitcase, and she was done. She hoped.

Daniel entered the room. "Here, don't forget the sleep mask." He tossed it in her direction, and she caught it with one hand. "The sun won't be setting the whole time we're there. I've already packed mine."

"Oh, honey, I don't think I'll need this."

"Sure you will. You just don't know it yet."

"Really? How do you know *you'll* want one?"

"How do you know *you* won't?"

She tried logic. "I don't need one when I take an occasional nap in the afternoon. The sun's out then, and I can still sleep."

When he gave her an exasperated look, Dakota heaved a sigh and tucked it in next to her mother's hat. "Okay, okay." She doubted she'd need the sleep mask, but she didn't want this to evolve into a tiff.

To change the subject, Daniel asked, "Read any good letters by your mother lately?"

"Actually, yes." She started taking things out of her suitcase to repack it. "Only it was one written to her, not by her."

"And?"

"And." She paused what she was doing and gave him a considering look. "It was probably the most romantic letter I can ever remember reading. Which brings up a question. Why haven't you ever written *me* a love letter?"

"Say what?" He looked over his shoulder like he should be making a getaway while he could.

"Love letters, they're a thing of the past. I think it's a shame nobody commits their love to paper anymore."

To deflect the direction of the conversation, Daniel said, "So tell me about this *oh so romantic letter* written to your mom."

"Well, it was written on notebook paper in pencil, and based on the content I surmised, it was from when Mom was in college. There was no context for the letter, so I kind of did some daydreaming and came up with a plausible backstory so the letter would make sense."

"This sounds fun. Give me the backstory then tell me about the letter."

"Well, the first line in the letter is two words; 'Green monstrosity?'"

"Wait, wait, wait! Didn't you say this was a love letter?"

"A romantic letter."

"Okay, so how does a green monstrosity equate to romance?" He sat down on the bed while she repacked the suitcase.

"That's where my backstory comes into play. It seems like the green monstrosity in question was a vehicle like a car or truck or van. Here's what I think happened prior to the letter being written. Mom was walking to school. This guy driving this ugly green vehicle pulls up to her and offers her a ride. She refuses to get into the *'green monstrosity.'* With me so far?"

Daniel nods. "With you."

"So she continues on to class, and he is not wealthy, based on the old beat-up vehicle he drives, so he is working in the library between classes to make some money. So Mom's class goes to the library to do research, and he is at the circulation desk. She walks past him, and because he is so smitten, he tears a piece of paper out of his notebook, grabs a pencil, and writes her this letter. As she walks past the circulation desk to leave the library after her class is over, he hands her the letter. That's my backstory."

"Okay, now I need to hear about the letter."

"Hang on." Dakota went into their home office, plucked the letter off her desk, and returned to the bedroom. "Listen… *Dearest Miss Blizzard—*"

"Stop there! 'Miss Blizzard'? Your mom's maiden name was Blizzard? I didn't know that."

"No reason why you would. Do you want me to go on?"
"Please."

Dearest Miss Blizzard,
  Green monstrosity?
  Would not a more accurate description be that of a superior mechanical instrument that is aesthetically pleasing, delightful, agreeable to the senses, and worthy of possession? Surely you hold no negative response for the only automobile, the only well-integrated unit of metal, rubber, glass, cloth, and plastic etc. that since 1951, when its glorious life began, has longed to have your bod as its passenger. Your extraordinary curvier linear properties placed in my

truck has been its ideal goal, and it has attempted to direct all its endeavors to this single purpose.

Would you deny my tuck and I the honor of your presence? Would you condemn that humble servant born to transport a buyer BUT TRANSFORMED *by your exquisite beauty and melting charm, to be your waiting chariot, your vehicle to life's worthiest destinations, your soft white cloud for ascending to lofty heaven's euphoria?*

Would you refuse to be sealed as a queen in the throne that has tried so long in vain to spin its wheels into your heart, to cleanse and soothe your luscious bod with its aromatic oils, and to thrust its pistons into—to put it's—to have it's pistons beat for you alone? Would you?

Surely such a lovely and generous goddess could not refuse this truck's humble request.

If he be green, then the color of reflected radiance of all the planet's life is contained within its warm, comforting walls and eagerly awaits your arrival.

And if he be green, then surely your swift ride in my truck shall be that of a leaf's journey propelled by gentle zephyrs floating to the earth to rest. If my truck be green and not in favor with your perception in beauty of hue, then grant its request that the green shroud might be lifted and replaced by the loveliest shade of blue, your eyes, or the soft warm color of your silky hair or the fresh pure splendor of your smile—surely the reincarnation of Helen's or Simonetta's that inspired Botticelli's Birth of Venus *or* Primavera. *Regardless of hue my green monstrosity's motor wishes no longer to be idle but rather to accelerate to the confirmation of your consent. Run away with me, Miss Blizzard.*

Yours in BURNING *passion,*
Wayne

For a moment there were no words spoken, then Daniel said, "You're right, that was romantic. The prose was a little purple, but even getting past the flowery writing, it seemed sincere. Do you think they ever got together?"

"I have no idea."

"I mean, she kept the letter all these years. It must have meant something to her."

"Maybe, but she kept *all* letters, so who knows."

"True, but this letter, I wonder what happened after she read it. I mean, you constructed a backstory, but what about what happens next? Did she go back into the library after reading the letter, and did they end up in a relationship?"

"I wish I knew."

"Grace never mentioned this Wayne guy when you were growing up?"

She shook her head. "It's a mystery. We'll likely never know."

Daniel, like a terrier with a bone, wasn't one to give up on something. "Maybe your Aunt Susie knows. Give her a call and ask her."

"That's an idea." Any excuse to be detoured from her repacking, she pulled out her phone and rang her aunt, who just happened to be handy. Dakota asked her about Wayne.

"Wayne, she never dated anybody named Wayne."

"Really?" She told her aunt about the letter. "It sounded like he was hot for her."

"So read me the letter." Dakota did. "Oh, yes, that guy, I remember now. No, they never dated. Grace was really bookish back in the day, intent on her studies, and not inclined to get sidetracked with the boy-girl thing. Oh, she'd go out with groups of friends, but not just one guy. Not until she met your father did she ever take the bull by the horns, so to speak."

"Wow. So I kind of feel sorry for Wayne. Sounds like he was pining away with this unrequited love thing."

"Sad story," her aunt went on. "He got over Grace and was dating a friend of mine. Lovely girl whose name I can't recall. Anyway, he had gone hiking in the mountains one day—alone—climbing up sheer sides of cliffs. Stuff like that. He fell, hit his head, and landed facedown in a little trickle of water. Drowned."

"You're kidding!" Dakota was appalled. "That is so horrible!"

"Some forest service guy spotted Wayne's vehicle parked in the same spot it had been for, well, I don't know how long. He investigated and found Wayne's body."

"How old was he when that happened?"

"I don't know. Maybe all of twenty."

"So he would have been nineteen or so when he wrote the letter to Mom?"

"I guess so."

"How tragic."

"I guess you could call it tragic."

"Well, it was tragic, Aunt Susie. Here was the young man, obviously bright and educated, at least according to his letter, and to die so young."

"You've heard the saying 'Only the good die young.'"

"Yes, I have." After a moment's consideration, Dakota added, "I'll tell you what an additional tragedy is, Aunt Susie. Not one of my students at the academy could write the equivalent of this letter at nineteen. Oh sure, there were a couple of grammatical errors in it. But overall it was so amazing. My students wouldn't even know the allusions Wayne made in the letter, let alone be able to use them correctly in a letter of their own."

"Just one more indictment of the public educational system in the country."

"I hear you."

"Hey, Call Waiting just buzzed, got to go. Have fun in Iceland."

As Dakota finished packing, her thoughts turned to young love. Love, of course, being one of the great themes of literature. Had this Wayne been desperately in love with her mother? Had her mother's cool indifference broken his heart? Had her mother ever thought back to that fork in the road that she did not take? And then she wondered about forks in the road she hadn't taken and those she had. The fork in the road that had led her to Daniel was one of the best choices she had ever made.

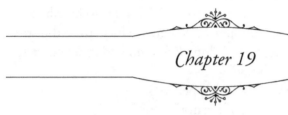

Chapter 19

Unlike a lot of modern families, Austin and Jill did agree that sitting down to a family dinner was one of the important things when it came to raising kids. No television, no phones, nothing but family eating and conversing with one another was on the agenda each suppertime. Mostly their conversations were mundane: What did you do in school today? Did you sell any Girl Scout cookies this weekend? Where do you want to go this summer for our family vacation? Don't forget to clean up your room before you head out for your sleepover. But every now and then they got into interesting topics, and those times made all the other sit-down meals worth it.

Tonight they could hear rain pattering against the window panes, giving them a nice, cozy indoor feeling. And the rain was very welcome as fires always blazed in the state this time of year. Hopefully the rain was widespread enough to help extinguish some of them.

Austin had been regaling the family about an occurrence at work.

"Speaking of work." Chelsea was scrunching up her face, which was what she did when she was thinking hard. "Are we rich?"

Austin bit his lip to keep from grinning at her. "What makes you ask that?"

"I don't know, are we?"

"We're...comfortable."

"'Cause if we're rich, how come we live like poor people?"

"What?"

"I mean, you make us make our beds and do the dishes, and if we are rich, why don't we have somebody doing that stuff?"

Austin sighed then told the family, "The best, most productive years in this country were when we had a strong middle class, which we don't anymore. Those middle-class people had values. Just because we no longer have a strong middle class, those values are still valuable, and I'll be damned if I will raise a couple of kids who shun those values. So you will pull weeds, make your beds, feed the dog, and etc. You are able-bodied girls, and you will learn the values that will turn you into well-grounded adults. Got it?"

Shannon kicked her sister under the table. Getting her attention, Shannon shook her head at her. "Sorry you asked?"

Chelsea wrinkled her nose at her sister.

"No one should ever be sorry for asking a question," Austin responded.

Since Shannon had her dad's attention, she decided to strike while the iron was hot and, once again, broached a sore subject. "So when are we going to be able to get our own phones?"

"Not for a while."

"But everyone has a phone. All our friends. We're like the oddballs."

"When you're older." And that tone of voice meant the subject was closed. Good Lord, was history repeating itself? He remembered having a discussion similar to this with his parents about getting a computer. He looked up to see Jill shaking her head at him. "What?"

"They aren't a couple of little Rapunzels. You can't lock them in a tower to protect them. Even if you did, you know how the story goes. Some prince would come along and help get them out."

Chelsea was frowning. "I don't need any prince to protect me!" She stood up and executed a spin, a kick, and a couple of punches in the air with her little dimpled fists.

Austin's impression with the little Tae Kwon Do demonstration notwithstanding, pointed to her chair. "Sit down and finish your broccoli."

She complied and picked up a little tree with her fingers and took a little nibble. Slanting a look at her mom, she said, "I like it better when it has cheese sauce on it."

"It's better for you without the cheese sauce."

"But—"

"But nothing," Jill cut in. "You can have cheese sauce on your broccoli on a special occasion."

"Like my birthday?"

"Sure. Now eat up. After you girls get the dishwasher loaded, if the rain lets up, we can head on over to Penney's and do some back-to-school shopping."

"And if we had smartphones," Shannon wasn't going to let that go, "we could do our shopping online."

"And *you* eat *your* broccoli."

The entire family could hear Shannon's fork tines clink against the plate as she stabbed the vegetable in question.

*   *   *   *   *

After tucking the kids into bed, Austin decided to get some work done. He flicked on the light in his home office then stood in the doorway. There it was, the box of his mother's writings. Sheesh. Not particularly in the mood for it, but not wanting all the reading he was supposed to be doing to get away from him, he decided there was no time like the present to finish up the trilogy he had started ages ago. After reading the first two parts of the Wyoming material, he had changed things up a bit and read some of the letters she'd written to him over the years. They were entertaining and blessedly short as she knew he didn't really have a long attention span when it came to things like that. Tonight, he settled in to read part three of the Wyoming articles his mother had written rather than do what he had come into the office to do. This one was entitled "Wildlife."

It didn't take long to finish, and the article reminded him of his own experiences with wildlife in Wyoming. There was that time he had gone hunting during antelope season with a friend of his and that guy's dad. His own father wasn't a hunter, and truth be told, he really wasn't either. But he was glad to have had the experience. He laughed at the memory of lining up the shot and pulling the trigger. There had been four antelope running one after the other: *running* being the operative word as they were swift. He had aimed for the lead antelope and pulled the trigger and waited and waited and watched as the fourth one crumpled and fell; so much for his marksmanship. But at least he didn't go home empty-handed, and the antelope steaks they had for dinner that winter were delicious. And the passages in the article about the reintroduction of wolves into Yellowstone had him remembering when that happened back when he was a kid. He also recalled reading something very recently about how the wolves reintroduced to Yellowstone back in 1995 has resulted in rebalancing the ecosystem in a much more far-reaching way than anyone could even have guessed when the experiment was first launched.

Austin had to admit that he found all his mother's articles on Wyoming interesting. But as his roots there had never been deep, he could also admit to himself that he didn't feel all that nostalgic when he read them. Or not completely, anyway. He had become a Californian, and while not born and bred in the state, well, most Californians were originally from somewhere else too, so he was in excellent company.

Putting the reading aside, he settled down in front of his computer and, deciding to check his email, discovered Dee had finally sent him some of the pictures she and Daniel had taken when they were in Iceland. That brought a smile to his face; he liked to live vicariously through her experiences. Oh, he took short family vacations and business trips, but actual journeys, not so much, unless you count journeying into cyberspace. Austin had spent most of his youth, and all his adult life, exploring the geography of cyberspace. That the internet had eclipsed anything that had ever come before was an understatement. Maybe Gutenberg and his printing press, which ushered in the Renaissance and the rebirth of learning, came close. Riding the crest of the wave of the technological tsunami was his passion and his job, and when the company he worked for went public and his stock quadrupled overnight, well, he never imagined he'd be rich, but he was now beyond stinkin' rich.

In the early years, to Austin cyberspace was a place to travel even a place to dream. Yes, cyberspace was where he went to get away. It was more than an information superhighway. A person could lose himself in cyberspace. The conventional rules of time, space, and physics didn't apply in that wonderland. You didn't have to walk to get from place to place. All you had to do was click a mouse, and *poof*, you were transported from one locale to another as easily as that. He had been young when he began a serious exploration of cyberspace; in fact, he and the internet had kind of grown up together. It was a place where you could try out different personas, be whoever you wanted to be, and no one was any the wiser. You could put on a mask, and no one knew who you were. But as he matured, he always suspected at some point that if one wasn't careful that the man became the mask, and that might not be a good thing. So rather than succumbing to the drug that surfing the internet could become, Austin learned early on to rely on detached objectivity when in this new environment. By the time he was out of adolescence, he was through with experimentation with alternate personalities in cyberspace. He had grown up, and he had more important work to do.

And as he matured and worked in the milieu he'd chosen for a career, he gained a healthy respect for all the things that could happen to people who didn't know how to traverse the boundless net. And when the dark net became a strong and ever-present reality, he knew that the mythic battle between good and evil had found its way even to this arena. He, like so many others in his field, enrolled his children in a private school that shunned electronics. No computers, no phones. Ironic? Not really. It was like that baby food mogul who refused to feed his children his product when his kids were babies because he knew firsthand how bad it was for them. Austin and his colleagues knew the evil that could befall children who got sucked into the world of electronics, and they weren't about to let that happen to their children.

His mother had probably been right. She had always treated her computer with mistrust, even suspicion. "That machine is out to get me!" were often her words of greeting when she called him with a computer problem. And the truth was if people weren't careful or knowledgeable, the machine could indeed be the tool that "got them." It had become so easy to steal a person's identity now. And that was just the tip of the iceberg.

When the phrase *The ghost in the machine* first came into being, it depicted the dualism of the fact that the human mind existed independently from the human brain. As far as computers, when the machine behaved with a will that was independent from the programmer's desire, well, there might be a ghost in *that* machine too. Little surprises happened often enough in his work that Austin did wonder about a, well, not a ghost per se, but a power greater than oneself that moved across the deep of cyberspace seeing to things. He wasn't exactly an agnostic. He hadn't discounted the idea of a God entirely. He did believe in something. But considering the state of the world, he often considered the fact that God could just as easily be malevolent as benevolent, and that possibility left him unsettled. And when unexpected and unexplained *things* happened in his work, he pondered the whys and hows and never really came to any satisfactory conclusions.

When Austin was growing up, he knew his mother had always worried that, with his all-encompassing interest in computers, his social skills would suffer. She'd tell him, "All that technology stuff doesn't serve as a substitute for real life." But he liked his solitary work, and the fact that the human element was removed from so much of what he did and what went on out there in the mysterious workings of the internet sucked him in. Austin knew firsthand and all too well the seductive and addicting qualities of cyberspace. That he had the fortitude to rise above an addiction and turn his knowledge into his life's work wasn't something everyone had the ability to do.

And yet, working with artificial intelligence had resulted in more than one sleepless night for him. He often had internal debates and worked diligently to stay on the side of what was best for humanity. He'd ask himself, will humans have to take a back seat as these intelligent thinking machines outthink their makers? He'd ponder the difference between information and intelligence. He'd read somewhere that it's wisdom, not knowledge that's important. Wisdom is what is needed to determine if knowledge is used properly. Artificial intelligence surely could never be wise. Could it?

On the one hand, he fully believed that machines were in fact as intelligent as the majority of the human population. But that was only part of the equation. What distinguished humankind from the machines were unconscious instincts. Those instinct Austin felt were one of the things that divided human intelligence from artificial intelligence; those instincts were something that couldn't be duplicated by a computer.

Austin had carved out a life for himself and his family, and mostly, that life was good. And it turned out that being a family man was a journey in and of itself as well. In the years before the kids (he could barely remember them—he thought of them as the Barbie-and-Ken years), life had been first-rate. Then suddenly it wasn't. When Jill became pregnant with Shannon, she metamorphosed into a different woman than the one he'd married. At first he blamed it on pregnancy hormones, but after the baby was born, she never again turned back into the woman he had married, which was a shame. But his kids, wow, what could he say, they were his absolute pride and joy. From the moment the wiggling little bundles had been placed in his arms, he'd never known he was capable of that much love and awe. They were smart and clever, and they were growing up so fast, too fast. Shannon had a deep and questioning mind. She was sure to become some kind of scientist. Just last week at the supper table, she had asked about one of her observations. "It is just so interesting that when bread or cake or brownies go stale that they get hard and dried out, but when cookies, like Mom's gingersnaps go stale, they get soft and mushy. I wonder why that is?"

And then there was his adorable little Chelsea, who was an active bundle of energy. Recently she had balked at helping her mother pull weeds because she refused to believe a dandelion was a weed. "But it looks like a flower. It is a flower, and they are pretty and fun when they get puffy. And we make wishes when we blow on them."

"Yes, and make even more dandelions when you do that." Her mother's comeback didn't quell Chelsea's stubbornness. Crossing her little arms, she also dug in her heels; she wasn't about to help with the weeding. After locking horns, they had finally agreed on a compromise, that Chelsea would help keep the dandelions at bay in the font yard, and they would let them flourish in the backyard. Problem solved. And when Chelsea wasn't around, Jill went out back and dug up the majority of dandelions leaving only a few, so Chelsea wasn't any the wiser.

And Shannon, as far as her chores went, was a sly older sister. She was pretty good at Tom Sawyering her sister into whitewashing any number of fences for her. One thing Austin tried to instill in his children was that each person was defined by their actions. That lesson hadn't completely sunken in yet. Yes, watching the sibling dynamics not only amused him, it reminded him of how he and Savannah always interacted.

Even now, Austin loved bugging Savannah. Telling her that something was on a "need to know" basis and that she didn't need to know was sure to start something percolating. Those interactions with Savannah always kept him at the top of his game. Knowledge was his business, and he knew what he knew. But there were times he would ponder the deeper question, what does a person really know? What *should* we know? Are there things we *shouldn't* be allowed to know? Knowledge sure got Adam into Dutch with God, got him kicked out of Eden. And then there was poor, curious Faust, who sold his very soul—maybe not the best trade-off. Yes, the amount of knowledge available at anyone's fingertips today should give people pause. And Austin continued to wonder if a line should be drawn and, if so, where?

Chapter 20

Every so often Dakota and Daniel would indulge in some film noir on a lazy Sunday afternoon and watch an old black-and-white movie. When the credits for *Breakfast at Tiffany's* were rolling and the *Moon River* theme swelled, Dakota turned to her fiancé and asked, "Did you notice that Holly Golightly just never shut up? She just blathered on and on and on and on. Now why would anyone want to marry that?"

"I thought you liked Audrey Hepburn?"

"Oh, I don't blame Audrey Hepburn. It's Truman Capote's fault."

"And as there is really no arguing with that…" Daniel picked up the remote and changed the channel.

After supper, they found themselves on the couch once again, this time watching the news. Dakota wasn't really paying attention to the news as she had the first batch of papers of the semester to grade. She'd take one off the pile next to her and read it, marking it as she went along. She'd put the graded paper on the bottom of the pile and pick up the next paper off the top. She had kind of a routine going. Each essay was three pages long with an additional Work Cited page. One source. She'd check the Work Cited page first to see that the entry was done correctly. Then she'd read the paper, looking for the specific things she asked to be included. If students followed her very precise instructions, they did very well; if not, the grades fell where they may. She was making a correction on the in-text documentation of a paper when words penetrated her concentration.

She looked up at the TV screen in time to see a mangled car wrapped around a tree. She recognized the tree immediately as it was one on the curve of the road going into the small village where her academy resided. The newscaster stood in a drizzling rain, telling the audience two students were dead. Names were being withheld until notification of the families.

She was shaking her head. "Not good."

"It happens every year."

"Which is way too often. Something needs to be done."

"What more can be done, honey? There are speed limit signs and signs depicting the curve that is up ahead. What's more, the kids know it's there. It's not like they don't drive back and forth on that road all the time."

"I know. But those poor kids. They had their whole life before them, and now they don't."

"I guess we'll find out who they were tomorrow."

"It's just that accidents happen so fast. I mean, even this morning when I was taking my walk, a car, in the other lane coming from behind, swerved toward me and narrowly missed hitting me. The idiot was probably texting and not keeping eyes on the road! If I hadn't heard the vehicle and glanced back in time to step way out of his way, it might have been me on the six o'clock news."

"Good grief, honey, you be careful out there."

"Well, it wouldn't have been my fault if he had hit me. I was doing everything right. I was facing the traffic. And he was totally in the wrong lane to begin with to be so close to me. As I was just saying, accidents happen so fast."

The next item on the news was retrospective about a school shooting in Ohio that had happened a year ago.

Dakota and Daniel simply looked at each other and shook their heads.

When Dakota had told her mom she had decided to go into teaching, she thought her mom would be pleased, following in her dad's footsteps and all. The fact was she had never really considered teaching until she was finishing up graduate school. Her advisor had talked her into becoming a teaching assistant for a semester, and she discovered she really had an aptitude for it. When she had written to her mom telling her of her discovery and her desire to go into teaching, her mother had shot back a letter in record time. She had reread that letter not long ago. One line read, "Are you sure that's what you want to do with your life, sweetie? I have to admit, I'll worry myself sick. As a teacher in these turbulent days, you'll just have a big ole target on your back. At least if you were a cop, you'd have a gun to protect yourself. Not that I want you to consider law enforcement as a profession." After the news was over, Dakota went and got that letter and read part of the letter to Daniel.

He said, "You know, baby, we do take our lives in our hands as teachers. I mean, you never know when a student is going to go bonkers on us."

The next day he went to the military store in town and bought Dakota a stun gun.

When he handed it to her, she looked at it curiously. "What the heck?" It was a rather innocuous-looking thing, appearing more like a cell phone then a weapon. "I'm not taking this to school with me." She put it on the kitchen counter.

He picked it up and handed it to her again. Instead of taking it, she put her hands behind her back. "Here, you just flick on this switch and it's activated. Then if someone accosts you, you just touch this end to their flesh, it has to touch the person, and press this button." He depressed the button, and an electrical charge issued from the end of the case. "It needs to be recharged every couple of months or so. That's it." The upshot was that he insisted that she bring it with her to school.

"What about you? Don't you need one too?" When he just raised an eyebrow at her, she asked, "What, real men don't use stun guns?" But to avoid an argument, she'd put it in her school tote bag. And after a few days passed, she forgot it was there. Well, mostly forgot, until those times when Daniel reminded her to charge it.

*　　*　　*　　*　　*

It was a beautiful Indian summer day. The autumn leaves were a blaze of color and hadn't yet fallen from the trees. Midterms all graded, Dakota decided she'd sop up some sun and get some recreational reading in before collecting papers to grade from her students the next day. But instead of reading, she just sat admiring the fall colors and started thinking about the stun gun in her school bag that she'd been toting back and forth with her to school. Back when her mother had first written her that worried letter when she'd first decided to go into teaching, she'd called her mom and talked to her to reassure her that she knew what she was doing. "Mom, I'll be teaching at this lovely little college-level academy tucked away from the crazy hustle and bustle of the rest of the world. It's an idyllic place, Mom, Shangri-La. Not even graffiti to mar its perfection, nothing. A throwback to a kinder and gentler time."

"People are people," her mom had said. "And they have issues, and they get crazy. Does the word *Columbine* have any meaning for you? That happened in our own backyard, Dakota."

"Mom, that was an aberration."

"Not as aberrant as you think. It happens all the time, several times a year anyway. Students are just percolating away at school, getting ready to blow when one least expects it. Everyone's temper is short."

"Mooooom," she drew out the word.

"And you, missy, have a temper too. It doesn't fly often, but when it does, it does. I hope you never lock horns with a student."

Her comeback was "Did you ever lock horns with a student?"

That was the icebreaker causing her mother to laugh. "Well, not per se, but I had a mouth, and I was lucky it didn't get me into trouble. It might have."

"Tell me."

"One time I was teaching high school seniors how to write a 'bad news' letter. The trick was to bury the bad news so the letter wouldn't be too upsetting to the person on the receiving end. So in preparation, I wanted to get the students into the right mind-set. We were having a class discussion about times people told us no and how we felt about that. So one snotty little gal in the back of the class said,

'Nobody ever told me no.' My response was 'Your mom never said, "No, you can't have that puppy"? Your dad never said, "No, you can't have the car keys"?' and she was just shaking her head. So I quipped, 'Well, honey, I hope you've said no a time or two.' The boys in the class lost it, cracking up, while she just sat there trying to figure out what I'd just said."

"What happened?"

"Essentially nothing happened, but it might have. And in today's climate, it probably would have. So, honey, just be careful what you say in the classroom."

Oh, how she missed her conversations with her mother, but having her mother's letters and her articles was the next best thing. Dakota glanced down at the article in her lap. Picking it up, she started reading:

> For many years I was a substitute teacher working for the Albany County school district in Laramie, Wyoming. Now, from the students' perspective, a substitute is the least important person in their lives. Not only that, but with Wyoming's hunting mentality, it is open season on substitutes for the entire nine months of the school year. My son used to come home from the junior high school and regale us at the dinner table about how long it took the students to get a new sub to cry. It was usually before the end of first period.
>
> I can only thank God that I didn't start substituting right out of college. When I started substituting after my children had started school, I am pleased to say, barring one close call, the junior high school students never did make me break down and cry. The fact of the matter is, a thick skin and a no-nonsense attitude are much more important to substitutes than a flimsy piece of paper declaring that they are certified to teach. I might add, with my tongue not really in my cheek, that substituting

is an occupation that may also make one certifiable on another level.

The first thing students will do when a sub walks into the classroom is to see how far she can be pushed. In order to determine her boundaries, they barrage her with questions: Can I go to the bathroom? May I go get a drink of water? I left my homework in my locker, can I go get it? I feel sick, will you sign my pass so I can go to the nurse? The answer to all those questions is a firm no! Now, I have nothing against a student who shows a little spunk and is willing to spar, but that student needs to keep in mind which one of us is the boss.

Granted, teaching is still one of the noblest professions, but today it has also become one of the most dangerous. Teachers literally take their lives into their hands each and every time they go to school. It is a war zone full of enemies and enmity.

In addition to students' drug and alcohol abuse, which we won't go into here, kids will take weapons to school regardless of the rules. This country-wide phenomenon of students taking guns to school to shoot teachers and fellow classmates should concern everyone, not just educators. The alarming increase in these types of incidents demands that something be done now. It takes courage to go to school today for both teachers and students.

The classroom isn't always a war zone, although it is still far from being the best of all possible worlds. When observing the students, one discovers there is no innocence there, nor yet enough maturity to help them temper the passions which run amok and destroy lives. Seeing a young junior high school girl being escorted from campus in handcuffs only reinforces my point. These kids are so much more street savvy, ballsy, and informed than I was at that age. Take seventh graders. In one class, students are required to write their vocabulary words in a sentence so that it can be determined if they can use them in the correct context. Using the word lubricate, one girl wrote, "You can buy lubricated condoms at Walmart." Whoa! I guess all that sex education in the elementary schools is actually sinking in. Another student put a whole new spin on the phrase carpe diem for me. His word was seethe. He wrote, "I seethed the opportunity." Now, I must admit, I myself have seethed the day on more than one occasion in my life, so I gave him credit for a unique, albeit accidental, interpretation of the word seethe.

Few students respect the teachers or the policies of the school, and the verbal abuse students hurl at the teachers is both unbelievable and commonplace. A teacher I know at the high school deals with such insults philosophically. When she saw a message regarding herself scrawled on a locker near her room reading "Mrs. Smyth is a fuck," she pulled a marker out of her pocket, placed a caret between the words a and fuck and changed the sentence to read. "Mrs. Smyth is a good fuck." What a grand sense of humor she has. I, on the other hand, tend to take things personally. One junior high school student called me a "ho" simply because I expected her to do nothing more than to abide by the rules. Another student, this one at the high school, threatened to hire a hit man because I wouldn't let him out of the classroom before the dismissal bell rang. How should one react to a threat like that? In the "old days," teachers could take the bull by the horns and deal with students who were out of line. But what about today? One of my favorite scenes found on page 70 in a. manette ansay's book river angel is when a teacher loses it during her stint at yard duty. Several bullies are picking on a kid, and the teacher intervenes: "'I don't have patience for this,' she screamed at the boys. 'If you're still here in three seconds, I'll slap your goddamn little punk faces bloody, do you understand English?' They did."

The purpose of going to school, of course, is to acquire an education, but the fact of the matter is, most of the education students get is acquired outside the classroom. This is not necessarily a bad thing. Mark Twain, Huck Finn's creator, refused to let his schooling interfere with his education. Maybe we should all take a page out of that book.

Chapter 21

The afternoon was waning quickly, as it was wont to do in the fall of every year, but Dakota wasn't yet ready to head indoors. A creature of light, the sunlight nourished her, body and soul. Before she knew it, the first snowfall of the season would commence, and it would be winter again. The seasons flew by so quickly. When there was a blanket of whiteness spreading across the lawn, she didn't exactly have SAD (seasonal affective disorder), but it was close. Neither did she have claustrophobia, but again that was close. Her brother and sister were named after bustling cities, but she'd been named after a territory—Dakota—a wide open space, wild and free. Perhaps that was why she often needed space to gain equilibrium. And she felt perfectly justified in exercising her freedom by taking the time and space just to be lazy and do some reading. So sifting through the folder she'd brought outside with her, she found something else interesting that snagged her attention.

It was a packet full of sad little testimonials about students who had died young. The rather lengthy preamble to the readings had been titled *Journey's Cut Short*.

> *In one year's time, four young people who touched my life have died. One fifteen-year-old girl, Dana, was bludgeoned and stabbed to death by a thirty-eight-year-old man suspected to be her lover; one young man, Charles, gave up the will to live and committed suicide by shooting himself in the heart—a very telling symbolic statement, doubly so as his suicide*

took place on Valentine's Day; one recent high school graduate, Colt, was the victim of a traffic accident that resulted in a broken neck and the loss of his life; and one young woman, Ingrid, simply disappeared off the face of the earth one beautiful July afternoon, and while the search for her continues, she is presumed to have been the victim of an abduction and, most likely, dead.

At one time or another, over the past few years each one of these four people was a student of mine. I did not know them intimately, but I did know them. Each one of them reminded me of what it was like to be at the beginning of my life: past childhood, yearning for adulthood while waiting, waiting for the shot that would open the starting gate, waiting for their lives to begin. With one exception, they resided in that in-between time when nothing seems to go right. All of these young people were important. Their lives were important. Even their deaths were important, helping to define them specifically and individually.

Sometimes, after people have gone from our lives, it is as if we dreamed them. Did they really exist? While they were here, did they make an impact? Leave a mark? Touch anyone on any level? As with Pirandello's characters who were in search of an author, these four students of mine cry out to me to help validate and make sense of their lives. I feel their need not just on a soul level but on a visceral level as well. Years ago, as a young lactating mother, sometimes just the thought of my baby would bring warm, nourishing milk rushing into my breasts, filling them. My too-late need to nurture these four young people makes my breasts ache in an oh-so-familiar way. And so I must make the effort to connect with them by telling their stories. I've taken it upon myself to invest these four lives with meaning and significance. Ingrid, Colt, Charles, and Dana are not to be forgotten.

While they lived, not all my four students realized that they were on a journey, because life is a journey. In fact, two of them behaved as if their spirits had been slammed in a door, and they had yet to recover from the assault. Now that they are no longer with us, their individual journeys have become moot. And yet, as it turns out, the four of them now accompany me as I continue on my journey. For this, I thank them.

After that preamble, Dakota turned to the article simply entitled "Ingrid."

Picture a beautiful, willow-slim, long-legged blond marathon runner wearing shorts, a tank top, and with a sweatshirt tied about her waist. Scouting out a new training route, Ingrid was running on a loop road in the Snowy Mountains. That was the last anyone ever saw of her. People run for all kinds of reasons: for exercise, for health, or just running away from something. Ingrid's running becomes a metaphor shattering into fragments. Did she just keep on running, running away from husband, home, and family? Or as is the more likely case, did she find herself running for her very life, racing away from an attacker who pursued her with an agenda all his own?

Ingrid had been missing for five days before an article about her disappearance appeared in our local newspaper. The article was graced by her picture, and I recognized her immediately. Over the chasm of about six years, I recalled a bright sphere of sunshine in one of the senior English classes I taught back in the early 1990s. To put it succinctly, Ingrid glowed. To look at her was to see light and lightness. She was slim, graceful, pretty with blond hair that, as I recall, was highlighted with occasional strands of red, which only added to her fiery radiance. She was also pale. In fact, she was so pale I wondered if she shared my chronic struggle with anemia. She was bright, serious, wanted to do well in school, and she did. And now?

Dead or alive? My best guess is that Ingrid is dead. My best hope is that she is alive. If dead, I suspect she died heinously. If alive, she is a wish-fulfillment personified for millions of people who dream of chucking it all and disappearing into a new life. But such an occurrence isn't realistic in her case. To reinvent oneself and begin again after a renunciation should happen, on some level, in the second half of one's life. That is the time of evaluation, of taking stock of one's accomplishments. A renunciation of all that is not important, the getting rid of the things and ideas and ideals that don't really matter, that is what happens on the other side of forty if one is emotionally and psychologically healthy. At that time, if a renunciation doesn't occur, it simply means that the person has refused to answer the "call" and that his or her life has stalled.

But at twenty-four, it doesn't seem likely that Ingrid was at that point where renunciation would be important. The week before, she and her husband of less than a year had just purchased a house. Life, in these youthful years, is all about acquiring, not sloughing off.

And so in our mind's eye, we see Ingrid on that last day, in the first blush of the summer of her life, we see her running toward or away from something. The only thing is, we don't know which, and we don't know what. Missing in action, generating hundreds of unanswered questions, we are left with the not knowing. Her disappearance is an unsolved mystery. In Ingrid's case, abduction is suspected; her footprints were evident for more than three miles, then nothing. No sign of a struggle. She just disappeared.

Just as the sun races across the heavens from horizon to horizon, Ingrid raced through life at the speed of light, as fleet of foot and as gentle as a deer. When we were schoolchildren, we all dutifully learned that "nature is red in tooth and claw." And we all know, at least on a cerebral level, that the premise in this world is eat or be eaten. But we civilized beings put a gloss over those realities and pretend that things like abductions of young women don't happen. And yet we all recall that Little Red Riding Hood went into the woods alone and what happened to her. In the original story before it was sanitized for modern children, she was eaten by the wolf.

Was Ingrid abducted, taken by force? Was it one of those inexplicable random acts of violence? Did she disappear of her own volition? She is presumed dead by the authorities. However, a nationwide, even worldwide, search for her continues. A few weeks after her disappearance, the official case was reclassified from a missing person case to a criminal investigation. And her husband? Well, for one thing, the public hates a survivor.

Dakota looked up from the article and wondered if Ingrid had ever been found, dead or alive. She then wondered how to go about looking into it. And that got her thinking about Christine, her friend from high school. How would one go about looking for her? To assuage her curiosity, she spent a couple of hours before bedtime on her computer looking up information on both Ingrid and Christine and basically came up with zilch. Guess she wouldn't make a very good detective.

Feeling sad and wrung out, she crawled into bed and tossed and turned before sleep finally came.

Chapter 22

The semester was almost over, Thanksgiving was just a couple of days away, the trip to Catalina was imminent, and Dakota was clicking off chores on her to-do list. She had gotten the studded tires on the car as the forty-five minute commute to and from school in the winter on the hilly Maine roads demanded just that. With that chore behind her, she focused on her upcoming trip to meet the family. The sibs had each agreed to bring something they'd read of their mother's to share with each other, so that was already chosen and in her carry-on tote. She was locked and loaded and ready to roll.

"What's the holdup?" Daniel stood at the door with car keys in his hand. "We don't want to miss our flight."

"Just a minute, I'll be right there." She was pretty sure her mother must have written an article about Catalina, so here she was, at the last minute, flipping through the folders in her banker's box looking for it. Ah-ha, finally, the folder on California found its way into her hands. That was where it would be, if there was one. The folder contained several travel articles, and of course, none of them were alphabetized: Solvang, Moro Bay, Disneyland, Coronado Island, San Francisco, Wine Country, and finally, there it was, Catalina. Pulling out the article, which wasn't really an article per se but more of an advertising broacher her mom must have done, she crowed, "Eureka!"

When the entire family had all assembled in Long Beach for the trip from the mainland to the island, Dakota read to the group:

A smuggling and piracy base in days of yore, Catalina
Island, twenty-two miles off the coast of southern

California, is one of the eight Channel Islands dotting this stretch of the Pacific like scattered jewels. Today Catalina is a quaint resort destination and a sport fisherman's paradise. Arriving by sea will take approximately ninety minutes or less, depending on your point of departure. Or you can arrive via helicopter in a mere fifteen minutes.

The beaches are outstanding; there's hiking and camping and, of course, a beautifully manicured golf course for those so inclined. But it is the deep-sea fishing that's one of the island's biggest draws. Cars are restricted, but you can get around easily via bicycle or golf cart, which are available for rent in Avalon, the largest settlement on the island. Tourist favorites include island tours, a visit to the museum, and an excursion on the Glass Bottom Boat goes without saying. A tasting and cultural walking tour will appeal to some and parasailing to others. It is a pricy little vacation, but well worth it considering the memories you will have for a lifetime.

"So come on." Austin clapped his hands once. "Let's get on over to the chopper and get this little show on the road."

"Fly over!" Chelsea started in as only a seven-year-old could. "But I wanted to take the boat!"

"Yah, me too," her sister, who was a little girl one day and a young lady the next, seconded the boat notion.

Daniel just rolled his eyes and walked a little away from the group, while Austin and Jill tried reasoning with the kids. "Look, honey." Jill was focused on Chelsea. "We'll get there a lot faster if we fly." The little girl's reddened cheeks were a good indicator that a full-blown temper tantrum was about to erupt.

"Hey." Dakota stepped between the parents and the kids. "Why don't the girls and I take the boat over and you guys fly. By the time we get to the bed-and-breakfast, you'll have us all checked in and our bags in our rooms. What do you say?"

Disaster averted, Dakota took each niece by the hand and strolled away. As she passed Daniel, she asked, "With us or with them?" He pointed to the group of adults. "Coward," she tossed over her shoulder, and they went their separate ways.

The adults, all settled in for the flight over, gave Austin his opportunity to size Daniel up without Dakota all in his face. "So how is it that a philosopher—"

Daniel stopped him right there. "I study philosophy and teach the subject. I wouldn't call myself a philosopher."

"Okay, so how is it that a guy who studies and teaches such a serious subject is also a practical joker? It seems incongruous."

"The study of philosophy is all about wanting to know fundamental truths about humankind. One of the interesting things about humans is their sense of humor or lack thereof"—he looked Austin dead in the eye—"and it fascinates me. I did quite an extensive study of the practical joke and the practical joker, which has a very rich history, all the way back to ancient times. In fact, you will find it in all cultures, the point being that it's common to all cultures because we are all gullible. It's part of human nature."

"Uh-huh." In a perverse mood, Austin couldn't help the dig. "It still seems completely juvenile. I mean, practical jokes are sometimes funny, yes, but they are also often just bad taste."

Daniel, not the least put out by the conversation with his fiancée's brother, said, "Maybe so, but I'm in good company."

"What does that mean?"

"God is the best practical joker I know."

"I'm waiting…"

"God's best practical joke on humankind is that women need to feel loved to have sex. But men have to have sex to feel loved. I mean, how are the opposite sexes ever supposed to get it together? I think the Big Guy is having a great snicker at our expense, which is the heart and soul of a practical joke. It's all about causing the victim of the prank embarrassment, discomfort, or indignity."

After a beat, the stoic Austin cracked a smile and couldn't completely hold back his own snicker. "Whatever."

Savannah elbowed her brother in the ribs. "As I recall, you aren't beyond the occasional practical joke: whoopee cushions, the rubber snake in the refrigerator."

"Maybe when I was twelve. I grew out of it."

"Did you? I remember pictures you sent Dee and me one April Fool's day a few years back when you pulled a prank on the girls. They were little yet and you'd put Jell-O in their juice glasses."

"Oh yeah, that." He couldn't help himself from laughing, and she joined in. "That was funny."

Savannah explained to Daniel, "There was little Chelsea with that cute little baby hand with dimples across the back of it, tipping the glass over and poking at the Jell-O with a chubby little finger with a look of complete astonishment on her face."

Deciding this was a teachable moment, Daniel said, "See, a practical joke is funny as long as you aren't the one the joke is being played on. Did the girls think it was funny that their juice was inexplicably undrinkable? What shows a person's maturity is when, say, a joke is played on you, and you have the ability to put yourself in the practical joker's shoes, which isn't always easy, and end up laughing at yourself. I experiment with my jokes. I'm really testing people's reactions. It's very interesting. I've written more than one scholarly paper on the subject."

"Really?" Savannah was all ears.

"One paper was on the subject of jokes that can go horribly wrong. People have gotten hurt or even died as a result of a practical joke. For example, there are those who believe that Orson Welles's *War of the Worlds* is an example of a joke gone wrong."

"Wait a minute, that was a practical joke? Not just a horrible misunderstanding?"

"So some say."

*   *   *   *   *

Standing at the bow of the boat with the wind in their faces and a mist of salt spray in the air, Dakota decided now was the time to chide her niece. She was a firm believer that if a person who stepped out of line wasn't rebuffed, he or she would learn essentially nothing about boundaries. That was one reason why she saw discipline of youngsters as being so crucial. They need to learn there is a point beyond which one should not go. "Look, grasshopper, that temper tantrum you were about to have back there was not cool for someone with a yellow belt in Tae Kwon Do. Don't they teach you about self-control in your classes?"

"Sure."

"You need to control your temper, and you need to pick your battles. Got it?"

Chelsea nodded in agreement but secretly knew that she often got her way when she pouted or showed a little temper. Being smarter than the average kid, she decided to keep that to herself.

"Why'd you call her grasshopper?" Shannon wanted to know.

"When I was a kid, I used to watch reruns of a show about this kid who was learning martial arts, and his teacher called him grasshopper. It just seemed appropriate."

"Oh. So what would you call me?"

"I don't know. Maybe bumblebee?"

"How about butterfly." Shannon fluttered her eyelashes as if they were butterfly wings.

"That works." Dakota laughed, and before they knew it, the boat trip was over, and they were on the island.

Chapter 23

The family was gathered around the firepit out on the patio of the bed-and-breakfast where they were staying. Savannah was off to the side playing Cribbage with Shannon. She had Chelsea on her lap, and the three of them looked cozy as could be.

"You missed one." Savannah pointed to Shannon's cards. "You have the right Jack, so you have another point coming to you."

"Oh, that's right. Thanks." Shannon moved her peg another space.

Chelsea was playing with Savannah's phone, flipping it open and closed. "How come you don't have a phone like Auntie Dee? If you did, I could play games on it."

"Because I'm old-fashioned and a creature of habit. Your deal, Shan." She nuzzled Chelsea causing her to giggle.

The night was crisp, but the fire made it more than bearable to be outside. In the distance, boats bobbing gently in the bay were strung with lights, which sparkled in competition with the stars. All in all it was a perfect November night. The Cribbage game over and drinks all around, it wasn't long before Savannah and Austin fell into their old habit of landing on opposite sides of an issue.

Austin was saying, "Social media has one strong advantage. It disseminates information rapidly. In fact, Bill Gates said, 'The internet is becoming the town square for the global village of tomorrow.'"

"Oh please." Savannah wasn't about to let him get away with that old cliché. "The internet has become a huge toilet that needs serious flushing. It might have started out to be something else, but now it exists to promote commerce and, in particular, pornography."

"Not completely. Social media, which wouldn't exist without the internet, is a necessary and valuable tool."

"Maybe, but social media is one thing, surveillance is another. Privacy is at the heart of being a citizen of this free country. Blanket surveillance is criminal. It is beyond anything George Orwell could ever have dreamed up." Savannah was tapping the table with a fingertip.

"Surveillance is a reality, get used to it.

"Here we go again," Dakota mumbled to herself.

Savannah loved a good debate; you could see it in the flush on her cheeks. "You internet moguls are the government's handmaidens when it comes to surveillance. It stifles the ability to dissent, one of our most important rights. Sadly, the US government, with the help of *you* guys, is guilty of doing any number of reprehensible things under the guise of national security. For example, my job is to act in defense of basic human rights. What concerns me is that the line between private and public has become blurred. I am all about information privacy."

He tried not to sound condescending when he said, "We need idealists like you. People like you are the conscience of the nation, the rudder of the ship of state. But a rudder is such a small thing. Easily broken off."

"What does that mean?"

"Mixing metaphors here, the ship of state is beyond huge. It's like this octopus that had all these tentacles going off in all directions, and one tentacle doesn't know what the other seven are up to. Or better yet," he corrected himself, "a giant squid. Safeguards like checks and balances aren't up to handling this behemoth with multiple tentacles anymore."

Savannah, seeming more sad than upset at what he said, postulated, "Even the free press seems so impotent today. Watching the nightly news, all you see is reporters spouting the interests of the government—talk about fake news. Serving Washington's interests is not what a free press is supposed to be doing. And as a member of Congress, I am determined to safeguard the Constitution and the people's rights."

"Savvy, you are so naive. People like me"—he patted his chest with an open hand—"we are fighting a battle from within. If we don't do what we do, China and Russia will pull out ahead of us and whip us."

Her eyes slid from one side to the other as she digested what he'd just said…and not said. "Define what you're talking about." Her voice was suspicious.

Heaving a theatrical sigh, he simply said, "Need to know, Savvy."

That pushed her button, as he knew it would, and had her flushing scarlet. "Sometimes I think you are walking a fine line with treason just on the other side."

"Oh, grow up, Savannah! Grow up!" Austin had lost all patience with her. "Our forefathers, Savvy, they were what? They were treasonists, if that's even a word. If the revolution had gone the other way, they'd all have been executed for treason."

"And?" She didn't really know where he was heading with that line of reasoning.

"Contrary to what you believe, you have no idea what I do. It is the new group of patriots I'm associated with. We make things happen or not happen. It's all about communication, knowledge, information. Oh yes, a war is being waged, and we're winning. You guys in Congress, you're just a facade to keep the masses in check. It doesn't matter if you vote yes or no on anything. It doesn't even matter if the president signs a law or vetoes it. None of it matters because you all aren't in charge. There is a new type of revolution, it's an information revolution."

"You're insane."

"Then so was Thomas Jefferson. And look how that rebel is now respected and revered. It's a whole new world, Savannah. Your way of doing things is outmoded—dead. Just as fighting the way the British fought was outmoded in the eighteenth century. The patriots' way of fighting was to hide behind rocks and tree trunks, not standing in a line waiting for the bullet. Well, this is the new way of running a country, of running a world, of running a war. You're passé, Savvy, you're outdated."

"So then what?" She threw open her hands in question. "If I can't beat them, join them? I don't think so."

"You're swimming against the current, Savvy."

"Like a salmon? Some of them make it, you know!" She turned toward Daniel, hoping for an ally. "Aren't philosophers on the side of democracy?"

"Actually, Plato wasn't a fan of democracy. He considered it the second worst form of government after tyranny."

She just shook her head and rolled her eyes and quipped, "Thanks for nothing."

Dakota got Jill's attention, nodded her head toward the ocean, and mouthed, "Want to put the kids to bed then to go for a walk?"

Jill, apparently adept at reading lips, jumped up with alacrity and said, "Yes, please."

"You coming with us?" Dakota rested one hand on Daniel's shoulder.

"Are you kidding? I've got a front row seat to the best show in town. All I need is a fresh drink and I'm set." He held up his empty glass showing he was ready for a refill. "You girls have a nice walk." And he busied himself making another rum and coke.

The kids were asleep as soon as their heads hit the pillow. Leaving a night-light on, Dakota whispered, "Will they be okay alone?"

"This bed-and-breakfast is just like a home. And the bunch of us have basically taken all their rooms. If the girls need Daddy, he's right outside a hop, skip, and a jump away, just like he'd be at home. Let's go."

The streets were all but deserted, and with the dark of night blanketing them, the only sound was that of their footfalls on the road. Dakota could imagine being all alone on this little island in the middle of the ocean with water lapping at the shore and the mainland so far away. It was a nice, peaceful feeling. After walking a ways in silence, she asked her sister-in-law, "What *exactly* does my brother do for a living?"

"Other than making buckets of money, I don't *exactly* know."

"Well." She was mulling over the argument they had just witnessed between Savannah and Austin. "I know every time my sibs get together, they go off on politics. Something they never seem to agree about. I think they are both patriots, but they are two very different kinds of patriots. Savannah is status quo, and Austin is avant-garde."

"You know something," Jill said, "I don't really care one way or the other."

"So," Dakota quickly segued in a different direction, "what do you know about the restaurant where we'll be having our Thanksgiving dinner tomorrow?"

"I guess we'll find out what it's like tomorrow."

Okay, so much for conversation, Dakota thought. They continued their walk in silence, which had the added benefit of giving her time to let her mind wander. Strolling with no purpose other than fresh air and exercise, she focused on the night sky. She and her mom used to sit out on the deck at night and look at the stars and find the dippers. Tonight, spotting first the big one then the little one made her think about her mom, which in turn made her think about all the great Thanksgiving dinners her mom had cooked over the years. All the Thanksgivings pretty much blended together into one great family feast, but one in particular, the year she'd been fifteen, stood out as being both typical and eventful. She let the memory of that Thanksgiving wash over her as she walked under the stars listening to the nearby lapping water.

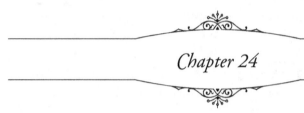

Chapter 24

They weren't an overly religious family, but they always said grace before Thanksgiving dinner. It was tradition. They held hands around the table, and Grace said grace, reciting an old Scottish blessing in honor of their ancestry. "Some hae meat and cannae eat. Some nae meat but want it. We hae meat and we can eat and sae the Lord be thankit."

"Now in English, please." It was tradition that Dakota always said that too.

So Grace would then say, "Some have meat and cannot eat. Some no meat but want it. We have meat, and we can eat, and so the Lord be thanked."

Then after plates were full and dining had commenced, each of them would share with the group something that they were thankful for.

"So what are you thankful for, bro?" Dakota looked at her brother with worshipful eyes. He had always been her hero.

"I guess I'm thankful I was able to talk Jill into staying on the pill for a couple more years at least. She got the big idea a few months ago that it was time to start a family, and I'm just not ready. I've got so much going on at work. We're expanding so fast that it would be more accurate to call it an explosion instead of an expansion. I just don't have time for kids."

"And she's okay with waiting?" Savannah was curious.

"We're young yet. There's no hurry. That's what I finally managed to point out to her after she calmed down enough to listen to reason when I told her, no, I wasn't ready to jump on board the baby train."

"How it is possible that she managed to keep that temper of hers a secret until after you guys got married? That's what I'd like to know." Savannah was gesturing at her brother with her fork.

His response was just a heartfelt sigh.

Grace stepped in, saying, "That fact is, people wear masks hiding behind them while dating, and it isn't until after the wedding vows that the masks come off, as do the gloves. I'm sure Jill was just as surprised to find out who the real you is as you were surprised to find out who she really is."

Dakota had been listening to her mother's words, and she'd started to frown. "Well, that sounds dishonest."

"Do you want to hear some words of wisdom?"

"Not really." That was Austin.

"Be nice." Savannah kicked him under the table.

"I want to hear them, Mom." Dakota's frown had disappeared, and she was looking intently at her mother.

"Okay." Grace focused on Austin. "Age, maturity, provides perspective that you just won't have for a while."

In an effort to get the focus off himself, Austin interrupted what he was pretty sure was turning into a lecture. "Now it's Dee's turn to tell us what she's thankful for."

Dakota, who had just started high school, said, "Well, it's embarrassing to admit, but I'm thankful for the C I got on my geometry test last week. Sheesh. Last year when I had Algebra, it was a breeze. I had no problem acing that class. But geometry, I'm really having to work to get it. I can't wait until this class is over."

"It was just the opposite for me." Savannah was helping herself to another scoop of stuffing and drowning it in gravy. "I had to work my butt off in algebra, but geometry came easily to me."

"And then there was your brother, who aced them both." Grace smiled at her son.

"Hey, I aced them both too. I just had to work harder in algebra than usual for me."

Austin reached over to Dakota's plate with his fork. "You don't need that, do you?" Stabbing an olive, it disappeared into his mouth.

Dakota laughed. "Keep your fork away from my food."

"Man, I can't believe you're in high school, Dee Dee. Tenth grade." Austin smiled fondly at Dakota. Then he looked over at Savannah. "I remember the Thanksgiving you were in tenth grade. Spent the whole mealtime in the bathroom barfing."

Dakota looked over at her sister. "Dinner made you sick?"

"No." Savannah was looking down at her plate, a bite of green bean casserole hovering on her fork between her plate and her mouth. "I guess I had the flu or something."

"As I recall, that was a crappy year all around for you. Didn't you have mono that year too?"

"Mono?" Dakota looked surprised. "Isn't that the kissing disease?"

Grace chided, "There's more than one way to get mononucleosis, not just from kissing."

"But that would be the fun way to get it. Was that how you got it, Savvy? Kissing somebody?"

Savannah set the fork with the uneaten bite of food on her plate and glared at her brother. "What I remember is that tenth grade after you got your car."

"My Charger! Yes!"

Savannah continued as if she had not been interrupted, "You ended up in trouble with Dad on more than one occasion. And it took a lot to get a rise out of Dad."

"What happened?" Dakota loved it when she heard tales about when her siblings were younger and their dad was still alive.

"I'll tell you what happened," Savannah still held forth, "first, Mr. Smarty Pants had been given a gas credit card. But he took advantage, and whenever he had a bunch of his friends in the car with him and they stopped for gas, they'd all go into the mini mart to pay for the gas and get all kinds of drinks and snacks and charged them on the card too. When Dad got the credit card bill, he hit the roof! Took the card away from Austin with lightning speed. But that wasn't all."

Dakota was all ears. "What else?"

"He didn't bother to tell Mom or Dad about all the speeding tickets he was racking up. Five, wasn't it? When they got the insurance premium, it had more than doubled. And that's when Dad went ballistic. Took Austin off the policy and made him pay for his own."

"Yeah, that was a lesson learned. I was twenty-five before my car insurance became anything close to affordable again."

"That was a case of out of the frying pan and into the fire."

"What do you mean?"

"You turned twenty-five and the insurance went down, but then you got married and took on a whole new batch of expenses. And if babies are in the future, start saving for college and braces now because—"

"Hey! How did we start talking about me? Weren't we talking about when *you* had mono?" Austin was a master at redirecting when necessary. "What I do remember about that time is being so jealous because I had to go to school and Savvy got to stay home. And I'm talking about staying home for weeks and weeks and weeks! Man, what a rip-off." He focused on Dakota. "Mom homeschooled her and everything."

"Wow, cool." She looked at Grace. "If I get mono, would you homeschool me too?"

"You're not going to get mono."

"How do you know? I do kiss boys, you know."

That was a conversation stopper. They all focused on Dakota.

Austin broke the silence by getting all big brotherly on her. "You better not be kissing any boys on my watch. You're too young for that."

Grace laughed at her son's reaction. "Don't worry about Dee. She and I have already had a few serious 'birds and bees' talks." Then she focused on Dee. "Want to tell us about this kissing?"

"Well, it's not *boys* plural," she amended, "just the one." She looked around the table at each family member, all of whom had given her their undivided attention. "And it was two years ago."

"Two years ago! You were still a baby in junior high school." Austin's eyes blazed.

Dakota was enjoying getting a rise out of her brother. "Remember Sammy, across the street? He and his family were moving, and that creepy Mrs. Rutherford was moving in. I went over to say goodbye as we'd played together for forever since I can remember. So I cried because I was sad he was leaving, and he hugged me. Then he kissed me. End of story. Now." She was a master at throwing someone else under the bus as she had learned that from her siblings. "I want to hear more about Savvy missing so much school because of the mono."

"Well," Grace picked up the conversational ball, "when a person has mono, she, or he, needs plenty of bed rest to recuperate. That's all. And that's what happened. Savvy spent a couple months laying low and finally bounced back. And now"—Grace looked around the table and just beamed—"I can tell you what I'm thankful for. That you were all able to make it home for the holiday."

Savannah jumped in, "I still think Jill could have made an effort to come too. After all," she focused on her brother, "last year you spent *both* Thanksgiving and Christmas with *her* family."

"Which is why I wasn't going to miss out on Mom's turkey, stuffing, and pie this year."

Grace added, "What else I was going to say before I got interrupted"—she looked at Savannah then toward her son—"was what I'm not thankful for is that darned computer. It's giving me grief again."

"How so?" Austin, doing the boarding house reach, stabbed another piece of turkey on the platter and transferred it to his plate.

"It's running sluggishly again for some reason. I took it into the shop awhile back to get it fixed. And it was okay for a short while, but now it's just not. Will you look at it later today?"

"Sure. No problem. Now it's Savannah's turn to tell us what she's thankful for."

Savannah considered then said, "I'm thankful that the literacy program I implemented is so successful. Right now we're focusing on the kids who are so far behind. But we're slated to start working with the illiterate adults too. The program will really make a difference."

Dinner was behind them, and Grace and Dakota, with the routine down pat, were on kitchen duty. Savannah stretched out on the couch in her mother's office, replete from the turkey and stuffing, not to mention the pumpkin pie. She lazily skimmed a magazine. Austin was sitting at Grace's desk dickering around with the computer. "I keep telling her it's time to get rid of the desktop. A laptop will do everything this will and more."

Savannah, ignoring him, flipped another page.

"Still doing that pro bono crap, Savvy?"

"It's not crap."

"When are you going to get a good-paying job?"

Still focused on the magazine, she tossed out, "Are you through harping on me?"

"I'm not harping on you."

"Yes, you are."

"Well, I'm sorry."

"No, you're not."

Throughout their bickering, she continued to flip through the magazine. She had just turned another page when Austin said, "Well, I'll be a son of a..."

That got her attention. "What?"

"Somebody put spyware on Mom's computer. If she knew that, she'd have a hissy fit."

Savannah sat up and was just staring at her brother. "Who would even be in a position to do that? You are basically the only other person who even touches it besides her."

"Those guys at the computer store most likely. I mean, who else? Nobody else has access."

"Can you fix it?" Savannah had gotten up and was looking over Austin's shoulder, not having a clue at what she was seeing.

"Just did."

"What? I mean, why?"

"Someone was probably hoping to get passwords and bank account information to clean out her account. Lucky thing Mom is too old-fashioned to do online banking."

"Can that happen?"

"Happens all the time. You just have to be savvy enough to prevent it."

"Are you going to tell Mom about this?"

"Not on your life! It would freak her out, and I fixed it, like I said."

"What now? Are you going to go to the computer store and tell them you busted them?"

"Whoever did it isn't going to fess up."

"But surely they have records as to who worked on her computer when it was there. That person would be the culprit."

"The guy would still deny it. I have a better way to fix their asses over there."

"What are you talking about?"

He glanced at her still hovering over his shoulder and left his explanation at "Never mind."

"Don't give me that! What are you going to do?"

"Suffice to say what they did here is really old school. Idiots. I can do things to them remotely that will really mess them up, and they won't have a clue."

"What? What you are talking about? Is that even possible?"

"Sure, if someone knows what he's doing, happens all the time."

*　　*　　*　　*　　*

When they got back to the bed-and-breakfast, Jill headed off to her room, and Dakota detoured to the firepit area. Daniel must have retired too. Austin and Savannah were now sitting on opposite sides of the Cribbage board. Savannah was chuckling at something her brother had said, and Dakota felt a warmth swimming around her heart. How she loved her big brother and sister.

Chapter 25

They'd made the reservation for eight at one in the afternoon. Austin sat at the foot of the table. Jill, flanked by her daughters, sat on one side of the table, and Dakota sat in the middle on the other side between Savannah and Daniel. They'd all agreed to wear one of Grace's T-shirts. Austin was wearing the one that said, "You can't scare me. I have two daughters." Jill's said, "To save some time, let's just assume I'm always right." David proudly wore the one that said, "Cleverly disguised as a responsible adult." Savannah's said, "WTF Wine Time Finally," and Dakota had carefully chosen the one with her mother in mind that read, "I haven't been everywhere, but it's on my list." Shannon had picked one that said, "Classy, Sassy & a Bit Smart Assy." It was big on her, but she had cinched it with a belt and turned it into a dress, and she looked so very grown up that when she entered the room, Austin had to turn away for a moment when tears filmed his eyes. Little Chelsea got a charge out of wearing a shirt that said, "Dear Math: I am not a therapist. Solve your own problems." Like her sister, she cinched it and wore it as a dress, but as she just looked like a little girl playing grown-up, Austin didn't have to deal with another emotional earthquake to the heart.

"Waiting for one more?" the waitress asked.

"We're all here," Austin told her.

"Well, then, I'll just clear this setting."

She had barely begun to clear the space at the head of the table when everyone all but shouted, "No!" Stepping back startled, she looked like a rabbit ready to bolt into the woods. Austin explained, "This is our first Thanksgiving since Mom died. Our first Thanksgiving without her. So we just want a place set for her."

"I see." It didn't really sound like the waitress did see, but at least she left the place setting where it belonged, at the head of the table.

When the plates of turkey dinner had been served, they all held hands around the table, and Austin said grace, reciting the traditional "Some hae meat and cannae eat. Some nae meat but want it. We hae meat and we can eat and sae the Lord be thankit."

"Now in English, please." Dakota, Shannon, and Chelsea all chorused in unison.

So Savannah then said, "Some have meat and cannot eat. Some no meat but want it. We have meat, and we can eat, and so the Lord be thanked."

After the first few bites, Savannah said, "Well, it's not as good as Mom's, but it's not half bad either."

"So who wants to go first?" Austin asked.

Dakota swallowed a mouthful and said, "I'll tell you what I'm thankful for. After reading a copy of one of Mom's letters written to a friend of mine from high school, I became worried about her. Her name was Christine, and her mom died when she was a senior. She was really messed up, into alcohol big time, and well, Mom wrote her a letter. After she graduated, she moved away, and I never heard from her again. So after reading Mom's letter to her, I wondered what had happened to her. Couldn't find her anywhere on the internet. So I hired a private investigator, and he found her. Happy ending. She had gotten married and has a couple of kids. I'm just thankful that the letter Mom wrote her apparently served the purpose of helping her get on the right track with her life."

"So did you contact her?" Savannah wanted to know.

"I haven't. I didn't want to dredge up any bad memories of that time in her life."

"Well, if it was Mom's letter that helped her turn her life around, maybe she'd be happy to hear from you."

"Maybe. I'll think about it."

Savannah kept looking over at Dakota as they conversed and finally broke down and asked, "What's different about you? I can't put my finger on it."

"What do you mean?"

"I don't know. It's just something."

"God, Dee, you aren't pregnant, are you?" Austin tossed out that grenade and had Daniel choking.

"No! I'm not pregnant." She slapped her fiancé on the back until he got his breath back.

"Well, there *is* something different about you." Savannah wasn't backing down.

"She's not wearing any makeup," Shannon offered. "That's what's different."

That had everybody looking at her.

"Well, pardon me for not wearing makeup."

"Why'd you stop?" Shannon wanted to know, particularly as she had been sneaking on mascara lately.

"I haven't worn any since we went to Iceland. It started out just to be something to make traveling easier. Less stuff to pack. But I realized I liked not having to put the goop on in the morning. Throwing my makeup out has turned out to be one of the most liberating things I've ever done. So after we got home, I just never got back in the habit. I slather on my moisturizer and that's that. Easy peasy."

"And Daniel doesn't mind?" Jill was frowning.

"I don't think he even noticed."

Daniel was giving her the once-over now, then he shrugged. "Well, it's not like guys really notice a woman's makeup when there are so many other nice things to notice."

"Like what?" Shannon was intrigued.

Daniel's eyebrows literally flew upward as he realized what he'd been thinking wasn't appropriate for a ten-year-old to hear. "Ahhh?"

Filling the breach, Austin said, "Like her mind. That's why you go to school to learn things. So you'll be smart and be able to carry on good conversations and impress someone with your mind."

"You and Mom don't have conversations." Chelsea sure looked innocent, but Dakota wondered if that was just a sly little dig.

Jill just crossed her arms, shooting her husband a *look*, while Austin spread open his hands, not knowing what to do after walking right into that one.

To fill the void, Dakota said, "Well, Chelsea, once a couple has been together for a long time, it's called a comfortable silence. Like when Daniel and I were first dating, we had so much to talk about, but over a year later, we still talk, but we also have long comfortable silences."

As Chelsea thought about that, a comfortable silence fell on the table while everyone shoveled food into their mouths.

Chapter 26

Coming up for air and barely restraining himself from loosening his pants as he slid a little back from the table, Daniel asked Austin, "Could you flesh out for me one thing you were talking about last night?"

"Sure, what thing?"

"You said, 'If we don't do what we do, China and Russia will pull out ahead of us and whip us.' Are you talking about cyber wars?"

"In a manner of speaking. The thing is, the United States needs to be able to disrupt cyberattacks from elsewhere before they happen. Or at least before they reach US networks. This is what we call *active defense* in cyber security parlance."

"Cyber security? That's what you do for a living?"

"In a manner of speaking."

"That's kind of vague."

"That's the closest you'll get to an answer from him." Savannah had been listening to their exchange and needed to add her two cents worth.

Ignoring his sister, Austin told Daniel, "The thing we have to keep on top of is that attacks from any quarter, be it Russia or China or an eighth-grade geek, consist of a progression of escalating access capabilities, and we can't drop our guard for an instant."

"But what does what you do have to do with the government?"

"Silicon Valley's research and development is crucial to the operation of the government. Whether you believe it or not, we've become the backbone of this country."

"But are you really addressing the issue of possible war. I mean out-and-out war?"

"Cyberattacks, which put the entire system at risk, are the new tanks or fighter jets of our time. They can destroy a city just as assuredly as the bombs dropped on Dresden or Nagasaki or Hiroshima destroyed cites. It can destroy a country by bringing it to its knees in an instant. And what has happened is that our bumbling NSA is falling behind in its role of defense from this new form of warfare. And that's where my company comes in."

"So," Savannah butted in, "how come Daniel gets a straightforward civilized response from you and all I ever get is lip?"

"Well, I'm sorry."

"No, you're not."

"Why don't you like Auntie Savvy?" Shannon wanted to know.

"What? Of course I like her!" Austin, who was usually so in control, looked flabbergasted. "Why would you say something like that?"

"Because you always fight with her."

"We just like to argue sometimes, that's all."

Chelsea was nodding in agreement with her sister. "But you yell at her. Like last night, you were yelling." Chelsea's little lip was almost quivering. "Sometimes it makes my tummy hurt and makes me feel like crying for her."

"Honey!" Austin knelt down in front of her chair. "Don't you argue with your sister?" Chelsea nodded. "So that's what siblings do." Austin floundered about, looking for words to explain to his daughter.

"So you do *like* Auntie Savvy?"

"Of course I do." Austin hugged his daughter. "I *love* Auntie Savvy. Between you and me." He looked around and noticed everyone at the table was taking in every word he was saying. "I really respect Auntie Savvy very much. She is someone who walks the talk, and not many people do that."

"What does that mean?"

"It means she backs up what she says with action."

"Thank you, girls." Savannah pushed back her chair, stood, and took a bow before sitting back down. "If it hadn't been for you two, I never would have gotten that compliment."

Chelsea looked back at her dad then looked over at her mom, and a glint of determination came into her eyes. "I still don't like it when you and Auntie Savvy fight." She had reiterated Auntie Savvy, but pretty much everyone at the table knew she meant she didn't like it when her parents fought. Austin and Jill's arguments were legend, but apparently Daniel wasn't in that loop, so he took Chelsea's words as face value.

"May I?" Daniel raised an eyebrow toward Austin, asking for permission.

Austin looked at Daniel as if he were a buttinski. "What?"

"As an impartial observer, I have to say that watching you and Savannah go at it last night was invigorating, but to a child, it might have seemed terrifying. So I thought maybe I could put things in perspective for Chelsea."

"Have at it." Austin sat back down in his chair, and Daniel focused on the little girl. "One of the classes I teach is an introduction to philosophy class. And one of the things my students learn in that class is a dialectic form of discussion. Now those sound like big words, don't they?"

"Yes." Chelsea's voice was cautious as she didn't really know Auntie Dee's fiancé, which was also kind of a big word.

"Dialectic is simply a form of conversation between two people, conversations like your dad and your aunt often have. But dialectic isn't just any old conversation. It is about important things. For example, let me ask you a question."

"Okay."

"Is it right or wrong to kill a person?"

She glanced at her mom and dad then looked back at Daniel. She hadn't been expecting her questions to suck her into this *conversation*, but being the center of attention was kind of fun. "It's wrong."

"Okay. That's a good answer. Your answer is an opinion. Now let me ask you this. If someone was very sick and was going to die and that person was in a lot of pain, and the person wanted to be out of all that pain, would it be okay for a doctor to help the person die sooner rather than later?"

Chelsea was thinking very hard. She looked over at her dad again then asked him, "Like when we took Button to the vet because he was so sick and we had to put him to sleep?"

"Yes, that's what Daniel's talking about, honey."

Looking back at Daniel, she said, "I guess that's okay."

"So on the one hand we know killing is wrong, but on the other hand, we have a situation where killing isn't wrong. Now there are going to be some people who will say killing is wrong under all circumstances all the time no matter what. That's an opinion. There will be other people who say that euthanasia, which is helping a very sick and dying person go to sleep, like Button, is okay. That's an opinion too. Both those opinions are valid. Are you with me so far, kiddo?"

She nodded, looking around the table, and realized that everybody was with him as well.

"So now we have two people with two different opinions, and if they start to have a conversation about the subject, what's going to happen?"

"They are going to fight about it?"

Chuckling, he said, "Well, let's not call it fighting. They are going to have a dialectical discussion about it. A conversation. Each will try to argue his or her case. And as people really believe in their opinions, sometimes these arguments get heated. If a person is really passionate about the subject, then it might even start to sound like a fight even though it really isn't. And what sometimes happens is that one person is so passionate and has so many good reasons to back up his or her opinions that that person is able to change the other person's mind."

Chelsea looked first at her Aunt Savannah, who was smiling at her father and who said, "Hmmm? So that's what we do, have dialectical discussions, who knew?" and that made her dad laugh. Savannah then turned to Chelsea and said, "I've learned a lot by batting ideas back and forth with your dad. He brings up things that make me think more deeply than just on the surface of a subject.

Which is a good thing because, and you might as well learn this now, *everything* is a lot more complicated than you think it is."

"So you like it when you fight…argue…have conversations?"

"When we *argue*," she emphasized the word, "your dad is challenging me to think deeper and wider and higher and in a more all-encompassing way."

"And do you change your opinions the way Uncle Daniel said some people do?"

"Not usually. But just talking about things helps you to examine your ideas and maybe readjust them. When you examine your ideas, you can refine them and make them stronger, so all the *arguing* helps."

Shannon, who wanted to be included because after all she'd started this whole ball rolling, said, "I think sometimes when Dad and Aunt Savvy are arguing…I mean, having a conversation, that Dad is just playing the devil's advocate to get her goat." She looked pretty proud of herself.

That had both Austin and Savannah cracking up. Austin saluted his daughter, holding his water glass up for a toast. "Here's to dialectical debates, no matter what side of the issue someone is on." Austin then turned to Chelsea and gave her a wink. "Did you understand all that, kiddo?"

"Yes, but…"

"But?"

"So it's conversation. And like Auntie Dee said before, people talk when they are first dating and then they end up with comfortable silences. So my question is"—she looked at Dakota—"when you were first dating, you had conversations?" She was like a little dog with a bone.

"Yes, when people are newly in love, there is always something to talk about."

Chelsea looked over at her mom. "So what did you and *Dad* talk about when you were first dating?"

Jill and Austin focused on one another, and it looked like both of them were drawing complete blanks. Then Jill kind of gave a small laugh and smiled at her daughter. "Well, I don't remember what we talked about per se, but I can tell you that when I met your father, he was kind of like the knight in shining armor rescuing the damsel in distress."

The little girl looked over at her father in astonishment and then back to her mom. "He was?"

"What happened?" Shannon was all on board with wanting to know.

Jill gestured to Austin giving him the floor. "Well." Austin focused on his daughters and fell into storytelling mode. "My friends and I had gone out for a couple of beers after work one Friday. There was this nice restaurant not far from where we worked. So as we're walking through the restaurant heading for the bar in the back, I noticed your mom immediately." He looked over at Jill and smiled. "Wearing this pretty red dress with her blond hair falling down her back like a waterfall."

Savannah played an invisible violin while he continued on with the story.

"She was on a date with someone, but she didn't look happy. So I was sitting at the bar but kept looking back at her. And this guy kept reaching out and touching her with his big mitts, and she kept pulling back as he was kind of repellant."

"Who was he?" Shannon asked her mom.

"A blind date."

"He was blind?" Chelsea asked.

"No, stupid." Shannon frowned at her sister. "That means it was a setup date with someone she'd never met before. Right?"

Jill nodded. "Exactly. I'd been set up by a friend, and this guy was drinking heavily, and he did keep reaching out, as your dad said, and grabbing at me. He had these hairy knuckles." She shuddered. "Well, I had no idea how to get away gracefully. That's when your dad helped out."

Austin resumed his tale. "I called her waiter over and asked him to go see if she wanted me to run interference. I mean, if she didn't want me butting in, I wouldn't have. So when the guy goes to the restroom, the waiter goes over, and he and your mom have a chat, and he points to me, and she looks over at me. She realized I wasn't alone but with a group, and there were some women in the group, so I guess she felt it was safe enough. So she nods. The waiter comes over and says, 'Her name is Jill, and she'd love some help.' So when the guy comes back from the restroom, I go over to their table and rescue the damsel."

"How did you do it?" Shannon was really lapping up this story of her parents that she'd never heard before.

"I'd had a lot of experience being big brother." He looked over at Dakota, who just rolled her eyes. "So I went over to the table like I was Jill's big brother and got all in this guy's face telling him to stop mauling my little sister. Then I told him to take a hike. He got up to leave, and I had to holler after him, 'Hey, don't forget to take the check with you!' That gave the waiter a head's up to intercept the guy as he headed for the door. Your mom joined my friends and me, and the rest is history."

"Hmmmm." Shannon thought about that.

"So why the heck didn't you just get up and leave? Why did you have to wait for some random guy to rescue you?" Dakota winked at her brother when she said "random guy."

"I guess because I hadn't planned ahead for any emergency. My friend and her husband talked me into a double date. They really played me. I'd refused to go out with her cousin a couple of times, and well, I arrived with them and was going to go home with them, but when we got there, they suddenly got a phone call from their babysitter and had to bail. There I was in the city with no car, no credit card, and not very much cash, so no cab fare for a ride home. I was stuck and really unhappy, believe me."

"So then," Chelsea wouldn't let it go, "when you were with Dad, on your first date, what did you talk about?"

"Enough." Savannah ran interference. "We have to keep this show going if we're going to get through everybody, so who wants to go next? How about you, Chelsea, what were you thankful for this year?"

After scrunching up her face and thinking, she looked at her Auntie Dakota and flashed a grin, exposing two front teeth just barely coming in. "I'm thankful for my new nickname that Auntie Dakota gave me?"

Everyone looked over at Dakota, who looked confused. "I did?"

Chelsea vigorously nodded. "Grasshopper."

That made Daniel laugh. "I like it."

"That works, but what about your old nickname?" Austin turned toward Daniel and explained, "We call Chelsea rosebud, not because she is pretty, which she is, but because of those sharp, painful thorns. She sure can get prickly at times."

Wrinkling her nose at her dad, she proclaimed, "I'm no longer rosebud, I'm grasshopper."

"And I'm butterfly." Shannon wasn't about to be left out.

Savannah looked closely at her niece and nodded in agreement. "I like it as you sure are as pretty as a butterfly." Which made Shannon blush prettily.

"Well, excuse me." Austin was indignant. "Butterflies are… flighty, and you, Shannon, are the antithesis of flighty."

"I like butterflies." Shannon mirrored her father's indignation.

"There's also the negative connotation with Madame But—"

"She likes butterflies, Austin." Jill's voice interrupted where he was going with that and brooked no resistance. "So let's leave it alone."

"Butterfly it is." Austin shook his head while smiling at his daughter.

Chapter 27

It had been a great day. They had taken a long, rambling walk after the huge meal in the bright, crisp November sunshine, then they hauled board games out and set them up in the sitting room and played Monopoly, Scrabble, Cribbage, and Spades. Shannon kept trying to run the spades, and she got shot down almost every time. When her Auntie Savvy choked on the queen just to stop her, she said, "Shit," which had everybody at the table cracking up.

"Hey, no profanity from the peanut gallery." Austin was laughing just as hard as the rest of them.

"I'll give her this," Savannah spoke to her brother, "that daughter of yours is a definite risk-taker."

"Which is a double-edged sword," Austin said. He looked over at Shannon, who was arranging her new deal of cards in a particular order. "Going to try it again, Shan?"

Her aloof response was "Maybe."

By nightfall they were hungry again. They had brought all the leftovers home in doggy bags, and the day before Savannah had been forethoughtful enough to buy a couple loaves of fresh Italian bread. They made heaping turkey, stuffing, and cranberry sandwiches for supper and began chowing down like they hadn't eaten in days.

Chelsea was complaining, "So the teacher said we each have to memorize a poem. I mean, *memorize*, that's hard."

"It's not that hard," Jill was saying. "You sing songs all the time, and that's memorization."

She was shaking her head. "It's not the same thing, and this teacher is really serious about this."

"Well, bravo for her." Savannah received a frown from her niece. "Memorization is one the basics as far as I'm concerned: The three Rs—reading, 'riting, 'rithmetic, and add to that, memorization. So have you picked something to memorize yet?"

Chelsea shook her head.

"How about this? Shakespeare." Dakota stood and struck a dramatic pose: "'Tis now the very witching time of night / When churchyards yawn and hell itself breathes out / Contagion to this very world: now could I drink hot blood / And do such bitter business as the day would quake to look on.' The bard himself wrote that, *Hamlet*, act III scene II."

Chelsea's response was "Ewwwwuuu."

"What does that mean?" Shannon asked.

"It means that Hamlet is so ticked off that his father has been murdered that he wants to revenge that death by doing things you can only do in the dark of night."

"Like drink hot blood?"

"Among other things. But that's just an example of something I memorized when I was in high school. And I still remember it. Anyone else? Any more Shakespeare aficionados?"

"How about this one?" Austin cited, "'As flies to wanton boys are we to the' gods / They kill us for their sport.' *King Lear*, act IV scene I."

Shannon wrinkled up her nose at that one. "How come all these things you guys memorized are so dark and yucky? Didn't anyone ever memorize anything nice?"

"What about this one, Shannon?" Daniel cleared his throat and cited, "'The mystery of human existence lies not in just staying alive, but in finding something to live for.' That wasn't a poem, but it was said by Fyodor Dostoyevsky in 1880."

"'Finding something to live for.'" Shannon, looking thoughtful, repeated the words. "That makes sense."

"Hey." Chelsea was put out. "I'm the one who has to memorize something. And it's not going to be any stupid Shakespeare or that Frodo guy."

Jill brushed her hand over her daughter's hair. "We'll come up with something appropriate for you, honey. It will be fine." Then to the group, "What gets my goat about the kids' school is that they have fallen on board with this ridiculous curriculum that has moved away from giving the students weekly spelling tests. What next!" Her disgust with the school was evident.

"I've read studies on that." Savannah whose literacy program was her baby was up-to-date on all literacy studies. "This school in Ohio started bragging that not giving the students weekly spelling tests, that teaching them word patterns instead, has helped with rising test scores in that state. But then an independent source looked into their claim. The reality is fifth graders can no longer read words that are on a second-grade level! That school system is praising a policy that isn't working. It's like"—she turned to Austin—"remember the new math they were starting to teach when we were kids, and we all discovered that learning it the old way was better. It's the same thing. Not teaching spelling is just another harebrained scheme that won't work."

Shannon had lost interest in what the adults were talking about now but liked being part of the conversation, so she jumped in and asked Daniel a question, "Will you tell us some more philosophy stuff like you did earlier today?"

"Sure." He considered a couple of things then nodded. "How about a mind teaser?"

"Okay."

"I'm going to tell you a sentence. Then I want you to think about the sentence. After that, I want you to tell me if the sentence is true or not. Ready?" She nodded. "Here's the sentence: *Everything I say is a lie*. Now, is that a true or a false statement?"

Looking confused, she glanced at her father. Then she looked back at Daniel. She was thinking so hard that everyone in the room could almost hear the wheels turning in her head.

"So," Daniel prodded, "was my statement a lie or the truth?"

"Well, if everything you say is a lie, then the sentence you said, 'Everything I say is a lie,' is the truth. But because you were telling the truth, you weren't telling a lie. So the sentence is a lie. I think.

But if you don't always lie, then saying everything you say is a lie, is a…lie. I think."

"Good girl! You did a good job of reasoning through that bog and came up with something that makes sense. Sort of." He looked over at Austin, who was beaming with pride at his daughter, and told him, "This one has a lot on the ball." Turning back to Shannon, he said, "And here's something else that circles back around to what your mom was saying about the school not teaching spelling words anymore. Philosophy is all about thinking, and in order to think, we need words, and in order to think deep thoughts like you just did, we need lots of words. The richer our vocabulary, the better thinkers we will be. As an aside, this is why we know our illustrious president isn't a deep thinker, because his vocabulary is so limited. But be that as it may, let's get back to our topic at hand: a rich vocabulary to help us be deeper thinkers. This is why it's a disgrace the school is doing what it's doing. You kids need to start doing your own spelling words each week and, in addition to learning new words, put them into contexts and use them if you want to understand philosophy. And"—he looked around at the group—"I'll get off the soapbox now."

Austin grumbled, "As much tuition as we pay to that school, they will be getting a phone call from me regarding this spelling business."

"Do you really think that will do any good?" Jill didn't sound convinced.

"Hey, when money talks, bullshit walks."

"Austin!" She tipped her head toward the kids.

"I'm just saying, they want their $10,000 tuition each semester, per kid, they'll listen to who pays it. Savannah, will you send me copies of those studies you were talking about? It won't hurt me to go in there armed."

After a while they started playing the "What do you want to be when you grow up" game with the kids. Shannon, sitting next to Dee, leaning in to her with her head on Dee's shoulder, said she wanted to be a college professor like Auntie Dee. Chelsea jumped up and did a little Tae Kwon Do demonstration and said she wanted to own a studio and teach little kids.

"So you both want to be teachers? A very noble calling."

The kids turned the tables and asked the adults what they had wanted to be when they grew up. "Did you end up what you wanted to be?"

Austin nodded. "Pretty much. From the time I was twelve, I knew what I wanted to be doing."

"Really?" Savannah looked at her brother in surprise. "I never really knew I was going to end up a politician. Even when I was in college. At one point I thought I'd like to be an investigative reporter. Traveling around the world writing important exposés."

"Like Gordon Foxe?" Dee gave a heartfelt sigh. "Now that guy is a *fox*. And so smart. Didn't he just get a Pulitzer for that story he did in Afghanistan? Something about the opium trade and all those poppy fields. And the real reason behind the power struggle there."

Chapter 28

Before long, the kids were yawning, and Jill, exhausted too, bundled them off to bed. Daniel wandered over and hunkered down in front of the television, watching a game that didn't interest the siblings, so they relaxed with a glass of wine and conversation. Dakota had polished off one glass and was refilling it. "Do you guys ever think that the fishes and the loaves thing is happening now, in this day and age?"

"Where did that come from?" Savannah wanted to know.

She waggled the almost empty bottle of wine at her sister. "I was just thinking about all the bottles of wine that are consumed every day in every city *and* town *and* country worldwide. That would be a lot of bottles of wine. Are there really that many grapes grown each year? It doesn't seem possible."

"So you think some great spirit is turning water into wine?"

Dakota was just tipsy enough to think that was funny and giggled. "Why not?"

"Why not indeed." But Austin wasn't really paying attention to what had been said. He was looking over at the back of Daniel's head with a little frown on his face.

"What's the matter with you, bro?" Dakota kicked him in the shin with her toe.

"What? Oh, I'm hoping that Shannon isn't developing a crush on Daniel. She kept looking at him with those big blue eyes of hers and...well..."

"Don't be silly." Savannah was shaking her head. "It's just admiration, kind of like the big brother worship Dee always showered on you whenever you were around when she was growing up. That's all it is."

Dakota nodded and took another sip of wine. "That's right. I sure did worship my big brother. But"—she turned to Savannah—"I worshiped you too. You were so good to me but also a disciplinarian. There were times it was almost like I had two mothers."

"Wh…what?" Savannah looked stunned.

"You and Mom were both good at giving me the 'Don't mess around and get knocked up speech.' And when I'd run into a brick wall with Mom over some issue, I'd run to you hoping to recruit you to my side. More often than not, you'd concurred with Mom, leaving me stewing at both of you. You'd say things like, 'I'd have to agree with Mom on this one. You're too young to be making decisions about tattoos.'"

That made Savannah laugh. "I remember that phase. I also knew how to buy time. I knew that if we deferred a hard decision on that topic, that if you had to wait long enough, you might choose differently. And voila, as far as I know, no tattoos."

"Like I said, it was like having two moms."

"So." To change the subject, Savannah decided to drop the bomb she'd discovered when reading their mother's articles. "Did either of you know that Mom had a boyfriend in the last few years of her life?"

"No way!" Dakota's voice showed immediate interest.

"She never said anything to any of us about a guy." Austin's voice was laced with suspicion.

"Guess she wanted to keep him to herself. Do you suppose he was that gentleman with the goatee who was at the funeral? The guy who was sitting in the back pew and looking so…lost?"

"I remember that guy." Dakota took a thoughtful sip of wine. "He did seem so sad, but then it was a funeral, all her friends were sad."

"So what did you read that gave you this information?" Austin was still trying to sort through his feelings on the subject.

"It was an article she'd written and published in one of those retirement magazines, like an AARP thing. She'd met this guy on an online dating service, of all things."

"Humph" was the sound that came out of Austin.

"Go, Mom" was Dakota's reaction. Savannah looked like she was about to say something then didn't. Dakota wasn't about to let her get away with that. "Spill, Savvy, what were you about to say?"

"Well, after reading the article, it got me thinking about online dating."

"Really?" Austin sounded protective. "Considering your profession, that might not be the best idea."

"I didn't say I was going to do it."

"But you were thinking about it? Really?" Dee was all over that.

"It was just a passing thought, but anyway." She focused on Austin. "Have you read anything interesting from Mom lately?"

"Not so fast." He was looking at her closely. "While the online thing wouldn't be a good idea, there are other options. What about a matchmaker?"

"Say what?" She hadn't a clue where he was going with this.

"You know." He broke into song. "'Matchmaker, Matchmaker, make me a match, find me a find, catch me a catch,' why not use a matchmaker to help you find someone?"

"Are you crazy?" Savannah was laughing. "First of all, I'd forgotten that you have a really good singing voice. That was great. But I was just joking. I'm not looking for a...match. Now, as I said, have you read anything interesting from Mom lately?"

"Actually I have. I reread a letter she wrote to me after we found out Jill was pregnant with Chelsea." He looked over his shoulder to be sure that Jill was nowhere around. "We'd had a pretty tempestuous year back then, and I was seriously thinking of bolting. Becoming the divorced Dad, the whole nine yards. I had called Mom and dumped a whole bunch of stuff on her. Telling her I'd gone to the lawyer and was getting my little ducks in a row before telling Jill my decision. Well! Here I am getting ready to lower the boom and tell Jill I want a divorce, and instead she's the one who lowers the boom, and she tells me she's pregnant. Talk about pulling the rug out from under a guy.

So then Jill wants me to call Mom right away and give her the news. So here it is like two days later from my earlier phone call to Mom, and I don't have time to give her a heads-up to this new development. So we call, and we are both on the phone telling her the news. I can just imagine what Mom was thinking and how thankful I was that she wasn't letting any cats out of that bag, as they would have been very angry cats indeed. Anyway, after that phone call with the baby news, she wrote me a letter." He pulled it out of his back pocket.

"Hey, I thought you were going to get all Mom's stuff scanned into your computer?"

"Haven't gotten around to it. Life happens. So knowing you'd bring up the subject, I brought this to share."

>*Dear Austin,*
>
>*I expect you are still overwhelmed by the news yesterday. Just remember that things turn out the way they are supposed to. And I also want you to remember that there is something very special about second children. I was a second child. You were a second child. And this second child will turn out to be the light of your life! He or she won't take anything away from Shannon, of course. A first child always holds a special place in the family and in your heart. And yes, two is a lot more work than one. My dad used to say the work doesn't double, it square roots. But my advice to you is to take only one day at a time and only deal with what is necessary to deal with that one day, and all will be well! And pretty soon (and I mean pretty soon), one of your kids will be calling you on the phone telling you that you will be a granddad! Time will fly; enjoy it while it does.*
>
>*And speaking of being a dad! Happy Father's Day!*
>
>*Love,*
>*Mom*

"Well, was Mom right? Did things turn out the way there were supposed to?"

"I suppose they did. Life certainly has its ups and downs, but that's true for anyone. So, Dee, your turn. What have you read lately?"

"Lots of stuff actually. But one article I read recently really got to me. I'd been reading articles about when Mom was teaching. It turns out, she had a few students who died, and she wrote about each one of them, and each story is one that will tug at the heartstrings, but this one in particular really hit me. This young girl named Dana was murdered." She recapped the story she'd read:

> Late one October, I was called in to take over a ninth-grade English class. The teacher's father was dying, and he would be gone for a number of weeks. I took over the class on October 29, a Wednesday, and on Thursday, I assigned some homework. A little girl in the front row, third or fourth from the door, immediately took umbrage. "Homework? We don't have homework in this class. We don't have to do any homework."
>
> I paused and took note of my surroundings. Yes, just as I suspected. I saw desks, computers, shelves full of books, a blackboard (green, actually), chalk, all the accoutrements of, you guessed it, school. I looked at the girl and repeated the homework assignment. A few students in the class were the compliant type; they wrote the assignment in their notebooks and waited for the bell to release them from second period. The rest listened raptly to the girl in front and followed her lead of obstinacy.
>
> She tried another tactic. "You're a sub, and subs can't assign homework." As a substitute, I set my own boundaries the first day or two of a long-term stint. Those who opted not to turn in the assignment the next day would suffer the consequences, a zero in

the grade book. I shared this with the students who joined Dana in considering a coup d'etat.

"I'm not going to do any homework," the girl, once again, huffed in protest as she crossed her arms over her ample chest; her lower lip extended into a full-blown pout. I looked at the seating chart to see who she was. Dana Brood. The fact that her last name was Brood, I found amusing. Our very names do indeed help to define us.

Looking out over a sea of belligerent faces, I realized that a portion of my ninth-grade students were more likely to tell me to go fly a kite than to agree to do something as basic and simple as a homework assignment. A lot of them did get that promised zero in the grade book. And when I averaged points at the end of several weeks, many of them asked if they couldn't please do that assignment and turn it in late for at least partial credit. Live and learn.

Of course, by that time, their ring leader was no longer a part of our class. In fact, the day of Dana's coup d'etat was the last day she ever attended school.

She missed school the following day and the rest of the following week as well. At one point I asked the class, "Where's Dana?"

"Oh, she ran away from home," I was told.

On November 13, I was reading the morning paper before getting ready for school, and my eye fell on an article toward the bottom of the front page. "Frozen body found in Laramie." At this point the body was unidentified. No name, age, or cause of death was given. The undertones of foul play were there, and as I sat there shaking my head at yet one more instance of man's inhumanity to man, the range hood light over my stove clicked on. Now this had never happened before or since. I was a good fifteen feet away on the other side of the room, and no one else was in the house. I sat there, staring at the stove light while goose flesh popped up all over my arms. Some will laugh at the coincidence, the light clicking on unaided as I pondered this article, but I know that there is more unseen than seen in this world, and I wondered what this meant.

The next day, the cops showed up at school. My fifteen-year-old student Dana had been murdered: bludgeoned, brutally beaten, stabbed, and hidden in the snow-covered mountains to the east of town. When we got the news, all I could see in my mind's eye was her sulky little mouth as she pouted about the homework assignment. As a substitute, I knew very little about Dana. In retrospect, however, I am glad we had our clash of wills. The incident showed me her spunk, a facet of her makeup revealed once again in her autopsy report, which detailed the number and depth of defense wounds slashed across her hands and arms as she fought for her life against her killer.

It is human folly to presume to know what our futures will bring. The patterns that we weave into our lives lead us to our individual destinations, and ultimately we have to take the responsibility for the choices we make. If Dana had known how short her life was going to be, I wonder what, if anything, she might have done differently.

"I remember when that happened." Savannah spoke in low tones.

"So do I," Austin said, and thinking about his daughters, he added, "and it gives me the willies."

"So sad." Dakota looked pensive. "And yet, we had such a happy life there in Laramie."

"It was a good life," Savannah agreed. "A very good life indeed."

After setting their mother's writing aside, Dakota said, "I think we have all been avoiding the elephant in the room for the past couple of days, but isn't it time to talk about that offer we got on the house?" Savannah almost shook her head no, and Austin got a little frown line between his eyebrows. "This lack of enthusiasm leads me to believe that you guys feel like I do."

"And how's that?" Austin asked.

"That we've changed our minds about wanting to sell the house?"

Austin was jiggling one leg. Savannah remembered that as a kind of nervous or stressful habit he used to exhibit when he was a small boy. She hadn't seen it in decades. "You have reservations about selling, bro?"

"It's funny, because I didn't think I had any deep attachment to Laramie or Wyoming, but after reading some of Mom's articles about the place, I guess my roots run deeper than I thought they did. So to answer your questions, yes, I am having some regrets about listing the house."

Savannah said, "Nothing is in stone yet as far as the offer. We don't have to accept it. We can take the property off the market. It's not like we need to sell it for financial reasons."

"But," Austin pointed out, "an empty house isn't a happy house."

"We could keep it and rent it." It sounded like Dakota had just been waiting to toss that idea into the mix.

"Hmmm." Austin seemed to be warming to that idea. "What do you think about that, Savvy?"

"I like it. We don't sell for now as we all kind of have reservations about that. And if later on down the road, if we change our minds, well, we can revisit the situation. Yes, I like the idea of renting it."

Dakota pointed out, "It's a college town, so maybe we can get a new professor or adjunct and his family interested in it. That would be a better bet than a bunch of college students."

"Good idea, Dee. We all have Laramie connections, so we can start putting out feelers, and we'll get somebody in there before school starts in the fall. Probably late summer at the latest."

"Which kind of ties in perfectly with what I have in mind."

"Which is?"

She looked over at the back of her fiancé's head, as he was still wrapped up in the game, and said, "We talked about getting married in our backyard in Maine. But I think I'd rather get married at home in Laramie. We have a great backyard there with the deck and the fountain, and there's that little archway. We could get married under the archway, and we could have chairs set up on the lawn. Not that there will be that many people, just family and maybe a few friends from Laramie. What do you think?"

"I think that sounds lovely, Dee." Savannah reached out and took her hand.

"Bro?"

"Works for me. Do you have someone in mind who will officiate?"

"Haven't gotten that far."

"Do you remember Erik? We were on the golf team together back in the day? He's a pastor of one of the local churches there. He'd probably be willing to do that."

"See?" Dakota beamed at both her siblings. "Everything is just falling into place."

"Okay." Austin clapped his hands, sensing all was settled. "I'll just contact the Realtor and have him tell the people who offered, sorry, no deal, and we pull the listing. Then we have a wedding this summer. And hopefully have renters in there by August."

"There's one more thing." Dee sounded a little breathless. Savannah was still holding her hand, and she reached out for her brother's hand. When he put his hand in hers, she said, "I'd like both of you to walk me down the aisle. Not that there will exactly be an aisle, but down the steps of the deck and to the archway. What do you guys say?"

PART III

Reaping the Whirlwind

I'm for truth no matter who tells it.
——Malcolm X

Chapter 29

"Well, somebody got up out of the wrong side of the bed this morning." Savannah's chief of staff set a sheaf of papers in front of her boss and crossed her arms. "You want to tell me why you're in such a grumpy mood today?"

"Not particularly." Savannah reached for the papers.

A hand reached out and placed it on the back of hers, arresting it in midmotion. "Savannah, what's going on?"

"Nothing really. I just had an unsettling dream last night. Woke me up out of a sound sleep. That was at 3:00 a.m., and I wasn't able to get back to sleep. So I'm sleep deprived, that's all."

"Was it a nightmare?"

"No, just...unsettling." When Beatrice simply raised an eyebrow in question, Savannah sighed. "I was, I think I was shopping or something. At any rate, I was going in and out of stores. I was holding a baby on one hip and shopping. Suddenly I realized I was no longer holding the baby. In a panic, I started calling the baby's name and running in and out of stores, retracing my steps, trying to find the baby. But suddenly I am no longer exactly in stores looking for the baby. I'm running down cobblestone streets crying for the baby. Then running up crumbling stairs and into ancient doorways and out of other doorways just in a panic because I have no idea where the baby is. That's it. I woke up scared, winded, trembling, and exhausted and...well, as I said, that's it."

"Hmmm? What was the baby's name?"

"What?"

"You said you started calling the baby's name. What was it?"

A little frown line creased Savannah's forehead for a moment as she cast around in her deepest memory. "Funny, I don't remember."

"Ah, well, even not knowing the name, and even without ever having studied Freud, I can tell you what that was about." Savannah made a moue of exasperation. Ignoring that, Beatrice plowed right on. "Remember Occam's Razor—sometimes a cigar is just a cigar."

"That's not Occam's Razor."

"Actually, it kind of is, but regardless, here's what your dream was all about."

"Please don't."

Beatrice ran right over her plea and said, "Your biological clock had clunked. It's lying on the ground, cracked, and all the springs have sprung out of it. So your subconscious was just needling you by saying, you chose the path less traveled, and now aren't you sorry. No babies for you. That's what that was all about."

"Is that what I did, choose the path less traveled?"

"Well, most of us do have kids. And for me right now, with my teenagers making my life a living hell, I'm thinking you made the better choice."

That made them both chuckle. Beatrice was no-nonsense but had the ability to make her see the lighter side of life at times. That winning combination is what won her the job as Savannah's chief of staff. That and her sterling credentials. "Whatever" was Savannah's pithy response.

"So now that we've settled all that, how about getting to work and settling all the woes of the rest of the world as well."

"Or at least the country."

*   *   *   *   *

Savannah walked to work when the weather wasn't prohibitive. Then depending on when her day ended, Savannah either walked home again or took a cab. She didn't like walking alone after dark as DC wasn't the safest city in the world. And wasn't that a shame.

Yesterday after work, there was enough daylight left that she had walked and stopped to observe the kids playing at a playground not far from her townhouse. One young mother had been pushing a bundled-up little kid on a swing, and the kid was squealing with delight. She had watched while a memory of doing the very same thing with Dakota circled around in her brain. Little ones took such abundant joy in the moment, and wasn't that a joy just to observe. Her step had been light as she headed the rest of the way home, and the evening had been peaceful and relaxing. Then the dream.

Savannah hadn't chosen to enlighten Beatrice to the fact that she had been dead wrong in her interpretation of the dream. Oh, if this had been the first time she'd had the dream, it probably would have been an accurate explanation. But this particular dream had been a recurring one ever since her college days, long before her biological clock had gone clunk, as Beatrice had so inelegantly put it. The first time she'd had it, it was a lot more sinister and nightmarish. That time, she had inadvertently scared the bejesus out of her roommate. She had awakened with a start so afraid because she couldn't find the baby, and she'd had such an ache in her chest, a pain really, that she had cried out, but the cry was blocked by that pain so she'd barely been able to mew like a weak kitten, asking her roommate for some water. Even the few sips of tepid water didn't dissolve the pain. Back then, she had the dream about once a week; that is, until she started volunteering at Planned Parenthood. Working with the young women there had given Savannah a purpose, and the dream had taken a hiatus for a while. In the ensuing years, Savannah didn't have the dream often, but often enough that it was a familiar old acquaintance. And as was usual after the dream, melancholy decided to visit for a time. Her antidote was to dive headfirst into work to move past the rare but recurring depression, and that was what she spent the day doing.

After her busy day, once again heading home before dark, she didn't stop to observe the children as she had the day before. There was still a whiff of melancholy following her, and in an effort to thwart its presence, she veered off in the direction of The Squeaky Wheel for a light supper and a glass of wine. She could dine alone at her little table toward the back of the restaurant without exactly being alone; that was just what appealed to her for the time being.

She'd finished her usual, the spinach salad and glass of wine, and decided she still wasn't ready to go home. Catching the waiter's eye and holding up her empty glass, she dug out a folder of her mother's she'd been carrying around in her briefcase. It never hurt to have something to read when the opportunity presented itself. Settling down with her second glass of wine, she readied herself to slide into her mother's world. When she dipped into the folder, she was surprised to see it contained several poems. What a surprise! She had no idea that her mother had ever tried her hand at poetry. She pulled one out at random entitled "Monstrous Crime" and read it.

> 'Tis a monstrous crime not to follow your heart,
> To hide behind your ineptness and your cowardice.
> 'Tis a monstrous crime to leave your lover unloved,
> A virgin to be despoiled by another instead of taken perfectly.
> 'Tis a monstrous crime to live the wrong life with the wrong wife,
> Because you weren't man enough to claim and love the right one.
> 'Tis a monstrous crime never to make it right,
> Even when given chance after chance after chance.
> But crimes are punished, and your jailer, with your compliance,
> Has cast into the sea your only key to freedom and happiness.

Whoa! What was that all about? The poem had left her feeling an ache and at the same time wondering where in her mother's heart or psyche it had been born, and, well, Savannah decided to read another one. The next one was entitled "Why Fight?".

> All is fair in love and war;
> And now I find myself in the fight of my life.

All is fair in love and war;
When honesty doesn't work; lie.
All is fair in love and war;
Cowards cower making it hard for the strong one.
All is fair in love and war;
Words of love aren't enough; actions aren't enough.
What is?
All is fair in love and war;
But life isn't fair. And even those who win lose.
All is fair in love and war;
The battleground is wet with tears.
All is fair in love and war;
Fresh sheets on an empty bed.
All is fair in love and war;
Sometimes you lose no matter how hard you fight.

The tone of these poems was so unexpected that Savannah found herself stunned and even a little saddened, and she continued to wonder what these were all about. The next one was titled "Vulnerability."

Because of warm feelings,
The flower slowly uncurls her petals,
Opening her worn and bruised heart,
Exposing it to the bee.
Will the bee sting her?
Or tenderly nurture and sup,
Kissing the wounds and
Healing the hurt?

There were only a couple more in the folder; she reached for another. It was called "Entitlement."

What do you do with a generation (or 2 or 3) of
individuals
Who think they are entitled to everything?

What do you do with a generation (or 2 or 3) of
individuals
Who have never been spanked or even moderately
disciplined?
What do you do with a generation (or 2 or 3) of
individuals
Who have never been told "No!"?
What do you do when they ride roughshod over your
rights
Because those rights don't coincide with theirs?
What do you do with a generation (or 2 or 3) of
individuals
Who feels the world owes them everything on a silver
platter?
What do you do with a generation (or 2 or 3) of
individuals
Who will sue you over something your (and their)
parents would have accepted an apology for?
What do you do?

Well, that was a completely different sort of poem from the earlier ones. And then the last one titled, "In the Moment."

There is only now. This moment.
The past does not exist, it never was.
The future hasn't happened. It won't.
The now is all you have. It is real
But only just now, in this moment.
There is only now. This moment.
Soft as a gentle rain in spring when
Young green leaves unfurl slowly, sensuously
As they did last year and the year before,
But only just now, in this moment.
There is only now. This moment.
Deep in the night under a cloudless
Starlit sky that draws us into the heart

Of forever, lasting, lasting, lasting into eternity
But only just now, in this moment.
There is only now. This moment.
Lightning striking! Thunder rolling…
Terror mixed with awe
The surround sound of the storm vibrating in our souls
But only just now, in this moment.
There is only now. This moment.
Thrilling under a lover's caress
Returning a gentle pinch that feels so good
Making soft sounds of perfect contentment
But only just now, in this moment.
There is only now. This moment.
The past does not exist, it never was.
The future hasn't happened. It won't.
The now is all you have. It is real
But only just now, in this moment.

Not quite ready to go home yet, as she had another couple swallows of wine left, Savannah sat for a while, pondering her mother's poems. In a literature class a long time ago, an instructor had told her something a poet once claimed. He (or she?) had said that when he wrote a poem, only he and God knew what it was really about. Afterward, he added, now only God knows what it is really about. So speculating on what or who her mother's poems were about might be futile, but still she wondered. Were they to or about her father? Maybe the one about the bee was, but all of them? She didn't think so. It seemed there were aspects to her mother's life she knew nothing about. Secrets? Well, everyone had secrets; clearly her mother was very good at keeping them.

Chapter 30

When Jill graduated from college, she had no idea what she wanted to do with her life. The future was just a big, hazy, confusing place. When she met Austin, she gave an internal sigh of relief. Getting married solved so much. Austin had been an answer to the prayer of *"What's going to happen to me?"* She fell into marriage with him in such relief that it was years before she surfaced enough to realize she was still hollow—the vacancy hadn't been filled.

Her daughters had such a talent for living in the moment. And Shannon, my God, she was ten, nearly eleven, and she already had a clear sense of self. It was obvious to Jill that Shannon would probably go into some kind of science or engineering field. When Austin tinkered on the car or even just changed the oil, she would be right there with him with her head peeking under the hood or flat on her back on a dolly rolling under the car with him. And that time when the vacuum stopped working, Shannon took it apart, found the problem, and put it back together before Austin had gotten home from work so she could dump that problem on him. How did Shannon know those things? It was like she was born knowing what she wanted to be when she grew up.

Jill thought back to when she was ten. What had she wanted to be back then? An actress, maybe? At any rate, something so unrealistic as to be laughable. And later, what then? Not only had she never really known what she wanted to be when she grew up, she didn't know what she wanted to be when her children grew up! Maybe she was just one of those people who peaked in high school. Now that was a depressing thought! What thrilled her? Did anything interest or thrill her? *I mean, my God,* she thought to herself, *the highlight of my life is when I find a perfectly ripe avocado or plump red tomato at the farmer's market, and how pathetic is that?*

She wondered what was suited to the landscape of her heart. She felt so left out of real life that eddied around her like an outgoing tide sucking at her ankles. She felt that she'd missed some boat or taken some wrong turn somewhere, but she had no idea where. She began wondering, once again, if leaving this life that she knew and starting afresh would be the answer. Answer, ha! She didn't even know the question that needed answering. Her father had always talked about greener pastures, but the fact was, her pasture was really, *really* green. So why was she so...not unhappy, but not happy either? Just a bland, bland blah. She wanted to be excited by something; just for once in her life she wanted to be at the very epicenter of something. She couldn't even bother to put on a mask of contentment anymore. So what next? She was back to the question of what to do with the rest of her life after her children grew up. She was still going to be young, relatively speaking, when they flew out of the nest off to college. If she wanted to do something with her life, make something of herself, be someone, she should probably start now. But where to begin? Because she could think better when she was in motion, she grabbed a sweater and headed out the door to walk.

Jill didn't remember walking home, but there she was, standing in her husband's home office. Her eye fell on a box of Grace's writings. Austin had said repeatedly that he was going to take them to work and have his assistant scan them. He'd said that months ago and repeated it again just last week, and it hadn't happened yet. But it could happen any day. She hadn't even considered reading any of Grace's writing. But..."Hmmmm?" If she was going to read any of the articles, it probably should be now.

Out of curiosity, she started flipping through the folders. A photograph of Grace had fallen between two folders. Pulling it out of the box, Jill held it up and examined it. Grace was standing in her driveway with her hands on her hips and her head thrown back in laughter. Whoever had snapped the picture had timed it perfectly. Here was a woman who always lived in the moment and made the most of everything that came her way. She hadn't brushed her hair before the photo had been taken, but that didn't detract from her prettiness. The T-shirt she wore said, "Sainthood is not required." One thing about her mother-in-law, she had raised three amazing children. Savannah, Austin, and Dakota were all doers. Maybe that was the trick. Maybe she needed to be *doing* something. But what? Jill slipped the photograph back where it had been and, closing her eyes, let her fingers walk through the folders. Almost of its own volition, a letter found itself in her hands, and as the kids were off to school, and Austin was at work, and she didn't have anything better to do, she settled in to read. The letter was a couple of pages long, front and back. At the top, Grace had written, "To Sarah, a student in my memoir class."

> *Dear Sarah,*
>
> *Your writings over the course of this class have been very poignant even to the point of sorrow. I feel your pain through your words. You are floundering, and I can't just sit by and let you continue to flounder without offering assistance. If you were in the ocean caught in a riptide and I was a life guard, it would by my duty to save you. So please ignore my being a buttinski here; just think of me as a lifeguard doing her duty.*
>
> *Those of us living in the United States in the latter days of the twentieth century are a people devoid of myth. We look for facts, not truth. We focus on reality, not symbol. We claim that the intellectual is far superior to the emotional. We also know that we are lost, flailing around as we search for meaning in our meaningless lives. I see you as one of those lost souls. Myth, when it is allowed to, provides a culture, or even an individual, with a context, a pattern, and a reason for all experience. Being robbed of a contextual framework within which to place our experience renders us vacant and diminished,*

and that is why we feel lost. We are much less than we should be because we fail to recognize the hows and whys of our very existence.

Understanding that each person is living out his or her own "hero's journey" can help place a life in context. Carl Gustav Jung, a well-known psychologist, wrote about the hero's journey, the best-known myth in the world. The hero's journey is an archetypal representation of a person's life journey during which one evolves from stage to stage until all the fragmented parts of the self are reunited in complete unity. The classic journey consists of three distinct parts: a separation, an initiation, and a return. The separation begins with the all-important Call to Adventure. Not all people, for a variety of reason, answer the call and even begin their journey, let alone complete them. Think about how sad that is. when someone chooses not to answer the call to adventure and his or her journey never begins.

I believe this is what has happened to you. Your journey has yet to begin. You need to listen closely, hear that call to adventure, then follow where it leads.

One purpose of the hero's journey is to unify all the fragmented parts of the personality. Think about what happens when you mix together a variety of ingredients such as flour, butter, eggs, milk, etc. and proceed to bake them in the oven. The end product, once all the component parts are integrated, is a cake—something completely different than the individual ingredients. The making of a cake could be a simplistic, symbolic representation of the hero's journey. The hero's journey does just that, unifies all parts of the psyche into a whole. Even our use of language points us in the right direction. How many times have you heard the expression "Get it together!"?

Men and women are faced with an incredibly huge challenge because they aren't just dealing with that sexual polarity between them. In addition, they are also faced with coping with the polarity of consciousness and unconsciousness, and the even more challenging aspect of the polarity is that there isn't so much a division they are dealing with but a shattering of all the parts of the personality (ego, shadow, mentor, anima or animus, etc.), which will require reintegration. This is where the hero's journey comes into play. For a journey means to wander, and to wander suggests a searching, a yearning for something that is lost. What the hero is searching for is all the fragmented parts of the personality which need to be reunited.

Part of what the hero's journey is all about is giving us the opportunity (note the word unity *within the word* opportunity*) to wrestle with our shadow aspects. The purpose of which is not so much to conquer them as to integrate them into our personalities. A shadow in and of itself isn't bad, it just is. The point is not to repress it. Look to literature to see that ignoring the shadow is not the way to go. From* Beowulf, *to* Saint George and the Dragon, *to* Moby Dick, *we see that the shadow has to be faced and fought, the end purpose of course being integration. Does everyone confront his or her shadow? No. At least you are beginning to confront your shadow; I see you wrestling with it in your dark writings in this class.*

Step by step the hero's journey is a process by which we become whole. The shadow isn't the only fragment that needs to be reintegrated into the personality. It is just one of many. The journey is fraught with frustrations and dangers, but the end result is well worth it. To accomplish the goal is to win the pearl of great price, which is a unity of personality.

And so the theme of one's life is tied up with the hero's journey and its overwhelming importance in integrating the various disparate parts of the psyche. The journey isn't so much a going toward something new but a returning to what was: unity, completeness, wholeness. It's time to listen for your Call to Adventure and Answer that Call.

I hope these words help put some things into perspective for you.

Your loving mentor,
Grace

Jill found herself deep in thought. Had she ever received a call? She didn't think so. And why not! Once again, she felt that life just wasn't fair. Suddenly struck by a lightning bolt of realization, the last page of the article she held slipped out of her hand and drifted to the floor. She needed a course of action! But what should that action be? Should it begin with a divorce? She didn't hate her husband, her house, her children, her life, not really, but she existed in an environment of indifference. And wasn't that even worse than hate? Hate would galvanize her to some kind of action. Maybe action was what she needed. But to what end?

At dinner she surprised her family by announcing, "I've been thinking about going back to school. The only thing is..." She looked embarrassed. "I have no idea what kind of classes I'd take. My liberal arts undergraduate degree isn't really worth much more than the paper it's printed on. I'm not really interested in any one thing in particular. So if I go back, I don't really know what kind of classes to take."

Austin hid his surprise and tried for nonchalance. "Well, maybe focus on what you're good at."

"Like what, laundry? I'm not really good at anything really."

"Sure you are. You're a wiz at balancing the checkbook. And at tax time, you have all our ducks in a row way before deadline."

"That's just because it's so easy."

"It's easy because you have an aptitude for it. If you got deeper into stuff to do with finance, it might become challenging and interesting."

Jill wasn't sure if she'd just heard a click or not. "Hmm? I don't know. It's something to think about."

"Speaking of finance." Austin cleared his throat, and the family knew he was about to hold forth. "There is something I've been thinking about for a long time. I think we, as a family, should do something…philanthropic."

"What does that mean?" Chelsea was suspicious.

Shannon, quick to answer, said, "It means giving money away."

"Not exactly. It's doing good. Years ago when Danny Thomas, a famous actor, made buckets of money, he started St. Jude's Children's Hospital, that kind of thing."

"So we have buckets of money?" Chelsea was always interested in the topic of money.

"What we're talking about here," her father steered the conversation back to the direction he wanted it to go, "is doing something good."

"So open a hospital?" Chelsea liked it when her dad talked to her like she was a grown-up.

"Not necessarily, but do something so that people on our earth would benefit from it."

"Like what?"

"That's what we have to figure out. For example, the bees are dying at an alarming rate, that's not a good thing for many reasons."

"What can we do about that?" Chelsea was wearing her concentration frown.

"Actually," Jill piped up, "I recently read that the bees are making a comeback."

"Okay, scratch the bees. It doesn't have to be that. We need to start looking around, investigating ideas. For example, what do you see going on at school or in the news? Keep your eyes and ears open.

We don't have to make any snap decisions today. We can take years, literally. But if an idea comes to you, bring it up and we'll have a discussion and see if that's what we want to do."

Jill was happy the conversation had veered away from her. She had lots to think about, and yes, going back to school was feeling more and more like what she needed to be doing. And as the spring semester was about to begin, she thought she'd better make up her mind in a hurry.

Chapter 31

April had tiptoed in surprising all of them. It was almost cherry blossom time. So spring had sprung, and holy moly, it was already more than a year since her mother had died. Time was flying by. While she walked to work, Savannah was mulling over possible gifts to send Shannon for her birthday. Well, she had a week or so to figure that out. Beyond that, she had a couple of weeks of recess to look forward to midmonth too, so between the soon-to-arrive cherry blossoms and the lovely day and the upcoming recess, she was all smiles when she arrived at her office. It wasn't long before that smile disappeared.

It took a lot to dumbfound Savannah, but it appeared her chief of staff had managed to do just that. "Come again?" she found herself saying.

"Wendy Greene has spearheaded an investigation into misappropriations of your campaign funding."

"What in heaven's name does she think she will find?"

"It appears she is looking for irregularities."

"Well, she's not going to find any. I've never used funds for personal purposes." Savannah hadn't been so flummoxed in she didn't know when. "What a waste of time, energy, and resources."

"Just wanted you to be prepared. You know this town."

"Oh, good grief." Savannah shook herself like a wet dog ridding itself of water, and now that her perfectly good mood had been dumped on, she turned her attention to her day's agenda. She couldn't even countenance how ridiculous this misguided investigation was, and she was already resenting the time and effort it was going to take to move beyond it.

Pushing nine o'clock that night, she found herself in The Squeaky Wheel alone at a table for two finishing her spinach salad and debating on a second glass of wine before heading back to her townhouse when her cell phone rang. This was one of her favorite haunts, a little place off the beaten path that catered to its regular clientele, who were mostly staffers but also scattered with a few recognizable faces: this congressman, that senator. She did see the broad back of Gordon Foxe, the Stealth Bomber, as he'd been dubbed by his fellow investigative journalists, taking up his customary stool at the bar. When she'd arrived, she had nodded to a few familiar faces as she made her way to *her* spot, as she thought of the little table near the back of the room, but like most others here, boundaries were respected. Everyone knew at the end of the day people here wanted to eat, drink, and be left alone. Digging her little flip phone out of her purse, she glanced at the readout expecting it to be Dakota or Austin as only family had this number. She frowned at the unrecognizable number. Shaking her head, assuming it was a wrong number, she let it go to voice mail and put the phone back in her purse without even checking to see if a message had been left. A minute later, it rang again, same number. Exasperated, she responded with a "Who *is* this?"

"Don't turn and look at me. It's Gordon."

"Really? How did you get this number?"

"Please." He purred the word, but it was still laced with sarcasm.

"Okay, whatever. What's up?"

"I've been listening to the rumor mill, Congresswoman. It isn't sounding too good for you right about now."

"Oh, for cripe's sake, Gordon, as often as we've crossed each other's paths these past few years, you know as well as I do that nothing is going to come of that."

"Where there's smoke, there's fire."

"Look, I take fiscal responsibility seriously, very seriously, and you can quote me on that. Now if you're trying—"

"Listen," he cut her off, "I'm on your side. You need to trust me. Let me look into it and report back to you so you'll be moving forward on this from a platform of knowledge. No point in being blindsided by something you aren't expecting."

A sigh escaped as she processed his words. "Then what? We skulk around and meet in parking garages a la Woodward, Bernstein, and Deep Throat?"

His chuckle was sincere. "We need to be smarter than that. I have an idea."

He let her mull on that for a moment.

"Okay, so what's your idea?" She motioned to the waiter to bring her another glass of wine.

"If we start having meetings, people will wonder what's what. But if we became known as an item, so to speak, it wouldn't raise any eyebrows when and if we are seen together. So here's the plan, we start tonight. I come over to your table, we give each other the usual hug, peck-on-the-cheek greeting and visit. I walk you home, and before you know it, the rumor mill starts seeing us as being in a relationship, and we can meet without anyone wondering why. Then I'll be able to fill you in on what I find out without having to be sneaky about it. We'd be hiding in plain sight, as it were."

She blew out her breath, emptying her lungs, inhaled deeply, then released her breath once again. Her mind had processed the whole scenario in seconds. She *would* like to know what Wendy was up to, and Gordon *was* certainly qualified to be able to ferret anything out. "Sure, that sounds like buckets of fun." She clicked off and put her phone back in her purse just as her wine arrived.

Taking a sip, she saw, out of the corner of her eye, Gordon sliding off his barstool and turning in her direction. He paused like he'd just spotted her, then he headed for her table. "Savannah, I didn't see you come in." She stood as he arrived, and they did the usual hug, peck-on-the-cheek thing.

"Would you like to join me?"

"That would be nice." He sat and smiled at her.

She smiled back, and after a moment, her smile became a chuckle. "It's been a while. What have you been up to lately?"

The waiter had come back to her table, and Gordon ordered another beer.

"Actually I just finished a piece on human trafficking." He sighed deeply and shook his head. "It's given me nightmares. Literally. Not writing the article. What came before. So I'd decided to take a breather for a bit and regain some equilibrium."

When his beer arrived, they mutually enjoyed their beverages in silence for a moment while Savannah mentally reviewed what she knew of Gordon Foxe.

She couldn't remember how many times over the past few years she recalled hearing him say, "I'm not a reporter, I'm a journalist." When he'd been asked to explain the difference, he'd elaborate. In his opinion, reporters catered to the lowest common denominator, giving people what they wanted, which was sensationalism. Reporters oversimplified the news and only reported superficially. Analysis was nothing more than a word in the dictionary to them. A journalist, on the other hand, instead of skimming the surface, knew how to unearth information, finding those the hidden nuggets of gold. To have credibility, a journalist had to be impartial, curious, courageous, broadminded, and certainly needed a definite degree of skepticism. One thing a true journalist never did was cater to the whims of those in power, settling for being a mouthpiece for their rhetoric, otherwise known as propaganda. Like all those reporting the evening news, he was sure to add for emphasis in case those listening to him missed the obvious.

Gordon Foxe wasn't a classically handsome man, there were too many rough edges for that, but he was certainly tall and dark. Whenever their paths crossed for some reason, James Fenimore Cooper's *The Last of the Mohicans* came to Savannah's mind. It might have been the hawklike bridge of the nose or the razor-sharp cheekbones, or maybe it was the burnished copper hint to his skin, whatever it was, it was a certainty that he had a pretty large splash of Native American blood flowing through his veins.

"So," Savannah broke into her own reverie, "sorry to hear about the nightmares. I guess human trafficking is really becoming almost epidemic."

"It's not like it hasn't been around forever." In an attempt to steer the focus off himself, he pointed out, "Even that movie from years ago with Julie Andrews and Mary Tyler Moore had an underlying theme dealing with human trafficking. But back in the era of that movie, it was called white slave trade."

"Really? What movie was that?"

"*Thoroughly Modern Millie.*"

"Wow. But wasn't that a musical?"

"Yes, but it was a lot more than that."

"Hmmm? Never saw it. Guess I'll have to see it. Sounds interesting. I mean, you're sure it was Julie Andrews?"

"Yep, the same one who played the woman playing a man playing a woman in *Victor/Victoria*."

"Wait! Wait! Wait! She played a transvestite?"

"In a manner of speaking."

"Okay, okay, wait a minute. Are we talking about the same actress? The one who played *Mary Poppins* and Maria in *The Sound of Music*?

"One and the same."

"Well, wow." She thought about it for a moment. "Yeah, her! Guess she's a real kick-ass woman, isn't she? I never knew all that about those movies you mentioned. How did we get talking about Julie Andrews?"

"Doesn't matter. Let's talk about your situation."

"Yeah, let's do that."

"As a politician, I assume you've developed a thick skin so as not to be daunted by criticism."

That sounded rhetorical, so she ignored it after rolling her eyes. "So what's the plan here?"

"Just let me do what I do. I'll find out what's at the root of Greene's accusations and let you know what's what."

"I suppose it goes without saying that you really do need to be discreet."

"I'm good at what I do, Savannah. They don't call me the Stealth Bomber for nothing."

"That's reassuring." They finished their drinks at the same time.

"Come on, let me walk you home so people will start to get the idea that we are on the way to becoming a couple."

Shutting the door, locking it, and kicking off her shoes, Savannah padded through her townhouse in the dark. She should be exhausted and ready for bed, but she wasn't. To say that today's events had been unexpected would have been an understatement. Wendy Greene, sad little pissant person that she was, had taken her dislike for Savannah one step too far this time. But what was she up to? Savannah knew it was all a tempest in a teacup; she wasn't worried, or not really worried. She just didn't like the idea of bad press, even if it turned out to be false news, because people being people would only remember the accusation and not the fact that it turned out to be a lie. Of course there were those who claimed that any publicity, even if it was bad, was better than no publicity at all. She didn't really buy into that. She just wanted this to be over with quickly, which it would be because there was nothing to find. In fact, she rather thought Gordon would become rapidly disenchanted when nothing exciting emerged from his sleuthing, and that would be the end of that.

After brewing a cup of sleepy time tea in the hopes of getting at least a little sleep tonight, Savannah crawled between the sheets and settled in to read something of her mother's to help take her mind off her own situation. She had been blasting through the readings over the months, and as of that morning, there were only a couple items left. That morning she had snatched up a shorter one and read it quickly as she had a full day. It was a letter to the editor that had been about a medley of things linked to social media, including the dumbing down of language as well as cyber bullying and its less sinister cousin, general harassment. It was a letter that had given her much food for thought, and she decided to reread it before bed. The letter ended as follows:

> *Archeologists dig for bits of broken pottery to piece together a culture. Historians read old letters to ferret out the culture of a time and place. But what will future historians do, now that people no longer write letters? A text or Twitter message, misspelled and so succinct, tells us nothing of the culture—or*

maybe it tells us too much of a culture. If we only still wrote letters telling it like it is.

What would Shakespeare, the greatest word-smith of all time, think of the bastardization of the English language, a language that is abused each and every day in texts and Twitter messages that fly through cyber space, written without thought or even a realization that words have meaning, weight, and will impact the person reading them?

Omar Khayyam wrote, "The moving finger writes / and having writ moves on / nor all the piety and wit / can move it back again / to cancel half a line / nor all thy tears / wash out a word of it." Perhaps if tweeters and texters thought of that before they hit send, the world would be a better place.

Most Earnestly,
Grace Quinn

"Well, you're not wrong, Mom." Savannah said as she turned off the light and rolled over on her side to sleep.

*   *   *   *   *

Two days later on her walk to work when a newscaster poked a microphone in her face, Savannah went into professional mode even before a question could be asked. "We need bills and laws that reflect the needs of the American people—for all Americans—that have nothing to do with party line divisions. Washington is so dependent upon this unseemly rigid partisan warfare. But if the red framework and the blue framework could be swept aside, and even transcended, there would be more hope for policymaking based on the actual interests of the people of this great country."

"All that aside, Congresswoman, what is your take on the investigation spearheaded by Wendy Greene?"

"I take fiscal responsibility seriously, very seriously, and you can quote me on that."

"And your current relationship with the investigative journalist Gordon Foxe?"

Turning her head, she looked right into the camera. The smile didn't reach her lips, but it was certainly in her eyes and that look, unintended on Savannah's part, was about as sexy as a look could get. "No comment." God that was fast, she thought. That drink at The Squeaky Wheel and the walk home that first night and the dinner they shared last night and the gossip mill was grinding away. Mission accomplished, she silently saluted the Stealth Bomber as he had been right. No one knew what they were really up to. Little did she realize that after that look into the camera, everyone *thought* they knew exactly what the two of them were up to.

Over the course of a week, the pseudo romance with Gordon Foxe had apparently gone viral as she'd had to field phone calls from the family. "Hey, big sis," Dakota's voice was all singsongy. "Anything new going on in your life you want to share?"

"Not really?" Savannah was having fun with this.

"I heard on the news that you have a beau."

"Well, you know that the president keeps warning us about fake news. So be careful what you listen to."

"Ha ha. Give. Tell me about you and the Stealth Bomber."

"Gordon and I are just friends. That's it. Finis."

"Hmmm." Dakota was thoughtful. "That you aren't willing to talk about it makes it all that much more intriguing and ergo that much more important. Interesting."

"So how's school going?"

"Just grading papers. Nothing fun."

"And the wedding plans?"

"Coming along. Let Gordon know he's invited."

"What?"

"You heard me. Now, I almost hate to bring this up, but what's that about the supposed financial irregularities?"

"That is just Wendy Greene trying to find something that doesn't exist."

"Too bad she's such a thorn in your side. But hey, don't you have a recess coming up? I bet you're looking forward to that."

"Going home to Denver to live in my own house for two weeks. Not that I don't like my townhouse here, but I really miss my real house."

Austin hadn't called Savannah, but Jill couldn't help herself. "You guys look like a nice couple. Is it serious?"

"We're just friends, Jill. The press likes to play things up, especially since he's one of their own."

Chapter 32

Austin wasn't looking forward to suppertime. Usually the family meal was pleasant, but last night he and Shannon had gotten into a real bona fide argument. She'd gotten back on the kick about wanting a phone, and she wasn't about to give up. She wanted a phone, and she wanted it now.

"Everyone has a phone, and all my friends can text one another, and I'm the only one who doesn't have one. They think I'm a freak!"

"Shannon—"

"I just want a phone!"

"What people want," her father had told her, "isn't always what they should have. Wanting something is dictated by popular opinion rather than judgment. People want too many damned things."

Jill had had enough. "Austin, you are turning this into a forbidden fruit situation. And we all know how that turned out. What's the big deal?"

"See, Mom is on my side."

Without giving any reasons, he opted for dictatorial instead. "The answer is NO! Capital *N*, capital *O*, NO!"

The rest of the meal was eaten in silence, and Shannon slunk off to her room soon afterward.

Chelsea asked if she could watch *America's Funniest Home Videos* before going to bed, and Jill said only if she'd gotten all her homework finished over the weekend. As she'd finished it Friday after school, she was allowed to watch her show before heading off to bed.

Shannon, still completely miffed, didn't speak to anyone the next morning before she left for school. No one could do the silent treatment like she could. And now it was time to sit down to another dinner. Whoopee!

Jill tried to keep exasperation out of her voice. She'd been beyond busy all day, had to drop off and pick up Chelsea for her Tae Kwon Do lesson, was in the middle of studying for a challenging test in her graduate school class, and had to get dinner on the table to boot as it was her day. She knew why Shannon was so moody and just picking at her food, but she didn't have patience for it. "Shannon, what's the matter?"

"Nothing."

"Is this about getting a phone?"

"No." She kept talking to her dinner plate.

"If not that, what?"

"Nothing."

"Did you and Sadie have a falling out?"

"No!"

Jill looked over to Austin and just raised her eyebrows as if to say, *You pissed her off, you deal with her.* Austin picked up the ball and ran with it. "Hey, kiddo, clearly something is bothering you. You sure you aren't still upset about last night?"

Shannon put down her fork and looked like she was about to cry. "When Sadie and I got to her house after school, the police were there."

That came out of left field and took both her parents by surprise. "Was everything okay?"

"Sadie's sister has been gone all weekend. She's just…gone."

"Tell me?" He tried to keep the fear he suddenly felt out of his voice. A parent's worst nightmare is that his or her child disappears.

"The police were talking to Sadie's mom. She hadn't gone to work at the post office today because of Rose. Rose is just gone. She'd been gone since some time on Saturday and all day Sunday and now all of today."

"What did the police officer say?"

"I don't know. She told us to go upstairs and play in Sadie's room. But we left the door open so we could listen. All we could hear was that they figured she'd been abducted and they would see what they could do."

Austin knew his daughter very well, and he was pretty sure Shannon was holding on to a nugget of something. "But?"

"I don't think she was abducted. Sadie and I think she ran away to be with her boyfriend."

"What?" Jill interjected. "Rose is maybe fourteen, what boyfriend? Does her mother know about a boyfriend?"

Shannon shook her head.

"Her mother doesn't know she had a boyfriend, but you do?" Austin didn't want his daughter to feel his fear for the girl so he kept his voice neutral and light.

"She met him online. When Sadie and I play after school, Rose is always in her room on her computer with him. She showed us a picture. He's really…" she started to say *hot* but amended it to "cute."

"What do you know about all this, Shan?"

"She told us he was going to send her money so she could go where he lives."

"Do you know where that is?"

"Not really. She said he goes to school at Harvard."

"Oh, for goodness sake." Jill had heard enough. "She clearly doesn't have a boyfriend who goes to Harvard. She's just a child."

"Honey." Austin was shaking his head. "This is serious. You and Sadie didn't tell any of this to the police or Sadie's mom?"

Shannon was looking down at her plate. "No." Her voice was small.

"Come on, kiddo." Austin stood up and held his hand out for his daughter. "You and I are going over there to talk to, what's Sadie's mom's name anyway?"

"Margie," Jill supplied.

"Can I come?" Chelsea was feeling really left out of all this adventure.

"No, grasshopper, you stay home and take care of Mom."

That nickname always puffed up the little yellow belt's chest. "Okay," she agreed then turned to her mother. "Can we have some ice cream for dessert?"

On the drive over, Austin quizzed his daughter so he'd have as much information as possible before they arrived. "Is there a father in the picture here?"

"Sadie's mom and dad are divorced. I think he lives in Sacramento."

"Do you know if he's been contacted?"

"I think the police called him when they were at the house today."

"Speaking of calling, does Rose have a phone?"

"Yes, but she left it at home. Her mom said when she tried to call her Saturday when she never came home for dinner, she heard the phone ringing up in her room."

Well, *that* certainly wasn't good, but he didn't share that with Shannon. Rose had been coached to leave her phone behind so it couldn't be pinged and let anyone know where to find her. Whoever was orchestrating this wasn't stupid.

Sadie answered the door when Shannon and Austin rang the bell. "Mom," she hollered over her shoulder. "Shannon's here with her dad."

Margie came out of the kitchen drying her hands on a dishtowel. It was clear she had spent the day crying. "Margie." He held out both hands and took one of hers. "Austin. Sorry to meet you under such trying circumstances. Shannon was telling me about Sadie's sister, and I thought maybe I could be of some help."

"In what way?" She was too exhausted to be confused or even curious.

"First of all, has it been determined she hasn't ended up with her father?"

"She's not there."

"You're sure?"

Nodding, Margie put her fingers up to her lips. "She's not there. Foster is on his way down now. In fact, when I heard the doorbell, I thought it was him."

"Shannon was telling me that Rose has a boyfriend?"

"Boyfriend?" Margie sounded mystified as if she hadn't heard the word before.

"Shannon!" Sadie hissed. "That was a secret."

Austin elucidated, "Apparently, she met someone online, and Shannon thinks she ran away to meet him."

"Well, that's utterly absurd." Margie wasn't being haughty, just stumped.

"She has a computer?"

"Well, yes. A laptop."

"May I look at it? I might be able to find out what's going on, and you would be able to give the police a solid lead."

Margie motioned for them to follow her. Trooping upstairs and into Rose's room, she pointed. "I'm sure it's password protected."

Austin sat down at the desk and booted up the laptop. "What's the boyfriend's name?"

"I didn't even know she had one, which I still doubt. How would I know his name?"

"Shannon? Sadie?" Austin's voice brooked no resistance.

"Brandon," they both said.

He typed it in. "Voila, cracked the password." His fingers flew over the keys as if he were a warrior. After a short time, he sat back. "He sent her money, cash. It apparently arrived on Friday. She's on her way to Boston."

"What?"

"She left quite a trail of breadcrumbs in her emails. Call the police and see if they have a tech expert who can come over. Or we can bring the laptop to them."

By the time the police had arrived, Austin had researched both Greyhound and Amtrak. As succinctly as possible he filled everyone in. "My educated guess is that there is no Brandon."

"But you found his picture online," Shannon interrupted.

"A decoy. There is no Brandon," Austin repeated then focused on the cops. "This is a predator who knows his stuff. Best guess, he's probably between forty and sixty. These are the two routes she'd take to Boston: one via Greyhound, one via Amtrak. I've found the likely ones she could have gotten on late Saturday afternoon or evening as that was the last anyone saw of her." He handed a piece of notebook paper to the cops. "Here are the various stops. Worst-case scenario, she's almost there by now. If you can have the authorities in those cities intercept her before she gets to Boston and get her off the bus or the train, your counterparts in whatever city can put an undercover woman with the same build and coloring in her place and catch this guy before he knows he's been made."

After an exhausting hour that for the first time in two days left Margie with some hope, Austin gave his business card to the police, and he and Shannon took their leave. On the ride home, Shannon kept taking sidelong glances at her father. She had seen him in a different light, and she wasn't sure how to interpret what she'd seen, but she was pretty sure he was the equivalent of a superhero.

"How did you figure out her password?" was the only question she could think to ask him.

"I could say because I'm smart and leave it at that. But the truth is, I could have gotten into her stuff without the password, easy enough to bypass, but I didn't want to freak out her mom and sister. So I asked for something that might have been the password, and it turned out it was. So…lucky guess."

"How did you learn all that stuff?"

"Took a lot of years."

"Humph. You can really get into a computer without knowing the password?" That was a bit unsettling to her. "Good to know."

He looked over at her, doing a double take. "Good grief, were you just channeling your grandmother? You sounded just like her!" Then he added, "Yes, it is good to know. And don't you ever forget it. Because when you and your sister get on social media, and that won't be for a long time, I am going to be checking up on you."

That was some real food for thought. After mulling it over for a bit, she said, "Auntie Savvy says privacy is an inalienable right."

He looked her dead in the eye. "For adults. Not for kids. If you were in Rose's place right now, Auntie Savvy would be the very first one with her foot up my ass seeing to it that I found you. And you want to know why? Because she loves you. And don't tell your mother I said 'ass.'"

"Dad?"

"Hmmm?"

"Sadie said I was a tattletale."

Peers! How to handle this? "So how do you feel about what she said?"

"I'm not sure."

"Do you remember when we were reading those Beverly Cleary books at bedtime? And Ramona in one of them was wondering what was worse, being a tattletale or a copycat?"

"Oh, yeah?"

"In the adult world, both of those things have a counterpart. Someone who is a copycat is called a plagiarist. A plagiarist is someone who steals someone's ideas or words and it is a crime. But a tattletale in adult parlance is called a whistleblower. This person isn't a criminal but rather someone who sees something that is wrong and tells the world that it's wrong. It's not a bad thing at all."

"Oh." She thought about that for a few minutes. "So I was kind of like a whistleblower?"

"Kind of."

"Dad?"

"Yes?"

"Is Rose going to be okay?"

"If they find her before she gets to Boston. If they don't…" He was at a red light, so he looked over and made eye contact with his daughter. "If they don't, no one will ever hear from her again. That man, who was not a boy in college, is what is called a predator. He is a…he knows what he is his doing…he knows how to hunt on the internet and find young, vulnerable girls." The light changed, and the car behind him had to beep to get him to break eye contact with Shannon and move. "I won't even pollute your mind with what will happen to her if the police don't find her. But I will tell you this, and I hope it scares you. There are right now, this minute, today, hundreds, maybe thousands of girls just like Rose. Gone. Never to be heard from again because of something just like this."

"I get it now. That's why you're so strict. About letting Chelsea and me have computers and smartphones?"

"See? I knew you were smart."

"How did that predator find her?"

215

What to tell his young and innocent daughter? That the internet had become a Petri dish allowing sick perverts (who once hid their disgusting obsessions in shamed seclusion) to gather into diseased covens feeding each other's ugly needs and providing all kinds of assistance in the fulfillment of base and horrible desires.

"Before the internet," he told Shannon, "towns had railroad stations, and the railroad tracks went through town. And on one side of the tracks, the well-to-do people lived and life was good. Kids didn't go to bed hungry and everybody had fun. But on the other side of the tracks, life was not so good. The poor people lived on the other side of the tracks, and they sometimes robbed people because they needed money. And there were lots of fights, and often their children went to bed hungry. Bad things happened on the other side of the tracks. The people who lived on the good side of the tracks knew better than to go over to the other side of the tracks, especially at night, because they didn't want bad things to happen to them." Shannon was listening intently, so he went on.

"Today in this place called the internet, there is also a bad side of the tracks, but it's not obvious. There is no actual railroad track to cross so you will know when you have crossed to the bad side. You need to become very aware that people you meet or communicate with on the net are often not who they claim to be. A predator can pretend to be Brandon, a college student at Harvard, but he is really something else something very sinister. You understand?"

"I do."

"And here's something else. Tonight you became my hero, Shannon, and that is because you did everything right. You told Mom and me what was going on. If you see something, say something. We need people who will do that, and you did it. You are the one who saved Rose."

"If she gets saved."

"Yes. If she gets saved. If anything were to happen to you or your sister, it would kill me, Shannon. You girls have no idea how much love I have for you."

"I get it, Dad. You are just trying to protect Chelsea and me and that's why we can't have access to the internet, but if I got a phone like Auntie Savvy's that doesn't connect to the internet, wouldn't that be okay? I mean, at least I could text."

Laughter was his only response. "You are *not* going to let that go, are you?"

"I think it would be a good compromise." She liked using grown-up words. "Besides, then I could call you immediately if I needed you for any reason. Wouldn't that be a good thing?"

He turned to the little girl he loved more than his own life and thought about the most recent school shooting he'd heard about on the news the week before. Yes, maybe a phone would be a good idea so she could get in contact with him. "When's your birthday?" he asked her, pretending he didn't remember it was just around the corner.

"Next week."

"And you'd settle for a phone like Auntie Savvy's for a birthday present?"

"Yes, yes, yes." She was literally bouncing in the car seat. Then she got a little gleam in her eye. "Are you still *able* to buy phones that old-fashioned?"

"Don't you worry your—" He stopped himself from saying *your pretty little head*, thanks to a committee he'd be sucked into last fall. "Self about that. I can get my hands on one."

"Will I be able to take pictures with it?"

"Don't push your luck, missy," he told her.

He parked the car in the driveway, but as he was reaching for the door handle, Shannon, once again, said, "Dad?"

"Yes?"

"Have you noticed how Mom is different since she started graduate school? She seems happier. I mean, not tonight because she was stressing over her test, but she just seems happier."

The fact was, Austin had noticed. For years Jill had been an unhappy woman. She was like a car stuck in soft sand. The more she tried to move forward, the faster her wheels spun, going nowhere, just spitting sand in everyone's eyes to the sound of an angry revving engine. But since she started school, she was making forward momentum, and while she still often got frustrated, it was coming from a different place. She was changing, and at times she was even happy. And for some odd reason, her libido had also kicked into overdrive, and Austin sure wasn't complaining about that. A tenderness, a closeness, and an intimacy they had never experienced before had emerged. It was still in the fragile beginning stages regardless of the years they'd been together, and when they whispered in the night together after making love, well, life had never been so good. Looking back, he knew the entire family had weathered some bleak times, and in the early years he'd thought more than once that abandoning ship was the only answer for him. But once their family of three had become a family of four, he had gone through a metamorphosis of his own. He had read somewhere that the best thing a father could do for his children was to love their mother, so he made a determined effort to do just that. There were times it was a challenge, but he did his best. And now, as Bob Dylan had pointed out many long years ago, the times they were a-changing, so he answered his daughter, "Yes, I have noticed that."

"If going back to school makes her happy, why didn't she do that a long time ago?"

"Well, I guess some people are what are called late bloomers. They don't really know what they want to do in life right away. It takes them a while to find their path. I think Mom was just a late bloomer."

"Is she going to stay happy?"

"I think so. Once a flower starts to bloom, it can't unbloom. So I think Mom is now on her way to being a much happier person."

"Well, I don't think I'm going to be a late bloomer." Those words made Austin's heart lubb-dupp. "I'm going to do what Auntie Dakota did and go to graduate school right away."

"And speaking of school, it's a school night, so time to get in the house and get ready for bed."

Chapter 33

To herself, Savannah admitted she was having fun with the deception. She and Gordon ate out often and did all the things that dating couples did. Went to art showings and browsed book stores, took long walks, and were seen going in and out of each other's homes. The doorman where Gordon lived always gave her a wink when she and Gordon entered or left the building. And all this in just two weeks! The first time she visited his apartment, she was surprised to see a cat stretched out on the couch taking a nap. It jumped off the sofa and trotted up to Gordon, winding itself in and out of his legs making chirpy little purrs. "Is somebody hungry?" he said as he bent down and scooped her up. "Meet Nellie," he said to Savannah, as she reached over and petted the cat's head.

"As in Bly?" she asked.

"One and the same. How did you guess?"

"Nellie Bly was my hero at one point. I wanted to be her when I grew up."

"Really? Why didn't you?"

"I have no idea."

This evening Savannah wandered around his living room. On an end table was a bronze sculpture of a hawk in flight descending with talons at the ready as if to grab some prey.

"Beautiful hawk," she told him when he entered the room handing her a glass of wine.

"I think of him as my totem animal."

"Because?"

"Because a hawk represents the truth, and as a journalist, I'm all about ferreting out the truth."

'Truth. That's a word with a lot of impact. It brings Pontius Pilot to mind."

"Yes, the old 'what is truth' debate. Then there is Winston Churchill, who once said, 'Men occasionally stumble over the truth, but most of them pick themselves up and hurry off as if nothing had happened.'"

"So as a journalist dedicated to ferreting out the truth, any progress on things?"

There wasn't. "This is a bit like chasing ghosts. There just isn't anything there."

"Then it's time to give it all a rest?"

"Let me follow up one last line of inquiry and we'll regroup tomorrow."

The next afternoon, Gordon stopped by her office, as he often did just to chat and make plans for the evening. "How about we eat in tonight?"

"Sure," she agreed. "Your place or mine?"

"How about mine? We can order out when you get there."

"Or I can fix something."

"Red meat?"

"If you insist."

"About seven?"

"Let's make it six as I have an early day tomorrow."

Savannah showed up with a sack full of groceries. While Vivaldi played in the background and the cat slept in a patch of setting sunlight that splashed across the floor from the west facing window, she made potato salad, bison burgers, and fresh green beans. She glanced over into the living room where Gordon sat absorbed in the evening news. What a nice, cozy domestic scene this was. At one point he looked up, caught her eye, and winked at her. She smiled to herself while at the same time chiding herself to stop acting like a schoolgirl with a crush. Past experience had taught her that fantasies like that didn't turn out well.

When it was time to eat, Gordon turned off the television. "Smells good," he told her.

"Tastes even better." And they both dug in with gusto while the classical music floated in the background.

After a while, Savannah pointed to the cat with her fork. "So what do you do with Nellie when you take off on assignment?"

With his thumb, he pointed first to the left then to the right. "Luckily for me both neighbors love her. She really belongs to all three of us and makes herself at home in all our apartments."

"A communal cat? How interesting."

"She just showed up one day on my balcony, so as I was the first one she adopted, I got to name her. Then she adopted the others, and she basically keeps us all in line attending to her needs."

"Doesn't look like her needs are many."

"They aren't. No dessert?"

"Sorry. Didn't even think of that. I usually have a second glass of wine for dessert." That said, he poured them each a second glass. "Thanks. The music reminds me of my father. He loved classical music."

"And your mother?"

"She always listened to what my brother, Austin, dubbed her *dead white males*: Elvis, Johnny Cash, Buddy Holly, Eddie Rabbit, that kind of music."

"And what about you? What do you prefer?"

"Honestly, I actually prefer nothing. I prefer peace and quiet. I'm not one of those who constantly needs to be hooked into something and listening to something. Music is fine, I don't mind it, but I don't go out of my way to listen to it."

Taking a long sip of wine, Gordon cleared his throat as if getting ready to hold forth. That got her attention, and she looked at him expectantly.

"Greene's got nothing except a grudge against you, apparently. Her investigation has petered out. It's essentially over. She'll try to keep it chugging along for appearance's sake for a little while. But nothing will come of it."

"I knew it." Savannah pumped a fist in the air. When he didn't smile or offer her a fist bump or even a congratulations but just looked her dead in the eye, she found herself saying, "But?"

"But I did find something you need to know about."

She picked up her wineglass then set it down without taking a sip. "This sounds ominous." When he just continued to stare at her, she added, "Hence why you suggested eating in tonight instead of out." She prepared herself for what, she didn't know, then said, "Okay, what is it?"

"I came across something, something on the very down low that, well, that probably nobody could ever trace. I even debated with myself about not bringing it up. But you really need to know this."

"What are you talking about?"

"You got significant campaign contributions from several organizations this past election. Organizations that hadn't contributed in the past."

"Yes, but it was all above board. They just, pretty much at the eleventh hour, decided to contribute. And the amounts were well within the legal bounds. And the fact of the matter is, if I hadn't had that surprising influx, I probably wouldn't have won the election."

"The sum of those monies taken together was significant. And I agree with your assessment, that the money they donated to your campaign was what actually helped put you back in the house. Without it, you definitely would have lost your seat."

"Yeah, I mean it was touch and go right up to the last minute." But she had won, even after her opponent had insisted on a recount, and well, all's well that ends well. "Where is this going?" She tried to keep confusion out of her voice, but the way he was laying all this out was starting to concern her.

"That money didn't actually come from those organizations. Well, it did, but not exactly. The money that *bought* you your seat in fact came from one individual." He hadn't taken his eyes off hers, and he could tell by her body language that she hadn't a clue what he was talking about or where this was going. That was a good thing. If there had been one single tell, he'd have known she wasn't the person he perceived her to be. But as he spoke those last words, he saw some small suspicion start to flicker way back in her eyes and an almost imperceptible shake of her head. "That individual who filtered money through those organizations into your campaign was your brother, Austin Quinn."

Savannah could actually feel the blood drain out of her face. She tried to shake her head but discovered she could barely breathe. "Wh…what?"

"It's buried deep, but it's there. I doubt anyone will ever be able to make any connection. It will never come out. Even if he was accused, it wouldn't stick. He's Teflon here. As are you."

"I…I can't believe it."

"I'm good, Savannah. I'm better than good. There's no question."

"It…doesn't…"

"Rest assured it wasn't illegal. Unethical, certainly, but he stayed on the right side of the line as far as any law. He actually just made *investments*"—he put finger quotes around the word investments—"and shortly thereafter the companies donated to your campaign." He handed her a list of the corporations. "If it had been one company…but there were too many for it to be coincidental."

"Okay." Her face was stone as she stood and slipped on her jacket, shoving the list into her jacket pocket.

"Look, Savannah, this all…what I'm trying to say is, you're good at what you do. And I don't—" She put up her hand to stop him, so he stopped.

"I'll take it from here. Thanks, Gordon." And she walked out of the door closing it firmly behind her.

First thing in the morning she called her chief of staff to cancel the next couple of days and then wasn't able to catch a flight heading west until afternoon. After making connections, it was early evening before she finally knocked on her brother's door.

Shannon answered it and squealed with delight to see her. "Auntie Savvy, guess what?" She pulled her little phone that was a clone of her aunt's out of her pocket. "See what Dad got me for my birthday! Oh, by the way, thank you for the book and the gift certificate. But could you give me your phone number? Then I'll be able to text you."

When her niece finally ran out of steam, Savannah herself was able to take a breath. She looked over Shannon's head and saw Austin, who was looking at her curiously, wondering what she was doing there. She gave him a warning shake of her head with eyes so full of fury that he literally took a step backward. "Hey, butterfly," she told Shannon, "I have rules that have to be followed if someone wants my number. Do you want to know what they are?"

"Yes! Yes! Yes!"

"Rule number one is I won't allow more than one text a week. Got that?"

"Okay. Is there a rule number two?"

"Yes. Don't be impatient for a response. Sometimes my phone is off for days at a time. So when I get to it, I'll answer your text. But that isn't an invitation to send me another text right away before the week is up. Got that?"

"Got it. But…"

Savannah sighed. "But what?"

"What if it's an emergency?"

"Then call me. If the phone is turned off, leave a voice mail."

"Okay."

They put each other's numbers in their respective phones, then Savannah said, "Now I've got to talk to your dad." She made eye contact with him from across the room and pointed to his office; he preceded her into his domain. She carefully shut the door behind her then turned to face her brother.

"What's up, Savvy?"

"Mom always said that people say things in the height of anger that are usually better left unsaid. And right now I am angrier with you than I have ever been before. So I don't want you to say a word. Not one word. Nor will I. Rather than saying anything, I'm just going to lay it out for you." She pulled some three-by-five index cards out of her pocket and laid one of them on his desk. Written on it was the name of one of the companies that had contributed to her campaign. He read it then looked up at her with caution in his eyes.

She laid out a second card with the name of another company who had contributed to her campaign. He looked at it then back at her. She could see he knew where this was going. So she quickly laid out four more cards each with the name of a different organization that had contributed to her campaign.

"Savvy…"

"Not one word."

"How did you find out? That new squeeze of yours?"

"I said *not* one word! I'm not speaking to you right now, and I don't want you to speak to me. I'll let you know when—if I'm ever ready to hear your voice again!"

As she headed toward the door, she turned and looked back at him. "Who are you? You're certainly not our mother's son. She wouldn't believe this!" She left the room shutting him in it, and for some reason, he knew better than to leave it while she was still in his home. She said her hellos and goodbyes to Chelsea and Jill and cautioned Shannon once again about not sending more than one text a week before leaving the house as quickly as she arrived.

Jill gave it about ten minutes, then she tapped on the office door and entered, closing it behind her. Austin was sitting in his office chair, spinning it slightly in one direction then reversing direction and going the other way. He was staring into space and didn't even look up when Jill sat on the corner of his desk, making it impossible for him to swivel back and forth as his knees were blocked by hers. With a fingertip, she moved the index cards around on the desktop, looking at each one with a quizzical expression.

"You want to tell me what that whirlwind visit from your sister was all about?"

"Not particularly."

"Let me rephrase that. Please tell me what's going on."

*　　*　　*　　*　　*

After her showdown with Austin, Savannah caught a flight home to Denver. She let herself into her house, tapped in the code on the alarm pad, then leaned back against the closed door. Home sweet home. She never slept as well as when she was here, at home in her own bed. She wondered if she'd be able to sleep tonight.

Chapter 34

The first week of her recess Savannah spent pampering herself by eating junk food, taking long walks, thinking long thoughts, and just puttering around her house. The next week, she spent two days at the legal aid office that had launched her, and she busied herself by helping a few clients. In the late afternoons when she got home, she'd wander around the backyard. It was early in the season yet, but she made some notes that she'd pass on to the gardener, who would probably be starting his weekly rounds next month, about some new plants and shrubs she wanted in the back.

Wednesday morning of the second week of her recess, she awoke thinking about Gordon. There had been a vital reciprocity in their short connection, and she found herself missing him, their conversations, even missing the anticipation she'd had during the day knowing she'd be seeing him that evening. True, their relationship had been a front to prevent inquiring minds from wondering what was really going on, and that, Savannah said to herself, as she tossed back the covers and got out of bed, was that!

When her housekeeper arrived to do her weekly duty, Savannah took off to catch up with her friends at Planned Parenthood. When she got home, the place was sparkling clean with the exception of one piece of furniture. Savannah had laid down the law early on: Flora was to leave the desk in her office alone. It was off-limits as far as dusting, straightening, polishing, or anything. "Don't touch it," she'd warned the housekeeper upon hiring her. "Don't even breathe near it." Flora had followed those instructions to the letter for the past five years of her employment.

Thursday morning when Savannah got up, she decided today was a day to be lazy. She pulled on some yoga pants and one of her mother's T-shirts. It read, "Always give 100%, unless you're giving blood." She skipped her oatmeal for breakfast, as she was out and didn't want to make a run to the store, and instead had a scrambled egg on toast then meandered through the house, ending up in her office. Once again noticing that her desk could use a good cleaning off, dusting, polishing, and buffing, she got busy with the chore. She cleared the desktop of clutter, placing it on the windowsill, and then emptied all the cubby holes and the drawers. The trash basket was filling up rapidly, and she was beginning to experience that sense of accomplishment one feels at giving something a cleaning down to the bone. When she lifted the blotter to set it aside to clean under it, she froze when she spotted the letter.

The *letter*!

She had been avoiding this letter for a year now. It was a letter that had been waiting for her when she got home from her mother's funeral. It was the last letter her mother had written to her and apparently mailed the day before her aunt had called her and told her to "get home now!" It must have been on its way to Denver via the United States Postal Service as she was speeding up Interstate 90 in a mad dash to try to make it to her mother's bedside before it was too late. She picked up the envelope addressed to her in her mother's handwriting, shaky handwriting, but still clearly her mother's. Her own hand started to tremble, and that made her give an exasperated snort.

When she'd gotten home after the funeral and saw the letter on her credenza where Flora always placed her mail when she was gone, something in her heart had stopped. These were the last words her mother had written to her, and she was afraid to read them. She wasn't a person who had ever experienced precognition, but from the first this letter felt different. It almost sent off a vibe, and that made Savannah more than cautious. It made her downright nervous and hesitant, and so she had resisted any inclination to open it and read it. She knew that inevitably she would have to at some point, but she also knew it wouldn't be immediately.

First a week went by, then two, and finally it was a month later and still she hadn't opened the letter. One day she slipped it under the blotter on her desk, and there it had remained all this time. It was now more than a year since it had been sent. She propped it up in front of the framed picture of her mother and her father that she had placed on the window ledge when she had begun her cleaning binge, then she sat back in her chair and just looked at the sealed envelope.

Shaking herself, she went back to the chore at hand and finished cleaning and polishing the desk. When everything was back in its place and the picture of her parents rested in its familiar spot on her desk, she once again propped the letter next to it. She reached out and caressed it with a finger. This was it. The last item she had left to read of her mother's. After staring at it for a moment, she retreated into the kitchen and made a soothing cup of chamomile tea. She always thought of Peter Rabbit when she sipped the steaming brew—a story her mother had read to her often in her childhood. Back in her office, sitting in her chair, she drank her tea while focusing on the envelope. She was certain she knew what the contents of the letter held, but there was only one way to find out. Setting the cup aside, she reached out her fingers, barely making contact with it when chimes filled the house. Saved by the bell, she thought to herself as she stood and headed for the front door.

When she looked at the security camera Austin had installed for her a couple of years ago and saw Gordon, she just stared for a minute. He was looking right at the camera. When he made a circling gesture with his finger as if to say get a move on and come and answer the door, she did just that.

"This is a surprise. To what do I owe the pleasure?" She held the door wide and gestured him in.

"I was in the neighborhood."

"Really?"

"Yes, really. And I thought I'd drop by."

She'd brought him into the living room, where they both sat on the sofa. "So what brings you to *this* neighborhood from Washington?"

"Actually the neighborhood I'm heading for is Estes as I have some property there. My property manager and I usually get together this time of the year to determine whether improvements or upkeep of some kind are necessary, and we get all that scheduled for the summer months. When I jumped in my rental at the airport, for some reason instead of heading to Estes, I drove over here."

"Did you find out something else I need to know about?"

He shook his head. "By the way, how did things go with your brother? Did you guys have a showdown?"

"Not exactly. Sort of. Suffice to say, he and I aren't speaking for the moment."

"I have to tell you, Savannah, being an only child, I have no understanding of sibling relationships, but I do know this. If I had a sibling, I never in a million years would have spent that sum of money on him or her. That was a butt-load of dollars he invested to see to it that you retained your seat. He must really care about you."

"Yeah. Well. Like I said, we're not speaking right now."

"You...you look a little different."

She looked down at her yoga pants and T-shirt then back at him. "I've been cleaning house."

"I don't mean what you're wearing, I mean, you just look like you have been thinking deep thoughts."

"I guess I have been." The way she said that sounded like the end of a conversation, not an opening. So he switched gears.

"On a different note." He cleared his throat and suddenly looked a bit nervous. "There is another reason I dropped by." When she didn't say anything, just looked at him expectantly, he said, "I missed you."

She opened her mouth to say something, but nothing came out.

"This is where you say, 'I missed you too, Gordon.'" He admitted to himself he was a bit unsettled coming right out with all this. To make naked his desires was not something he usually did as he was a private sort of individual, but what made all this seem right was that he suspected she kept much to herself as well.

She gave a little laugh. "Well, as a matter of fact, I did miss you too."

"Good. Now that that's established, I have a"—he started to say *proposition*, but realizing that would be the wrong word, finished with "suggestion."

"I can hardly wait to hear it."

"Now that our investigation is over, I say we go back to ground zero and start again, only this time we do it for real."

"Start what again?" She wasn't being obtuse, just cautious.

"A relationship." Their eyes were locked as she assessed exactly what he was saying. Then he singsonged, "Let's start at the very beginning. A very good place to start."

That made her laugh. "Julie Andrews again?"

"Hey, I think she's hot. What can I say?"

"Ah, well, apparently you have a type. And as I am nothing like Julie Andrews, why would you want to be in a relationship with me?" Now she was flirting, and it had been such a long time since she had done that she wasn't sure she was doing it correctly.

"Au contraire. I think you and Julie have a lot in common. You're both smart, kick-ass women who have risen to the top of your respective careers. And that is very attractive to me."

"I can honestly say that this is a conversation I didn't imagine having. But as a segue back to those deep thoughts I've been having, maybe this is the appropriate time to bring it up. I've been second-guessing my choices. My life in Washington."

"How so?"

"My brother has never hesitated to point out to me that I have succumbed to a Kafkaesque strangeness as far as the life I've chosen to live in our country's capitol. He claims the whole system is completely dysfunctional."

"And?"

"And I'm beginning to think he's right. Oh, not completely right. I'd never give him that satisfaction. I'm just thinking I might serve my constituents better here in Colorado than in Washington. The governor is making noises about stepping down and not seeking reelection."

He knew immediately where she was going with that but was still surprised. "Wow. I didn't see that coming."

"The fact is I'm not one for snap decisions. I'm just now these past few days starting to think about it. So it may not come to fruition, but if it were come to pass, I wouldn't be spending time in Washington. I'd be here at home. I mean, I'm just bringing this up, in light of what you brought up, about the relationship thing."

"I'm suddenly feeling that it's a good thing I have property in Colorado."

It seemed like he had more to say, so she jumped in to stop him. "Honestly, Gordon," she started speaking quickly, "I don't know if I'm the best bet."

"Don't sell yourself short, Savannah." Both just sat back and took a breath. Then Gordon added, "But another fact is that you aren't the only one thinking of new directions. I have my own plans. For instance, I have a couple of books on the backburner of my brain, and as I was flying out here and thinking of my condos in Estes, I was thinking Colorado is probably a better environment in which to get the creative juices flowing than my apartment back in Washington. I'd have no problem letting that apartment go."

Okay, this was sounding like something that was happening way too fast to suit her. She caught herself leaning back firmly into the couch while crossing her arms across her chest. "I…a…a book, huh? What about?"

Her body language wasn't lost on him. As an accomplished fencer, he knew when to parry and when to thrust. He gave her a gentle smile. "Yes, actually a couple of books. But when it comes to my writing, I don't talk about things until they are on paper, so…" He cleared his throat again. "So…circling back to our previous line of conversation, do you have a type?" And *that* made her laugh. "What kind of man are you attracted to?"

She looked off into space for a moment. When her mind lit on something, she looked back at Gordon, appraising him. "Did you ever watch those old reruns of *Have Gun, Will Travel*?"

"Palidan? That's your type? A vigilante gunslinger?"

"Au contraire," she tossed his own words back at him, "a hired gun, certainly, but never a hired killer. He was ever so much more than that. He was cut from a very moral piece of cloth. Kind of like the Jack Reacher of his time."

"Okay, Palidan and Jack Reacher. Now I get your type. Luckily for me, I kind of fill that bill."

And that made her laugh again. "Let me reiterate, this is a conversation I never imagined having."

Thinking it was time to make a bit of a retreat so she could think about all the cards he laid on the table, Gordon glanced at the clock on her wall and rose. "I've got to get going as I have that appointment in Estes. When are you heading back to Washington?"

"Friday. I've got a lot to do before I hit the ground running on Monday. What about you?"

"Sunday. What say, I knock on your door Sunday night and we go have some dinner and see if we click?"

He liked that she took the time to process what he said before she answered. When a slow smile lit her eyes and she said, "Sounds like a plan," he smiled back at her.

She walked with him down the driveway to his rental car parked at the curb. Standing in front of her, he ran his hands down her arms from shoulder to wrist, then taking her hands in his, he pulled her toward him for a kiss. When it was over, he winked at her, turned to open the car door, then, rethinking the situation, turned back. This time he pulled her snuggly into his arms and kissed her again. That she was kissing him back with her arms about him, he took as a good sign.

"You know," he spoke against her vibrating lips, "my appointment isn't in stone. It can wait until tomorrow."

She slid her eyes away from his and looked into his car, seeing his travel-worn duffel in the back seat. "Why don't you grab that and come back in the house?"

* * * * *

The top bedsheet lay knotted and tangled at the foot of the bed. Face-to-face with their legs just as entangled as the sheets, Gordon languidly stroked Savannah's upper arm as they both recuperated from a lusty bout of lovemaking. When her mind started to register things again, she said, "All this happened kind of fast." She wasn't complaining, just stating what she saw to be a fact.

"Not so fast for me." Gordon leaned back just enough to look at her face. "I've had my eye on you for a long, long time." He read the surprise in her eyes and leaned in and kissed the tip of her nose. "Almost from the moment you arrived in the Capitol. You were so smart and witty, didn't hurt that you were also pretty. Not to mention single. I was just getting ready to make my move and ask you out when you started socializing with the junior congressman from Georgia, or was it Alabama? That kind of put a hitch in my plans."

"Toby? I haven't seen him in a long while."

"I kept thinking you two were just casual friends. But whenever I'd see you together, you looked so comfortable, and, well, that lasted until the next election. What I'd deem to be a long-term relationship. So I never had that chance to make that move."

"Well, wow" was the only thing she could think to say.

"When he didn't regain his seat after that first term, I wondered if you two would end up in a long-distance relationship. So I continued to hold back. Then that didn't appear to happen, but I didn't want to be the rebound guy, the one that doesn't stick, so I held back some more. Then of course I had the occasional assignment that took me away for weeks at a time. Next thing I knew, more than a couple of years had passed."

She had a faraway look in her eyes. "I haven't thought of Toby for ages." She ran a finger over Gordon's jawline and rested her fingertip in the almost imperceptible cleft in his chin. "If it hadn't been for him, what you and I shared here today, well, it probably wouldn't have happened."

Now that was an interesting comment. "What do you mean?" He saw a shutter slid down in her eyes, and to play for time, he brushed a strand of hair off her cheek and leaned in and kissed the spot. "None of my business?"

A long few moments flowed by before she said, "I had a very... unhappy introduction to sex when I was very young. It took years before I was ready to try it again. Then after a couple of experiments in my twenties, which weren't that fabulous, I decided I wasn't relationship material. Toby and I were elected to the house the same year, both new kids on the block, so that was an immediate bond. And we served on some of the same committees, one having to do with battered women. Apparently, his sister had been in an abusive relationship, and it made him very sensitive to women who had been wounded whether inadvertently, as I had been, or deliberately, as many are. He was so kind, especially at first, gentle, never demanding. He healed me. I was the bird with the broken wing, and by the time our relationship had run its course, I could fly. Thanks to him. Before Toby, I would never have been able to be open to the...intensity...we shared here today."

When she fell silent, he knew it wasn't the time to press for more. But he felt that some recognition of her confession was necessary. "Well, then, if I ever cross paths with Toby, I'll be sure to shake his hand."

He had a habit of saying things that made her laugh. She liked that about him. "Yeah, you do that." She needed to change the subject so asked, "What about this condo of yours in Estes?"

"Condos, actually, plural. I own two buildings each about the size of a city block. Views from the condos are outstanding. Rather than sell the individual units, I rent them out as I like the monthly influx of capital. It's good investment property. In fact, it paid for itself in less than ten years, so it's pure profit now. In the last couple of years, my property manager and I opened up two of them to the Airbnb thing. I come out a few times a year to touch base with him, you know, keep my finger on the pulse of things."

"How's that Airbnb thing working out?"

"Pretty well. But it was a whole new learning curve in discovering how when people are transient, they don't give a rat's you-know-what about the property. For example, one tenant left spilled grease or oil in the bottom of the oven and didn't clean it up before leaving, so when the next tenant turned on the oven, well, the place filled with black smoke. So now my manager knows to run a check on the oven, turning it on before cleaning the place for the next tenants and turning it off afterward."

"Hope he has a checklist so he doesn't forget to turn it off."

"He's very capable."

"You have warmth in your voice when you speak of him."

"Thayne and I go way back. Buddies from when we were in school. I trust him implicitly."

"You mentioned being an only child. Sounds like he might be the brother you never had. Tell me about him."

"Well, he lives in one of the condos, rent-free I might add. As the manager, that's part of his salary. But as managing the property isn't at all a full-time job, he owns a bicycle/ski store in town. He pretty much has the life of Riley. I fly out a few times a year and stay in his guest room, and we catch up."

"You didn't lay claim to one of the condos as your own?"

"I have my eye on one, but for now it's rented. No point in not generating income when I'm only out there on occasion. And Thayne always has my room ready for me."

She lay in his arms listening to his voice and thinking to herself, yes, this friend of his sounded almost like a family member, when he took her by surprise by circling back to the earlier topic of relationships. "So why wasn't there anyone after Toby? You still crazy about him?"

"Toby and I were never in love, but I certainly loved him. He was just a good, sweet, kind man. But when we went our separate ways, well, before Toby, I'd already been many years without a significant other, and it wasn't like I was panting to replace him. Life just went back to my usual routine. That's all."

"You didn't miss sex?"

"Well, sex isn't the end all and be all of my life, but speaking of sex." She gave his shoulder a little push until he rolled onto his back, then she rolled on top of him. "Just for the record, one other thing Toby taught me was that men think it's very sexy when a woman takes the lead once in a while. He said that a woman being a little selfish in the bedroom really turns a guy on. So brace yourself, 'cause I'm about to get selfish."

"Yep. Definitely going to have to remember to shake Toby's hand." That was the last coherent thought he had for a lengthy block of time.

Chapter 35

Dakota sat at her desk in her office at school, resting her head on her arms. She had just ripped a student a new one and was berating herself. God, could she have been more unprofessional? Jason had come in complaining about the D he had gotten on a paper. The D had been a gift, and it never ceased to amaze her that the students had such elevated opinions of their obviously inferior work. They thought they should be getting As and Bs just because they turned the paper in on time. Hadn't they figured out by now that she didn't give grades; they earned them.

The student had missed at least twelve class periods over the course of the semester, and that translated to four weeks of missed time as they met three times a week. If students missed more than three days, she docked them half a letter grade. So he'd already blown those gimmie points, and now he'd blown this second to the final paper. He had gotten right in her face and told her that everyone knew her class was a blow-off class, that this was a math and science school and writing wasn't important in his future profession, and she'd better give him a B on that paper or else.

She snatched the paper out of his hand and said, "Look!" She put her finger on the word *to* and said, "'The water was to cold'? 'To cold'? Really? Do you see what's wrong there? What about this?" She put her finger on the word *there* and said, "'They grabbed there life-jackets'? 'There lifejackets'? Do you see what's wrong there? And what about this." She pointed to the word *fairy*. "'The fairy,' not *ferry*, 'was sinking at an alarming rate'! Sheesh! A third grader wouldn't make those mistakes."

Clearly not understanding what he'd done wrong and caring even less, he said, "That still doesn't mean the paper deserves a D."

"No, it deserves an F. What about this?" She pointed to his use of statistical information. "Where did that come from? It wasn't in your head, it had to come from somewhere, but do you give credit to the source by documenting in-text as we learned in class? No, you don't. That's called plagiarism."

"Hey, I put the source on the reference page."

"This is still plagiarism if you don't document it in-text! And plagiarism is cheating. Let's just hope when I get the final projects graded, which should happen this weekend, you didn't do the same thing. Because cheating twice in a row means your papers gets turned in to the dean's office."

That did it. The kid snapped. "Oh yeah? Well, let me tell you something. That's what we do around here. We cheat!"

"Thanks for the heads-up. I'll be sure to look closely at your final project. If you fail that, you'll fail the course as it's worth fully one-third of your grade."

Too angry even to volley the last word, he snatched up his paper and stormed out of the office.

It was only then that she noticed that her door hadn't been completely shut, and the few students in the hallway were looking in at her like she had two heads. Yep, she'd never lost it like that with a student before. What the upshot was going to be, she didn't know. Would he report her to the dean for behavior unbecoming? Or would he just snuff it up and that would be the end of it. Well, she'd deal with the fallout when it happened, which wouldn't be until Monday as this was blessedly Friday afternoon.

On the drive home, she told Daniel about the confrontation. "I just get so frustrated with students who think that just because they pay their college tuition that they are entitled to a passing grade. They sure want a college degree because with it they can get better-paying jobs, but a college *education*? God no, they don't want to bother studying or learning anything. Their attitude is 'I paid my tuition, now give me a degree.' When are they going to figure out it doesn't work that way? Laziness and entitlement have becomes their default setting."

"Unfortunately, with the whole dumbing down of America thing, more and more schools are actually passing failing students. It's the new normal, Dee. Schools need the tuition, and if all the students who were doing failing worked failed and were kicked out of college, schools wouldn't be able to get the tuition they need to keep afloat."

"Well, I'm not about to compromise my standards."

"As you teach a core class, you shouldn't."

"What about in your classes?"

"Well, the difference between our classes is that yours is a required course and mine in an elective. So it's a whole different dynamic. Don't get me wrong. My students still have to work for their grades."

"I'm just glad the semester is almost over."

"Me too. Still, your flying in the face of that student is very unlike you, Dee. Do you think you're more stressed than usual because of the wedding?"

Giving his comment due consideration, she made a moue of agreement. "Good grief, I'm turning into Bridezilla. I mean, late yesterday afternoon when I had my fitting for my dress, it wouldn't zip up properly. So back it goes for more alterations. And the shoes finally arrived, but they weren't the ones I ordered, so they had to send them back and try again, and good grief, it's already the end of April and the wedding is just a blink away. And I'm starting to rant, aren't I?"

"See, just wedding stress. That's all it is. You'll be fine and back to your old self once we tie the knot." He pulled into the driveway and parked behind the house.

"I sure hope so!"

Getting out of the car, he walked around to her side of the car, reached out, and took her hand, the one wearing his ring. "Have I told you lately that I love you?"

"You have. Have I told you lately that I love you?"

"You have."

They were both wearing smiles as they headed into the house to fix a cozy dinner for two.

Daniel, tired after the long week, went to bed early. Dakota was still charged up after her crazy afternoon at school, so she settled herself in their office and graded final projects. When she finished Jason's, she wasn't surprised, but she was heartsick. He had indeed plagiarized once again. He was definitely going to fail the class. Well, wasn't Monday going to be fun! She certainly wasn't looking forward to that conversation.

*   *   *   *   *

Late Saturday morning, Dakota lounged on the back deck reading. It was unseasonably warm for nearing the end of April, and she was taking advantage of that by sopping up some sun and fresh air. Over the months she'd gotten through all her mother's articles and most of the letters. There were only a few of those left. She had grabbed a couple and settled in to read. After finishing one, she reached for another. "Okay," she said to herself, "one more letter, then I must get up and do something or Daniel will wonder if he's marrying a slug." She slipped the letter out of an envelope and began to read:

> *Dearest Daughter,*
>   *The time has come for you to make a choice:*
> *will you be a mother or a sister?*

What? Dakota read that line again and then a third time. She glanced up at the date in the corner, and her world tipped. This letter was written when she was two months old. She read the first line of the letter again. A mother or a sister? The tingling started in her hands and worked its way up her arms. When spots formed before her eyes, she knew she was about to faint. Bending over at the waist and dropping her head between her spread knees, she tried to breathe, but she could only manage shallow breaths. That was how Daniel found her.

"Dakota?" He rushed over to her and took her by her upper arm. "Dakota, what's happening?"

She was barely able to say, "I think I'm going to throw up." Her voice was muffled coming from below her knees and being projected toward the deck.

"Can you make it to the bathroom?"

"Maybe."

With a firm grip on her upper arm, he pulled her up and, slipping an arm about her waist, helped her into the house. She stumbled on the steps but made it into the dining room. All she could see was a murky shade of gray. "If you puke on the floor, you clean it up." He said it in a bantering way. All she heard was buzzing in her ears. By the time they reached the bathroom, she sank onto the floor by the toilet and proceeded to lose her breakfast.

Daniel handed her a cool, damp towel. "Honey?" She reached up, flushed the toilet, and taking the towel in one hand, as she still held the letter in the other, pressed the dampness into her face. "Come on, let me help you to bed."

Lying down and rolling over on to her side, she once again pressed the towel to her face.

"Honey, talk to me. What's going on here?"

Realizing she still held the crumpled letter in one hand, she offered it to him. "I read the first line and…just…collapsed. I don't even know what's *really* in the letter."

Daniel took it and read the whole thing. "Well" was his only response. She reached out, and he gave it back to her. She slipped it under the pillow in no shape to deal with it but not wanting it out of her reach. "Look, honey, just lay here until you get your equilibrium back. Then we just put one foot in front of the other. That's all."

"I need to be alone for a while."

"Okay." He kissed her on the forehead before leaving the room.

Dakota had never collapsed in her life, and how embarrassing was that? She was as healthy as an ox. She power walked; she did yoga; she had hiked a glacier in Iceland, for Christ's Sake! And here she was swooning like some female character in a Victorian novel. How lame could she be? She turned her mind back to the moments before her world buckled. She had pulled a letter from the folder. It was the folder that had her name on it, and it contained letters from her mother written to her and even letters from her that she'd written to her mother. Those letters she'd read up until now had all been just the sheet of paper, no envelope. But this letter, she recalled it had been in an envelope, and she had slipped it out of the envelope. She didn't recall if anything had been written on the envelope, but she didn't think so. Okay, so she slid the letter out of the envelope, sat back, and read the first line and, *pow*, caught one right in the kisser! She could see the words written in her mind's eye: *The time has come for you to make a choice: will you be a mother or a sister?* A mother or a sister. A mother or a sister. The words reverberated around in her brain. A mother or a sister.

The letter was to Savannah. It had to be. Savannah hardly lived an uneventful life. She worked tirelessly, but beyond that? Savannah kept one guessing about her inner life. Her outer life was, well, was an open book. But she kept her public life public and her private life private. She not only valued her privacy, she cultivated it, which always intrigued and mystified Dee. But boy oh boy, were things becoming clearer now.

She pulled the letter out from under her pillow and, biting the bullet, read it.

> *Dearest Daughter,*
> *The time has come for you to make a choice: will you be a mother or a sister?*
> *There has been many a girl who had agreed to give her baby up for adoption but upon holding the baby after it was born couldn't go through with it. I know what a mother feels when holding her baby for the first time. There is no other love so deep and wide and all-encompassing. Motherly love is a wonderful and lofty thing. But when reality clomps into*

the room with its muddy boots, it's time to take stalk and to look it in the eye. What is our reality here?

It's now time for you to think about the choices you made before Dakota was born. You made those choices for a reason. And your father and I not only supported your decisions, but we agreed to the deception out of love. We agreed out of love for you and out of love for the baby who hadn't even been born yet. We three, all of us, you, your father, and I, we all went to great lengths to let the world believe it was me who was pregnant and who had the baby. And that's exactly what everyone believes.

These in-between months between Dakota's birth and the beginning of your junior year have been the limbo time. But that time has come to an end. I know you are resisting the thought of reentering your life as it was before you had this beautiful baby. But think. You have just turned sixteen, and you have your entire life ahead of you. A life you had planned out ages ago. You had your five-year plan and your ten-year plan. So what happens now? Will you be a mother or a sister? You can't be both.

I know you were consumed with shame and guilt when you discovered you were going to have a baby. I have done my best to help and guide you through this time. Facing facts is productive; cultivating that shame and guilt is not. But you need to know that there are many kinds of guilt. If you don't become the person you are meant to become, guilt will follow.

You may find it odd that I'm such a willing party to deception when I have always taught you to tell the truth. But I am looking at the bigger picture and seeing the person you always wanted to be, the person you were growing into becoming. My dearest daughter, if you don't become that person you were meant to be, if you take this other path, you will not become a whole person. You will end up resentful, and you will foster the resentments until they poison you and your baby. Rein all your scattered emotions in and think about what you always wanted to do and what you always wanted to be and then revisit your options. I am here for you (and her), and I will honor your decision, whatever it might be.

Just please remember, all this is written with love for both you and Dakota.

I'll abide by your choice because, after all, it's a woman's right to choose.

In Sorrow and in Joy,
Mom

Dakota had always been good at reading between the lines, but there was much that needed filling in. She was angry, hurt, confused, lost, betrayed, pissed, and wanted answers. And as a straight line was still the most direct connection between two points, she went online and found a flight out at the crack of dawn the next morning. She would land at LaGuardia and then catch a connection to DC. She was going to have a face-to-face with her…her…with Savannah.

After making her reservation, Dakota spent the next few minutes just staring at the wall, thinking about her "big sister" who had always been a puzzle to her with a few missing pieces. There was often an opaqueness about Savannah; she was never fully transparent, but boy howdy, things were becoming clearer now!

A little while later, Daniel found her sitting on the floor in front of the safe. It was open, and papers spilled out and were spread all around her. "What are you looking for?"

"My birth certificate. I swear I remember it says 'Grace' under mother's name. Were they so diabolical that they falsified my birth certificate?" She swiped at a few tears that rolled down her cheek. She pulled it out of the safe and just stared at it.

"Well?" Daniel squatted down next to her.

"S. Grace Quinn. Mom's name was Sylvia Grace. But she hated Sylvia, always went by Grace."

"The S. could be for Savannah. What is her middle name?"

After a pause, Dee said, "Grace."

Chapter 36

Savannah opened her purse to pull out the receipts she'd been carrying around to toss in the desk drawer when she spied the letter that she had tucked in there before leaving Denver. Taking a deep breath, Savannah decided it was time. Today was Sunday, the last day of her recess. Work began again first thing in the morning. So she decided it was time she read her mother's last words to her. She sat at her desk and picked up a silver letter opener that she rarely used, but ceremony seemed to be called for here. She slit the envelope and slid the sheet of paper out. There it was, her mother's nice, neat, precise handwriting with nary a crossed-out word marring the letter. She must have written it days or even weeks before her handwriting had become shaky. She must have planned this long before the end. The words flowed across the page, waiting to be read. One sentence buried in the middle of the letter jumped out at her. "Don't you just hate that cliché that the truth will set you free? But the one thing about clichés is that they are clichés for a reason, it's because they…" Savannah looked away. A cold sense of loneliness enveloped her. She didn't want to read her mother's last words to her, but she knew it was time to do so.

When she had been a little girl getting ready to graduate from elementary school and move on to the upper grades, she and her little friends all had autograph books that they had taken to the last day of class. They wrote silly little sayings in each other's books and signed their names. Things like, "Roses are red, violets are blue, you look like a monkey, and you act like one too." When she got home, she had showed her mom what all her friends had written, and Grace had asked if she could sign it too. She never forgot what her mother had written: "Love many, trust few, and always paddle your own canoe." Well, she had certainly been paddling her own canoe for as long as she could remember. As far as loving many, well, she loved her family, her friends, and her constituents. She loved the young mothers she worked with in an effort to better their lives.

Savannah wandered out to her small patio that was really just a slab of cement walled off on three sides by a wooden fence that was about eight feet high. She'd furnished it with a little metal table and two ice cream chairs as well as a few potted plants to brighten it up, but the patio was really more a suggestion than a functional space. Sitting down in one of the chairs, she thought about those things that shaped lives. She wondered, *If this had happened, or if that hadn't happened, how would my life have been different?* Who hasn't thought that a time or two? And yet, did she want her life to be different? Not really. She had a good and fulfilling life, a life that would have been very different if it hadn't been for her mother. Taking a deep breath, she plunged into the letter.

After reading it, she set it aside on the table. She found herself staring at a pink geranium that needed watering. Obediently she got up and, filling her watering can, set about methodically watering her plants. That chore finished, she picked up the letter and reread a portion of it.

> *We were partners in crime, Savannah. Who knew we were capable of pulling off what we did. But the truth will out. Dakota deserves to know the truth, and it's up to you to tell her the whole of it. I can hear your thoughts right now, your resistance, let sleeping dogs lie, you might be thinking. Leave well enough alone. But I have an unswerving faith and unconditional trust in the truth. I didn't always have that. It has come to me over the years, especially the years when I have been rattling around alone in this old house while you are out making the world a better place. My book club recently read a book full*

of the translations of Rumi's spiritual poetry. One passage hit me between the eyes: "That which is false troubles the heart, but truth brings joyous tranquility." *You know that saying that the road to hell is paved with good intentions. We both know our intentions were good, but...*

The doorbell broke her train of thought.

Savannah, too consumed in thoughts and memories to remember to look at the security camera to see who was ringing the bell, was holding the letter in her hand when she opened the door. For some reason, she wasn't at all surprised to see Dakota standing there looking at once like a thundercloud and a little girl. Dakota had worn one of the infamous T-shirts. She'd chosen the one that said, "She's my sister," but she'd taken a black Sharpie and written a huge question mark after the word sister. Savannah's expression went to a blank shock when she saw the question mark on the shirt. Dakota knew? Her eyes flew to Dakota's, and Savannah knew truth time had arrived. Dakota pointedly looked at the caption on the T-shirt Savannah wore. It read, "Seemed like a good idea at the time." Her response wasn't a word but a sound, "Humph." Then she added, "Appropriate?"

"Better come in." Savannah held the door wide, and after a nanosecond, Dakota entered the townhouse.

"How did you find out?"

Dakota took the letter out of her purse and offered it to Savannah. "It was in my folder of letters. It must have ended up in mine by accident as it was clearly written to you."

Savannah took the letter from Dakota while proffering the one she held in her hand. For the next few moments, they each read the letter they now held.

"Talk to me, Savannah."

"What do you want me to say?"

"Just tell me the truth."

"The truth? I memorized a poem back in high school. One line was 'Perhaps the truth depends on a walk around the lake.' Wallace Stevens." Savannah was staring at a spot on the living room floor.

"Well, I don't feel like taking a walk around the National Mall, and that's the closest thing to a lake here." They both just stared off into their respective distances, not ready or willing to look one another in the eye. To bring Savannah back from the faraway place she seemed to have found herself in, Dakota finally broke the silence with a question. "Will you tell me? Tell me about my...father?"

That got Savannah's attention. "*Father!*" She spat the word with such vengeance that Dakota literally took a step back. "He was nothing more than a sperm donor!"

"Well, just feel free to tell me *exactly* how you feel."

Savannah closed her eyes against a sudden sense of vertigo, but that only made it worse. She opened her eyes and slowly went further into the living room and sat in the nearest chair, a soft roomy rocker recliner. She sat back and rubbed the fingers of one hand over her forehead.

Dakota had followed her into the room and sat in the companion chair. "Of all that Mom"—she finger quoted the word *Mom*—"taught us, two things stand out: treat others as you wish to be treated and take responsibility for your own actions. Looks like you, with her sanction, dropped the ball on that last one."

Not really paying attention to Dakota, Savannah was lost in thoughts and memories. "I wondered what happened to that letter." She was really speaking to herself. "When I finished everything in my folder and it wasn't there, I just figured she didn't keep a copy of that one."

And so for the next block of time, Savannah relived that portion of her past that had nearly destroyed her and finally given her a new lease on life.

"I was fifteen. Christ! Was I ever fifteen? Anyway, I was head over heels for this new boy at school. A boy who didn't even know I existed. He was a year older than me."

"Did he have a name?"

Savannah looked blank for a minute then nodded. "Yes, Carmine. I don't know his last name, don't think I ever knew it. He'd showed up at school slightly after the beginning of the semester, *after* they'd already taken pictures for the yearbook. So he wasn't in the yearbook. And then he left again before the end of fall semester. Looking back, it's almost as if he was a ghost, someone who never really existed."

"But obviously he did exist."

"Yes, he did. He'd transferred to our school from New York City. I was a sophomore, and he was a junior, so we didn't have any classes together. We'd just pass in the hall. He was so exotic that I was immediately infatuated. He wore a leather jacket and had slicked-back black hair that curled around his shirt collar. He wore white T-shirts under the leather jacket. A real bad boy. And I was so smitten." Then she stopped talking. Oh god. It was everything coalescing into the perfect storm. Savannah linked the fingers of both hands and squeezed so hard her knuckles turned white. "Oh god, I don't want to think about this." Her voice shook as tears sheened her eyes. She blinked the wetness away and stood up. "I need a couple of minutes." She blindly walked out of the room.

After a few moments, Dakota went in search of her and found her curled up on the bed. "Was it rape?" Dakota wanted to know.

Savannah rolled over and looked at her...her daughter. "Maybe date rape. Maybe." Savannah took another deep breath then sat up and dove in. "I was fifteen and in the tenth grade. In fact, that Thanksgiving when you were fifteen, I almost came clean then. I almost did figuring that Mom would have been there to pick up all the pieces."

"Why didn't you?"

"When you and Austin took off to visit your friends, I told Mom that maybe this was the time. You know Mom, always pretty much a straight shooter, not often prone to sarcasm. Well, her comeback was 'Oh, sure, implode Dakota's life at fifteen too. What is this, history repeating itself?' Needless to say, that did give me pause. I mean, I ended up really messed up at fifteen, and I sure didn't want all that trauma and angst visited upon you. So...water under the bridge and over the dam, as Austin would say. Anyway, it was a different world back then, from when you were that age in that grade. I remember how savvy you were already by the tenth grade. Oh, I know you weren't sexually active then, but you knew things that I never knew until much later. I was very naive and very, well, I guess I was a romantic. I fell for this guy, fell like a ton of stupid bricks. *Stupid* being the operative word."

When Savannah paused, Dakota prodded, "Tell me."

"He was a guy who didn't even know I existed. I mooned after him in my own way, but he never even looked at me. Oh god, how my heart ached. I remember how devastated I was that he never even noticed me." Looking into the long ago past, Savannah sighed. "I said hi to him once in the hall. He stopped dead in his tracks, just stopped, looked at me, gave me that up-and-down look that only arrogant guys can do, then looked away and started walking again. Never even said hi back. I never felt so like a cipher, like a pile of dog shit as I did at that moment. I was nothing to him. I should have known then to give up. But feelings, well, they have their own way of controlling a person. He was my first real crush. I'd never even been on a date. Mom said I had to wait until I was sixteen before I could date. So…"

Savannah, sitting up on the edge of the bed, had stopped talking and was just starting at a print on the wall. Not seeing the print, maybe not seeing anything.

Dakota sat on the bed next to her…her mother. Savannah looked so fragile, like she was about to shatter into a million pieces. Dakota suddenly felt like she was the parent and Savannah was the child. Her voice was kind. "But he eventually did more than just look at you."

"One Friday after school, after debate club, I was walking home, and he pulled his car over and started talking to me. He asked where I was going. I was so stunned it took me a minute to be coherent. I told him I was going home. He asked if I'd like to go for pizza. It was like a dream come true for me. The guy I had worshiped asking me to go out for pizza. I got in his car and thought my heart would burst from the joy I couldn't contain."

Dakota had never seen Savannah so pale; she just stared at the print on the wall, and she didn't even seem to be aware that she wasn't alone. Dakota looked at the print too. It was of a lovely woman in a wooded area bursting with springtime wildflowers and new green leaves on the trees. The woman, wearing a flowing, diaphanous white dress, was dipping the toe of one bare foot into a pond or stream. It was a peaceful picture, perfect for a bedroom wall.

"Did you get pizza?"

"What? Oh, yeah. I remember there were some junior high kids in the pizza parlor playing some video games, and when they saw us come in, well, they saw him with his leather and chains and slicked-back hair, and they were all, 'Look! He looks like Fonzie.' And he was all, 'Yeah, and you look like a bunch of pimply faced junior high school kids.' What an ass. But I didn't register that then."

"Definitely sounds like a creep." Dakota wasn't sure how she felt about that.

"Yeah, well, I had a crush on the creep and couldn't believe my good luck that he had finally noticed me and asked me out. It was my first date." She swallowed. "And my last one until I was in my twenties."

It was Dakota's turn to swallow. "It happened that night?" Her words came out in a whisper.

"Oh, Dee, I was so inexperienced. We ended up parking out of town, and he ushered me into the back seat of his car. I thought we'd kiss and maybe neck a little bit. I had no idea what to expect. I'd never even been kissed before. I didn't even realize we were beyond the parameters of petting when it was all over." Tears were falling, but she didn't seem to notice.

"Was it rape?"

"No, not really. It was just some stupid girl who didn't know what was going on. You know those Nora Roberts novels Mom always devoured? Those love scenes that run pages and pages and pages long? It's all so romantic and tender and, well, my experience didn't run pages and pages. It wasn't even a page or a paragraph. It was more like a sentence fragment."

"Then what happened?"

"He drove me home and reached across me and opened the door and shoved it open. Never said a word. I got out and shut the door, and he drove off. He never even looked at me again at school. It was like he didn't even see me. I didn't have to put up with that silent treatment for long. His family decided Wyoming wasn't for them, and they hightailed it back to New York City."

They sat side by side in silence. Then from a deep well of memory, Savannah continued. "There was this other boy. I never really noticed him, he was just a quiet, really sweet boy. And years later, I'm talking years later, I realized that he'd had a crush on me. I remembered that he'd often chat with me in class, or sometimes at odd times I'd see him walking down the street by our house and just looking at the house. At the time I never realized that he must have been pining away for me in the way I was pining away for Carmine. How odd it was to realize all that years later, when at the time I was so unaware of that sweet, sweet boy. He's the boyfriend I should have had. But after all that with Carmine, after the pizza and the dumping me off at home like a sack of garbage, and then just ignoring me, well, I was heartsick. I can't begin to explain the heartache. He made me feel so inconsequential. Each day was torture."

Hearing all this was like having a hand squeeze her own heart. Dakota asked, "When did you realize you were pregnant?"

"By November, probably mid November."

"Were you scared?"

"Terrified. I ended up jolted out of my heart sickness and realized I was in a hell of a mess. I knew I was in no position to have a baby and raise it. But that wasn't the worst of it. I was just so ashamed and so humiliated and so hurt and bitter over the whole experience. The word *annihilation* gives you an idea of what had happened to me. I thought of abortion, but something in me rebelled. You know my stance about women's right to choose. But even now I fight for more than just that. I promote commonsense family planning and reproductive rights. My goal is to reduce unintended pregnancies so there won't be a need to decide about an abortion. But…but…back then I knew abortion was something I personally could never do.

So then I thought of adoption. I wanted all my little ducks in a row before I talked to Mom and Dad."

"Did they flip?"

"I went to Mom first but was so stressed…emotional, I couldn't come right out. I asked her to tell me about when I was a new-born baby. She was so amazing. She said when I was born and when they handed me to her, she—" Savannah sniffed and smiled a fragile smile. "She asked me if I remembered that scene in *How the Grinch Stole Christmas* when his heart expanded. She said when they put me in her arms, her heart filled her chest in just that way. She said never knew such love. Not that she'd ever been a grinch, but it was the bit about her heart expanding. It was then that I told her. I started crying, and I told her I was pregnant.

"The plan wasn't something that came about immediately. She and I and Dad looked at things from all angles. I was only few months along and had just seen a movie about a teenage girl giving her baby up for adoption so told them that's what I wanted to do, I would give the baby up for adoption. The next day she told me that she and Dad had talked about things late into the night.

"Mom told me that if I gave the baby up, that I'd be left with a hollow place in my heart for the rest of my life. I hadn't gotten to a place where I was thinking about that yet. All I knew was that I just wanted it all to go away. I wanted things to go back to the way they were before…before. A futile wish, certainly, which was what Dad pointed out to me. When I was little and I had a crisis and my world crumbled around me, Daddy always gathered me onto his lap and he'd rock me in the rocking chair. But this crisis wasn't going to be fixed so easily.

"The upshot was that Mom would tell all her friends that she was expecting—a menopause baby, they called it. And somehow we pulled it off. I was able to make it through most of the school year without anyone really noticing, then when I really started showing, Mom told them I had a serious case of mononucleosis that was compounded by acute anemia and that I needed to lay low and not be exposed to germs and things. Teachers would send lessons home with her, she'd see to it that I did them and take them back to the teachers.

She was subbing at the time. No one ever knew that I was the one who was pregnant, and everyone thought she was because she started wearing baggy tops."

"And where was Austin when all this was going on?"

"He was around but off in his own little universe: on the golf course and playing Nintendo. He was also told I had mono and to stay away from me as it was contagious. Whenever he was around, I just went into my room and stayed there. I'd be under the covers with a comforter over me if he even came in my room, so he never got a look at my belly."

"He was really that oblivious?"

"He was a twelve-year-old boy, Dee. Enough said. Then you were born, and everyone thought Mom had the baby. I did care for you and nursed you for a few weeks. Mom tried to talk to me as it got closer to school starting in the fall, but I would shut her out. I was so wrapped up in you and taking care of you that I'd just walk away from her when she tried to talk to me. But when my junior year was about to start, well, that was when Mom wrote that letter to me. The one you found and read. Basically I had to decide about my future. So I weaned you, went back to school, and you know the rest."

"Do I?"

"I became your sister. I went to school, came home, and soon went off to college."

"I remember when you came home from college for holidays. We would have so much fun. You'd read to me and take me to the park. It was almost like I had two moms back then. Austin was fun too, but it wasn't the same. He'd call me Squirt or Brat and tousle my hair or pull my braids and then take off with his golfing buddies. Then he was off to college too. It wasn't until I was older that he stepped up and became a real big brother, warning me about drinking and drugs and boys." After a moment she said, "Did you ever even consider telling this boy about me?"

"Not in a million, billion years. First of all, he was long gone before I realized I was pregnant. But if he had been found and told, he'd probably have denied ever having anything to do with me. He might not even have remembered me. I might have been just one of dozens! Plus, why open that can of worms? Mom and Dad were completely against that. What if he wanted custody? What if his parents had sued for grandparents rights? What a nightmare that would have been for us, you living half your life in New York City among strangers! You were ours, a Quinn! He was a nobody. He didn't deserve to know about you."

"That's one way of looking at it."

"Do you hate me? Well, before you decide if you hate me or not, just remember, there are times in life when your head may tell you to do one thing, but your heart tells you to do another. In the very beginning, my head told me to give the baby, you, up for adoption so you would be out of sight, out of mind. Oh, I cloaked that thought in 'It would be best for the baby.' But after you were born and I held you in my arms, my heart couldn't do that. I chose to keep you as close as I could. You were ours. No one else's. Ours." After a pause she asked again, "Do you hate me?"

"I...I don't know how I feel, but no, of course I don't hate you. But I do need time...to think. And I have a plane to catch as I have school in the morning. After I'm able to think, we'll talk again." She hugged Savannah then walked out of the room and out of the townhouse, leaving Savannah alone.

Chapter 37

Savannah stood in the middle of the room, not knowing what to do. Time passed before she came back to herself. How long she'd been standing there she didn't know. Her mind was a complete blank. A crazy lightning bolt had struck her twice, in such a short space of time, electrocuting the nerve center of her life, knocking the power out and leaving her shocked and weakened and unsure of her next move. One lightning bolt had left her at odds with her brother and the other had thrown her into odds with Dakota. She focused on the two letters lying side by side on her bed. Dakota hadn't taken the letter with her. Was that an oversight, or maybe a message for her? She picked them both up and wandered into the living room and sat in her comfy chair, placing the letters on the nearby end table. She needed to talk this out with someone, and her first thought was Austin, but then she remembered they weren't speaking. With no mother to talk to, thoughts of her Aunt Susi slowly came to her, her mother's sister. If anybody had been told about all this, it would have been her. Perhaps she'd have some words of wisdom for her.

When her aunt answered her phone, Savannah simply said, "Dakota found out."

"Found out what, honey?" her aunt asked matter-of-factly.

"That she's my daughter."

The dead silence on the other end of the line answered the question of if Grace had confided in her sister. Savannah filled in the blanks and listened to her aunt's soothing, comforting words of wisdom dispensed from that place of age and distance. Then after talking it out twice in a matter of a few short hours, Savannah, exhausted, said her goodbyes and hung up the phone. Wandering over to her knickknack shelf, she picked up her little Billiken, a ceramic statue about six inches tall of a little Buddha-like creature sitting with legs outstretched, wearing a beatific expression. A Billiken is the god of the way things ought to be, a good luck charm of sorts. Holding him gently she thought about the way things ought to be and they way things were and considered why there was usually such a chasm between the two. Lord she was exhausted. She would have loved to soak in her claw-foot tub, but that tub was back home in Denver. She settled for a hot shower instead.

* * * * *

Dakota's flight home wasn't for a couple of hours yet, but she hadn't wanted to spend any more time with Savannah. She had a lot to mull over, and she wanted to do that alone. She walked toward the mall and decided that walk around the lake was just what she needed. Clouds were starting to roll in, and it looked like rain was in the forecast, but for now it was nice. Cool but nice. After walking and pondering, and pondering and walking, she was ready to talk. She sat on the ledge of the reflecting pool, took out her phone, and called Austin.

"Did you know?"

"Know what?"

As Dee laid it out for him, it was as if a very bright light had just been snapped on in his brain. A room that had been shrouded in darkness was suddenly illuminated. He'd known, but he hadn't really known that he'd known. Pieces of a puzzle clicked, clicked, clicked into place.

"Are you sure you didn't know? I mean, you're a smart guy, why didn't you ever figure it out?"

"Probably because a person sees only what he expects to see. Over the years something would be said or I'd remember something, so half-guesses would slip into my mind, suspicions, speculations, but overall, no, I didn't know."

As they continued to talk, interestingly, his utmost concern at the moment wasn't for Dee. It was for Savannah. "Is Savvy okay?"

"She seemed pretty fragile when I left."

"God, I want to get my hands on that creep and beat him to a pulp."

"You are such a guy."

"A guy with an eleven-year-old daughter. In four short years, she'll be fifteen. Right now my heart is just broken, and I want to break something else in return, like that guy's legs."

"I wonder if Dad ever wanted to beat him up? And I just now fully realized, Dad wasn't my real dad."

"Stop that right now!" Austin's voice took on that parental timber. "Mom and Dad raised you, we all raised you. None of that changes."

"Well, anyway, I just can't imagine Dad getting all macho and in somebody's face."

"Remember, you were young when he died, so you never got to see him in his glory during your teenage years as I did. One time I was cocking off about something, pissed off at I don't remember what, and I was getting ready to storm out of the house, and he just grabbed me by the upper arm and held on and very sternly told me to calm down and stay put. He didn't get riled often, but he could hold his own when he did. I tell you, I stayed put that night. Didn't want to, but I did. So yeah, he could have gotten all macho in that guy's face and I wouldn't have wanted to be that guy. He was a good dad, Dee, and I learned how to be a good dad from him. And just for the record, because I know you were hit hard here and are still reeling, the reason you are such a grounded adult is because of Mom. If Savannah had been left alone to raise you and be the mom, she would have botched the job. Not because she wouldn't have loved you but because she wouldn't have been equal to the challenge. It really does take a village to raise a kid properly. And you were damn lucky you landed where you did."

"We were lucky in the parent department, weren't we?"

"Yes, we were. Speaking of parents, are you going back to Savvy's before you fly home?"

"No, we both need our space now." She and Austin had been talking for quite some time when Dee realized she was hearing weird city noises in the background. "But speaking of home, are you at home?"

"No, I have a meeting tomorrow afternoon so I flew into La Guardia a little while ago, and as of right now, I just paid off a cabbie and am in front of my hotel."

"Well then, I'll let you check in. I've got to get going to the airport before it starts to rain. And I'd better give Daniel a call so he'll know when to pick me up. Tomorrow is a school day."

After Austin clicked off, he spent about a nanosecond considering his plan of attack. Waiting until tomorrow wasn't an option he even considered, and a phone call would not suffice. Instead of checking into his hotel, he flagged down another cab and circled back to the airport.

*   *   *   *   *

Gordon's flight was late, so he didn't waste any time heading for the exit. He had just passed through the sliding glass doors in full stride when he did a double take, looking back at the crowd; a Savannah lookalike was just now passing through security. Upon closer inspection, even from the distance, he saw that she was younger and a bit slimmer.

*   *   *   *   *

After her shower, Savannah slipped into her yoga pants and a T-shirt that said, "There are 13 minerals that are essential to human life, and all of them are found in wine. Coincidence? I think not!"

She pulled a chilled white out of the fridge and stood there in front of the open door, looking at the nearly empty shelves, trying to decide what to have for supper when she remembered she was supposed to be going out with Gordon tonight. As if on cue, her doorbell chimed. She poured two glasses, padded from the kitchen to the entryway, and opened the door.

"You may want to rethink your notion about getting involved with me."

"Why would I do that?" He entered the townhouse, slipping off his coat that was lightly covered with raindrops, and hung it on the nearby coat tree.

"My life is crumbling around me right now, I'm a mess." She pushed the door shut with her hip, handed him one of the glasses of wine, and turned toward the living room.

Following her, he said, "Tell me."

"Well, first there was the Wendy Greene thing, then my confrontation with my brother. Then, shortly before you got here, I had another confrontation with my..." Shaking her head, she left the sentence hanging.

"Your sister?" he supplied.

When she looked up startled, he said, "I saw a woman at the airport going through security that, at first glance, I thought was you. So adding two and two..."

"Yes, Dakota and I had..." Picking up the two letters from the end table, she handed them to Gordon. "Here. I don't have the heart to go over this again right now. These will give you an idea of what happened."

He settled into a chair and read while she circled back to the kitchen and snagged the bottle of wine she'd left on the counter. By the time she had knocked back and refilled her glass and returned to the living room, he had finished both missives.

Standing, he went to her and took the wineglass out of her hand and set it on the end table. First he just held her in his arms, then he scooped her up and went back to the nice, cozy, roomy rocker recliner and held her on his lap, holding her close and rocking ever so slightly. Long minutes passed before he said, "I am so sorry, Savannah."

"No, you're not," she murmured against his chest.

"What?" He sat up straight so they were face-to-face, and his face read *Color me astonished!* "Why would you say something like that?"

It took her a moment to realize what she had said, "Oh. That's just what Austin and I automatically say to each other when one of us says we're sorry. We've been doing that since we were kids. It was just a reflex."

"Well, phew!"

She put her hand on his cheek and almost chuckled. "I'm really sorry. That must have sounded so snotty."

"I guess not having a sibling, I missed out on a lot of weird bonding nuances like that."

"I don't even know how that got started."

They had been conversing face-to-face while she still rested on his lap. He saw that some color was coming back into her cheeks that had been beyond pale when he'd arrived. "You hungry? We were going to have dinner."

"I could eat, but I'm not up for going out."

Nudging her off his lap they stood. "Then let's take a look at what you've got in the kitchen. I'm pretty good at throwing odds and ends together and turning it into a meal."

They stood in front of the open fridge door. "Doesn't look promising, does it?"

"This is the saddest excuse for anything I've ever seen. Eggs and not much more."

She'd wandered over to a cupboard and looked in. "When we were kids and Dad was off to a symposium or a conference so it was just Austin and me and Mom, we'd often have breakfast for dinner. It was fun and different, and to me eating breakfast at dinnertime is kind of like comfort food. So how about I mix up some waffle batter, and I know I have a very naughty package of bacon in the freezer. So we can have waffles and bacon and eggs for dinner?"

"That actually sounds really good." He shut the fridge door and opened the freezer door. Pulling out the bacon, he added, "Let me help."

The bacon was frying and the first waffle was cooking in the waffle iron when the doorbell chimed suddenly followed by knocking. "I sure am popular today." She looked at the monitor and in surprise said, "It's Austin."

"I thought you two weren't speaking."

"We're not." She sighed. "But I can't leave him out there in the rain."

After she opened the door, they just stared at each other. He looked so worried. She stepped back and gestured him in, closing the door behind him. Like Gordon before him, he slipped off his wet coat. She took it and hung it on the tree.

"Dee must have called you."

"I'd just arrived in New York for a meeting tomorrow when she did. I was worried about you, didn't think you should be alone."

Gordon stepped out of the kitchen. "She's not alone."

Doing the classic double take, he turned back to his sister. "I thought you told Jill you two weren't..."

"We weren't...then. We are...now. We're also in the middle of fixing breakfast for dinner. Want some?"

The three of them sat at the kitchen table wolfing down waffles and bacon and eggs.

After a moment of silence, Savannah turned to her brother and asked, "Did you know? I mean, before Dee told you what went down here today?"

"Not really. Not back then. Maybe subliminally. But, well, some things just clicked into place when I heard."

"Like?"

"I never really did know for sure. But one time, when Chelsea was about two months old, Jill was rocking her and nursing her in the living room when there was a knock on the door. She tossed one of Mom's crocheted baby blankets over her shoulder and the baby for modesty sake while I got the door. It was the UPS guy, and when I turned around with the box in my arms and saw her, superimposed on her was a time I saw you rocking Dee when she was a baby. I had knocked on your bedroom door and then entered before you said to come in, and I saw you in the process of tossing a similar baby blanket over your shoulder and the baby. I didn't think anything of it at the time. I mean, I was all of twelve. But when I saw that superimposed image of you and Dee over Jill and Chelsea, god, it was so... surreal. And I thought, 'Was Savvy nursing Dee?' Then I convinced myself I was wrong and pushed it out of my mind. But when Dee called me today, well, like I said, things clicked into place."

"Oh. How did she sound? I mean, I just wonder if Dee and I are going to be okay."

"Of course you are. Mom raised us to be forgiving people. So what happened to the guy? Did Dad beat the crap out of him?"

"No."

"No? I could still do that, you know. Tell me who he is and I'll clean his clock." His eyes shifted over to Gordon.

"Don't even think about it." Gordon straightened up and crossed arms over his chest.

Refocusing on his sister, Austin said, "Good grief, Savvy, you were just a kid. How did that all happen? Did Mom and Dad drop the ball on the birds and bees thing? Do I have to start talking to Shannon about all that *now*? Sheesh, she's only barely eleven."

"I was naive, Austin, stupid. Had no experience. And I was Mom's first. Maybe she thought she had lots of time before the 'speech.' It probably never occurred to her that that could happen me. I don't blame her."

"I really am sorry all that happened to you, Savvy."

"No, you're not." They grinned at each other across the table, while Gordon just rolled his eyes.

Chapter 38

After she got home from confronting Savannah, Dakota didn't know how she felt other than hollow and just a little unsettled. But Monday was a school day, and as is always the case, the week just clicked along. She didn't pass final projects back on Monday as she just didn't want to begin the week with a confrontation with a student. She was confrontationed out! So that was what she'd had on the agenda for Wednesday. Wednesday was now all but over, and she sat brooding in her office. The rap on her doorframe got her attention, and there was Jason glaring at her. She and Jason had had a showdown in the hallway after their last class. He had been genuinely shocked that he'd failed his final project and as a result would not be moving forward with the rest of his class. She had told him there was no point in showing up on Friday for their actual final exam as even if he passed it, he wouldn't pass the class. It was moot. They'd already been through all this earlier, why did he want to keep beating that dead horse by knocking on her office door now?

She rose and swung the door farther open. "Come on in, Jason."

He stepped into her office and closed the door behind him then stood between her and the door. The words *not good* flashed through Dakota's mind. When in her office, she usually kept her door open just a few inches, but the knob was also always locked, so if the door was shut, no one could get in. So now her locked door was shut tightly, and if this angry student got out of hand, no one could get into her locked office to help her. She decided sitting would be more relaxed and less threatening then standing in a face-off, so she sat at her desk and swiveled her chair around. She looked at him and waited.

"So it looks like I'm going to have to take this class again in the fall."

Dakota nodded, waiting for him to continue.

"So it looks like you are the only person teaching it in the fall."

"Yes."

"Perfect." His sarcasm didn't just drip, it flowed. "But none of the sections you are teaching are the hybrid-online section like you taught last fall that a friend of mine took. So students only had to go once a week and the rest of the class was done online?"

"That class has been discontinued. It was a dismal failure. Students didn't do the quality of work that was expected. Students perform much better in the type of class we had this semester, when they meet three times a week with the instructor. Providing, of course, they show up to class." The last sentence was a dig she couldn't resist as Jason had missed a huge chunk of the class meetings during the semester.

"But I'll only be able to come once a week in the fall. So I need the online class."

"It's not being offered."

"So then we need to make some arrangement so I only attend your class one day a week instead of three."

"No such arrangement is possible." And from that point on, the conversation devolved.

After Jason slammed out of her office, Dakota headed for the dean's office. She sat down and smiled a weary smile at the woman who had hired her a few years before.

"Everything all right, Dakota?"

"Just wondering if I ended up on your radar since Friday?"

The dean shook her head. "Did I miss something?"

"I stepped out of line with a student. We ended up in a bit of a verbal battle." She sighed. "He punched my buttons the wrong way, and I lit into him. Anyway, since that time, he failed another assignment, and well, he just showed up in my office again today, and we went at it again."

"Who was it?"

"Jason Pound."

The dean laughed. "Yes, you and every other instructor he has. I don't expect he'll come in to complain. He's failing most of his classes. It isn't just you."

"He seemed to think he was entitled to make up my class in the fall by showing up only one day a week."

The dean shook her head. "I don't expect he'll be back to make *any* of them up."

"Well, that's a relief."

The dean was looking at her closely. "Is everything else okay? You look pretty tuckered out."

"I guess I am." She heaved a great sigh. "End of the semester and all that."

"Yes, by this time in the semester, we all are whipped." After a pause she added, "No more snapping at students, okay?"

"No. I'll keep it under control."

*   *   *   *   *

Friday morning, yeah, Dakota could hardly wait until this day was over. She was feeling just ishy, as she had been for several days now, and experiencing those uncharacteristic mood swings, and she looked closely at herself in the mirror and saw suspicion written all over her face. "Why so pale and wan? Come on, snap out of this."

Trying to ignore the thought that kept knocking on the back door of her brain, she took another little nibble of the dry toast she'd made for breakfast in the hopes that it would settle her stomach when the light bulb slammed on in her head, and she suddenly realized that she'd missed her last period, maybe even her last two. She'd been so distracted with the wedding plans, the end-of-the-semester rush with the completion of all the major projects and the grading of them, not to mention her distraction over recent revelations with Savannah, that she hadn't even realized it until now that the time for her period had come and gone—and she meant *long* gone. She put her hand to her abdomen. "Morning sickness? Is that what all this is?" Then the sloppiest, silliest grin she had ever seen slid across her face. As she grinned at herself in the mirror, she said to her reflection, "I'll be damned." Well, this certainly wasn't in the plans. Observing her reflection, she saw her grin grow even wider. The wedding wasn't for a couple more months, but no matter. The only question was when and how to break it to Daniel.

*　　*　　*　　*　　*

One more final to go, and yeah, school would be out for the summer. What a relief! At the beginning of each term, she was always so optimistic. She'd reach all her students and teach them what they needed to know to get through their college classes successfully. By the time they got through her class, she was determined that they would know how to write an essay properly: research it properly, document it properly, and execute the whole thing properly. So when they moved on to other classes and were assigned a research paper or even an essay question on an exam, they could pull it off. That was the goal. But as each semester wore on, she'd once again come to realize that a segment of her students saw her class as the least important one they would ever take. And when she once again realized they were only doing just enough to get by and pass, and when she once again realized that no matter what she tried to do to reach them failed, she would begin to wonder if she was in the right profession after all. She had reached that point this semester, and that was what she contemplated sitting alone in her office. Well, at least it was the last day of the week coupled with being the last day of the semester and the blessed last day of the whole school year with summer break about to commence.

It was minutes before class, and Dakota was shoving finals into her pack when a tap on her office door got her attention; she looked over her shoulder and saw Samuel, her football player. He'd been

269

passing her class, just barely hanging on to a low C, until the final project that she passed back on Wednesday. Surprisingly the paper had been a B quality paper until she started checking the documentation. She found several instances of citing directly from a source without the necessary quotation marks or in-text documentation. If it had happened once or twice, it would have amounted to losing a few points in the area of documentation. But it had happened too often, and that turned the B paper into an F paper. Because of the grade on that project added to the rest of his points in class, he would be getting a D in the class, and a D was not considered passing. He'd have to take the course again in the fall. She had expected him to talk to her after class on Wednesday, but with Jason taking up all her time, that didn't happen.

"Sam, come in."

"I'm just wondering what I can do to pass this class."

"Sit down." She gestured to a nearby chair while taking a seat herself.

She told him that prior to the final project, he had a low C in the 72 percentile, and it dropped to a D in the 67 percentile because of the F on that paper.

"But it was a good paper! I took it to the writing center, and they even said it was a really good paper."

Dakota didn't want to get into another shouting match with another student, so she took a deep breath and tried for reasonable.

"It was a good paper, but you plagiarized. That makes it an automatic F. We went over the rules of documentation in class more than once."

"But why didn't the writing center tell me I needed to document those passages?"

"That's not their job, Sam. You need to know when you copy a sentence or two out of a source that it needs to be cited."

"But I didn't know. It wasn't a quote. I had changed things up a bit."

"That's called paraphrasing, and as discussed and practiced in class, paraphrases need documentation too." She talked to him about accountability, about taking responsibility for one's own actions. And

she said she was sorry, but rules were rules. "The first time you pla-
giarize, you get an F on the paper. That's what happened here. If it
happens again, you'll likely suffer worse consequences. You are learning a lesson here."

"But I didn't know…"

Instead of repeating that it had been discussed in class, she said,
"And now you do know."

Not really listening to her, he looked like he was doing some
math in his head. "So if I'd done better on all my other work and had
a higher grade in the class, getting an F on this paper, I still might
have gotten a C in the class and passed?"

"I suppose…"

"So somebody could have done what I did, although I didn't
know I was doing wrong, and still pass."

"Sam…"

"It's not fair, Ms. Quinn. I worked hard all semester. Maybe I
was just getting a C, but I was earning that C, and now this! And why
isn't a D passing? That's not fair either. It's passing in other courses."

"Look, Sam, it's almost time for class to begin. Let's go finish
out the semester and talk some more after class."

"If I do really, really well on the final, will that pull me back up
to a C?"

It probably wouldn't, but she just didn't have the heart to burst
any more bubbles. "It might."

When he left, she shut the door behind him and just sat back
down in her chair for a moment. She was recalling her sophomore
year in college. She had been taking a physics class, for the second
time, as she'd solidly failed it on the first go-around. She was working her butt off to pass the class, and she was, with a solid D. A D
was passing for that course in that school. So the last day to drop,
her teacher took her aside and told her as she was getting a D in the
course, she should probably drop it and try again later. She told him,
"You don't get it. A D is so much better than what I got last semester." She had managed to maintain her D average all semester long,
and when grades came out, she was stunned to see a C on her report
card. The teacher had given her a C because she had tried so hard

and—no, that was apples and oranges. She had not cheated, she had worked hard, and Sam had plagiarized. But inadvertently. But didn't people need to be held accountable? Damn! She realized she was on the horns of one of those philosophical dilemmas and decided to talk to Daniel before she made any decisions. That decided, she headed for class.

Dakota stood in the front of the classroom, pulling the finals out of her pack. Sam was not exactly glowering at her from the back row where he'd sat all semester. He was just watching her intently, perhaps trying to mentally get her to recognize he was determined to pull out all the stops and pass this course. His arms were crossed over his massive chest while he watched every move she made in setting things up, so he saw it before anyone else. The rest of the class was in their usual after lunch slump, not noticing anything. Sam saw Dakota glance out the window and blanch.

What Dakota saw had her blood running cold. Jason, carrying some kind of firearm, has just bounded up the stairs and into the building. Instinctively she knew where he was headed, just a few steps away, and who his target would be.

Sam, alert and curious, watched his teacher's arm disappear up to the elbow into her school bag and, as she reached for something and pulled it out of the bag, her voice took on a timber he'd never heard before. It was something that made the rest of the students freeze and listen.

"Hallway's off-limits as there's a shooter out there. Duncan"— she grabbed the room phone on the window ledge and tossed it to the kid in the first row—"phone security, *now*, number on the wall there!" To the group she said, "If you can get out the window, good, but remember you'll likely have a target on your back. The best place is the floor as I'm the one he wants. Sam, heads-up." She pitched whatever it was that she'd pulled from her bag to him. He caught the pass as easily as if he was on the football field. "Stun gun. It's on, just depress the blue button, be sure you're touching flesh, and hold the button down until he pees himself!" Less than ten seconds has passed since she had seen the shooter.

The door slammed open, and Jason entered the classroom. Most students sat in complete shock, but one was scrambling to climb out the window. "Floor, now!" Dakota screamed. In the three seconds it took for Sam to locate the correct button and get across to the doorway where Jason stood like an avenging dark angle, the madman had shot one student in the back. Chaos ensued as he then aimed at Dakota and screamed, "This is for fucking up my life!" His finger tightened on the trigger. That bullet passed through the shoulder of a student still sitting in the front row and lodged in Dakota's side. If she hadn't been making a horizontal dive for the floor, it would have hit her center mass. By now most of the students were on the floor. From behind Jason, Sam finally closed in close enough to act. He touched the stun gun to Jason's neck and depressed the blue button, sending electric fire jolting through the gunman's body. Jason fell to the ground, and while he was down for the count, Sam sat on him to make sure he wouldn't be getting up anytime soon.

The whole thing had begun and was over so quickly. Dakota lay shivering on the floor while one student applied pressure to her wound. Other students did likewise to the other two wounded students. It was minutes before security showed up wearing bullet-proof vests and carrying weapons of their own. Students answered questions explaining what had happened.

"Dakota!" Daniel burst into the room and saw her on the floor. A siren and then another came roaring up outside the building, so at least help was on the way. He knelt down beside her, careful not to bump the student applying pressure. He refused to see that the boy had blood all the way up his forearms. "Dee?" It was barely a whisper.

Their eyes met. "I'm pregnant," Dakota managed to say before her eyes rolled back into her head, and she knew blackness.

Those who had been shot were rushed to the hospital. Thankfully it was certain that they would all live.

Daniel paced in the little courtyard just off the waiting room in the hospital. He had called Savannah and Austin a while back. He told them both what details he knew. That the doctor was performing surgery but it didn't look too serious. The bullet had lodged in her side and she'd lost some blood, but it wasn't life-threatening.

Coming back into the waiting room, he sat in front of the television that was on a local news channel.

Sam, the football hero, as a reporter had dubbed him, was being interviewed. "Tell us about your instructor. What is she like?"

"Ms. Quinn, she is strict, but we appreciate that. We know there is a line beyond which we do not step. It's in our nature to toe that line, but very few of us cross it, we respect her too much. Just before class, we locked horns. I was pissed—"

"And yet you saved her life."

"Of course. Anyone would have."

Daniel jumped up as the doctor came through the doors. "Everything went well." He smiled at Daniel. "She's in recovery now. Give her a little time. We'll come get you in a few minutes so you can sit with her."

"And the baby?"

"Time will tell there."

*   *   *   *   *

Wasting no time heading for Dulles and the first flight to Bangor, Savannah was approached by one of the ubiquitous reporters who materialized whenever any public servant appeared. The woman stuck a microphone in Savannah's face and asked a question that the congresswoman didn't even hear so intent was she on flagging down a cab that had just pulled up to the curb. She turned toward the reporter with a face full of passion and fury and said, "Now is the time to have more than just a conversation about gun control. We've had that political dance before. Now is the time for action." With that she leaped into the cab and headed toward the airport and Dee.

*   *   *   *   *

Dakota surfaced in recovery, and the first thing she saw was Daniel's face. He asked her, "Do you remember what happened?"

She barely nodded and blinked a couple of times. "I've had that dream before, standing in front of a classroom when a gunman enters, only in the dream I was naked."

That made him smile. "Do you remember what you said to me just before you passed out?"

She thought for a moment then shook her head.

Chapter 39

Jill, Savannah, and Aunt Susi were in the kitchen shucking corn and looking out the window at the men jerry rigging a couple of make-shift lobster pots. Daniel had insisted on overnighting in fresh lobster for their dinner tonight, the night before the wedding. "Hey, we were going to have the lobster fest in our backyard in Maine, so no reason not to have it here in Wyoming" was his logical reasoning.

Jill watched as Gordon and Chelsea peered into the large cooler full of fresh live lobster. He picked one up and held it toward the little girl. When it started waving its banded claws around, she backed up with eyes as big as moon pies. "So?" Jill picked up another ear of corn and looked back out the window. "Is it serious?"

Savannah followed her gaze and felt her heart lift as it did now whenever she laid eyes on Gordon. "It's...nice. It's very nice and so new that sometimes I forget the relationship protocol."

"For instance?" her aunt asked.

"For instance, when I was zooming to the airport when I'd heard Dee was shot, I didn't give Gordon a second thought. I was getting ready to board the plane, and pow, I suddenly remembered him and realized I needed to call him and let him know what was going on. I mean, I've been so independent for so long with never the need to check in or let anyone know what was up that I dropped the ball on that one, or almost. His phone went to voice mail, and I was able to leave a message just as I got on the plane, and I did call him again later from the hospital."

Aunt Susi gave her a peck on the cheek. "Well, he seems very nice, and you look very happy, so a win-win, huh?"

Savannah agreed then reached for another ear of corn while giving her sister-in-law a good once-over. "You look happy too, Jill. Is it school that has put that glow in your cheeks?"

"It certainly is challenging. I don't know where I'm headed yet, but I'm enjoying the journey."

"Somebody once said the journey is as important as the destination."

Dropping the last ear of corn in the pot and drying her hands on a hand towel, Jill pointed out the obvious, "We're finished here. Let's go out and see how close they are to cooking the lobster."

Jill wandered over toward Chelsea, who had slipped one hand in Gordon's as she poked at the lobster he held. "How come he's got those rubber bands on?"

"Because his claws can pinch, and you don't want these little fingers pinched."

"Curiosity killed the cat, missy. She'll just keep bombarding you with questions if you let her."

"Well, as a journalist, I have to admit that I too continually ask questions. You need to if you want things clarified. In fact, it was Albert Einstein who said, 'The important thing is not to stop questioning. Curiosity has its own reason.'"

"And you just became her new BFF."

Meanwhile, Savannah peered over Daniel's shoulder as he lifted the lid off one cooking pot and assessed the interior before putting the lid back down. "Ready?" Savannah asked.

"Just about ready."

"There wasn't that much water in there."

"That's because you don't boil lobsters. You steam them."

"Ah yes, I've heard that before. I've also heard that lobsters squeal when they land in the boiling water."

"They do not squeal." Daniel brought the cooler closer to the steaming lobster pots, reached into the cooler for the biggest one he could find, got Savannah's attention, and dropped it in. "See, no squealing, nothing, that's just an old wives' tale." He dropped more lobsters into first one steaming pot and then the other pot, one at a time. None of them made a peep.

Meanwhile, Gordon saw Dakota bringing some folded chairs out of the garage. "Hold up there." He intercepted her and reached for the chairs.

"I've got it."

"Just let me."

"Gordon, I've got it."

"Well, I can think of several reasons why you should let me carry those chairs. One, you were recently shot, two, you're pregnant, three, you're the bride, and four, if I am not allowed to help you, it will bruise my fragile male ego."

Laughing she relented. "Can't have that ego bruised, now can we?"

"Just show me where you want them."

While others busied themselves with setting the table on the deck and bringing food out of the house, Gordon and Dee headed for the area where the chairs were going to be set up for tomorrow's ceremony. They passed Shannon who was deep in conversation with her father. "See, it's this mass of nonbiodegradable plastic that makes up this huge garbage patch, and it's unconscionable."

"Excuse me," Gordon asked Dakota, "did that little girl just use the word *unconscionable* in a sentence?"

"Looks like Daniel's pep talk over Thanksgiving about vocabulary building paid off." After placing the folded chairs next to the ones already leaning against a tree, she said, "See that box of tea lights over there? Let's start stringing them on that tree near Shannon and Austin. We can eavesdrop on them and see what they are talking about while doing something constructive at the same time."

"The biggest one is floating somewhere between California and Hawaii," Shannon seemed very passionate, "and it's mostly plastic. It's not just sea animals like turtles and seals that are being harmed from all this plastic. It's the algae and plankton too. The entire web of sea life could be damaged."

"So what's the plan?" Austin was listening to his daughter very seriously. "How can we help?"

"Well, I did some research, and by the way, it's real inconvenient to have to do it all on the computer at the library, if I had my own computer—"

"Get back on track." His voice held laughter, but he kept his face straight.

"Oh, well, there are a lot of organizations trying to help. Not so much in cleaning it up but in trying to stop it from getting bigger. I think we should help too."

"Out there at sea?"

"Maybe someday, I'd really like to do that, but we can start at home."

"How are we going to do that?"

"Simple! We can start getting people to take recycling more seriously. And stop using plastic when there are other alternatives."

"Good idea, Shan. It's too true that waste disposal is out of control in this country. We could start by blaming the manufactures who package goods so ridiculously."

"See, you get what I'm saying. There's so much that needs to be done!"

"The longest march begins with one little step."

"You know how Mom refuses to buy olive oil in plastic bottles? She insists on glass. We should get laws passed that they can no longer use plastic. They have to use glass. That would be a start."

Gordon stood on the stepladder, while Dee handed him the strands of lights. Looking down at Dee, he nodded his chin in the direction of Shannon and Austin. "Wow. Did you hear him quote Chairman Mao to his daughter? Time for a break." Descending from the stepladder, Gordon opened up a chair and nodded to it. "Have a seat."

Laughing, Dakota said, "What?"

"Sit down." He was smiling too, but Dakota noticed a seriousness around his eyes.

"Okay," she complied. "Why am I sitting down?"

He opened up another chair and sat next to her. "Earlier when I mentioned that you had been shot, I noticed it, just for an instant, you covered it quickly, but I noticed the flinch."

"Gordon—"

"Ah-ah. I'm talking now. Just listen. I'm not a stranger to post-traumatic stress. Been there, etc. So I just want to say to you that I could see that you are dealing with something. Want to share?"

A few seconds went by before Dakota dove in. "Yeah, I'm dealing with something. I've decided not to go back to teaching, at least for next year. I mean, everyone will think it's logical with the baby and all, but it's not just the baby." Gordon didn't say anything. Just waited. "And part of me is telling me that I'm crazy. I mean, I loved my job. I was good at it. And that school, it was so perfect. It was idyllic, a throwback to the 1900s. Then the real world intervened, and—"

"Well, give it a year, then maybe you'll be ready to go back."

She shook her head. "I really don't think I will be. And yet, and yet..."

"You love teaching?"

She nodded and worked at holding back tears. "I did—do. But even before I was shot. Even before I found out about...Savvy and me...I was starting to get snappy with students. Frustrated mostly. At their incompetence and the fact that they don't care. If they don't care about their education, why should I?"

"I guess it might be too late for them. I'm not humoring you, I mean it. They don't care. But if you are serious about teaching, maybe you need to be reaching them at an earlier age? Maybe you can make a difference with younger kids. I remember my second-grade teacher. She was the one that set me on my path. Just an idea." Sensing that it was time to change the subject, he pointed with his chin toward the deck. "Looks like somebody else just arrived. I wonder who that is?"

Looking over her shoulder, Dakota gave a holler in Daniel's direction. "Honey, your dad's here." Then to Gordon, "Looks like the whole wedding party is present and accounted for."

"Okay, gang!" Jill got everybody's attention. "Time to eat."

Once again the family members were wearing Grace's T-shirts. Savannah's favorite was the "WTF Wine Time Finally" T-shirt. She had decided this was her family gathering T-shirt. Austin wore the only one he had, as did Jill: "You can't scare me. I have two daughters" and "To save some time, let's just assume I'm always right." Daniel had gone through the shirts that Dakota had taken possession of and found one he liked better that the first one. This T-shirt simply said one word: "Ba-zinga!" Dakota's bore a quote by St. Augustin:

"The world is a book, and those who do not travel read only one page." The kids wore the same ones they'd worn at Thanksgiving. Shannon's said, "Classy, Sassy & a Bit Smart Assy." And Chelsea still got a big kick out of wearing the shirt that said, "Dear Math: I am not a therapist. Solve your own problems."

Everybody dove into the food like it was going to be their last meal on this earth. The sound of cracking lobster claws and the oohhing and ahhhing after they had extracted the sweet succulent meat, dipped it in melted butter, and slipped it between their lips was all that could be heard for the first few minutes; then slowly the casual and comforting conversation of family bantering commenced.

Gordon felt a bit like a fly on the wall. He'd always been an observer of the human condition. He liked people, in theory, but from a remove. He'd always managed to keep an intellectual distance. Being immersed in this family up to his eyebrows was a completely new experience for him. The family dynamics were so amazing. The people meshed so perfectly. They even liked one another. Not every family could say that.

"So I've got the music all lined up, but as Savvy and I are walking the brat down the aisle, I can't be running the equipment." Austin was still licking his lips from the buttery lobster.

"I can do it," Shannon offered.

"Ah, no, you can't." Dakota looked her dead in the eye. "Your job as maid of honor is to walk down the aisle before me. You can't be messing with the music."

"And because I'm the flower girl, I can't either." Chelsea wasn't about to be left out.

Aunt Susi came to the rescue. "I'm sure I can figure out how to push the on and off button on a boom box."

"What's a boom box?" Shannon and Chelsea asked simultaneously.

Everybody over forty laughed.

Gordon got Austin's attention. "That was a pretty heavy=duty conversation you and Shannon were having about the Great Pacific Garbage Patch. What was that all about?"

"Sounds like you've heard about it."

"Wrote about it a year or two ago. I spent some time out there on the ocean with a marine research foundation. Do you know their drones have revealed that there is one hundred times more plastic by weight in that patch than previously measured?"

"See," Shannon jumped in, "something really needs to be done!"

"And that's what we were discussing," Austin told Gordon. "A few months ago, the family and I started looking into different possible ways to do some good for others or for the earth."

"Yeah," Chelsea was thinking hard, "it's called faa-land-tropy."

Once again the adults laughed. "Close enough." Austin reached out and touched Chelsea's cheek.

As the conversation circled around and diners started pushing their chairs back from the table and stretching out their legs, Chelsea slid out of her chair and climbed up onto Gordon's lap. Twisting about, she pressed her little index finger into the almost imperceptible dent in his chin. Looking down into her little face so open and completely guileless, he felt this heart stutter and stumble. Never having thought about fatherhood—and knowing it wasn't going to happen for him in this lifetime—he was stunned to realize that what he suddenly felt was what a father must feel for a child: the need to care for, to protect, to love unconditionally. It was just a blessing he was sitting down because if he hadn't been, he'd have fallen to his knees. He looked over at Austin and said, "You are one lucky son of a gun, you know that?"

Austin looked from Gordon to his daughter and back to Gordon. "I do know that."

"She sure is a peach."

"Just wait until you witness one of her famous temper tantrums. She'll more likely remind you of a peach pit then. She gets all that from her mother." He tilted his head in Jill's direction.

Dakota and Savannah immediately mentally paraphrased the T-shirt Savannah was wearing. *WTF!* they thought simultaneously and looked first at each other then over to Jill, thinking that the fat was in the fire now. But to their surprise, Jill and Austin were sharing one of those smug and secret *looks* that married people share that means something only to them and to no one else. Dakota elbowed Savannah. "Look," she whispered.

"I see," Savannah whispered back.

For weeks everyone had been circling around the elephant in the room, that Dee was Savannah's daughter. By now every family member knew what was what. But no one knew just how touchy a subject it might be so evaded any direct discussion of it when both parties were present. Dakota, however, being Dakota had never been accused of just dancing around a subject. She liked to face things head-on and, as all family members were present and accounted for, she decided now was the time.

"So." She looked over at Savannah. "The last election was touch-and-go. If you have skeletons coming out of the closet…how's that going to affect the next election?"

Savannah took a deep breath while almost everyone else at the table held theirs. "Good question. What do you think?"

"I think it's going to come out. It's just a matter of when."

Austin stepped up to the plate and added his two cents worth. "In that case, the sooner it comes out the better. And"—he gestured to Savannah with his beer bottle in his hand—"it definitely needs to come from you. You've always been a straight shooter with your constituents. So you don't want to make this sound like it was a secret."

"Well, it was a secret."

"It needs to sound like it wasn't, like you were a single parent who had your family's support. Which you did, just all of us didn't know the extent of it. Be that as it may, you put the right spin on it and you'll end up the poster child for single parents everywhere. The 'See what you can achieve with a little hard work.'"

"And obviously a lot of help," Dakota added.

Gordon was in agreement with the rest of them. "You need to take the bull by the horns, Savannah, or Wendy Greene is going to get a whiff of this, and all you'll be doing is damage control at that point. If that happens, you can kiss the governorship goodbye."

"Wait? Wait? What? Wait a minute? Governorship?" Dakota was looking from Savannah to Gordon and back again.

Savannah was refilling her wineglass and realized all eyes were on her. "Yes. I'm getting ready to throw my hat in the ring."

"Well." Austin had a little frown between his eyes. "I thought you liked being part of the Washington inner circle."

"I do and I don't. It's not that I won't miss Washington, because I will. I'm just starting to feel that I can do more for Colorado by being governor than being a senator."

Austin said, "Then all the more reason to control this… revelation."

Savannah looked over at Dee. "Dee? It will be a roller-coaster ride with the press for a few weeks."

Their eyes held, and Dee nodded. "I'm equal to it. I say do it. The sooner the better."

"I have an idea about how to break it." All eyes turned to Gordon. "Picture this: Savannah being interviewed by Savannah on that morning news show."

Chuckling, Austin said, "I like the symmetry of that."

Gordon continued to paint the picture, "The interview begins with Savannah, the interviewer, touting our Savannah's work with single mothers both with Planned Parenthood and at the legal aid office and blah, blah, blah. Then it segues into our Savannah saying something like, 'They always held a place in my heart because I was one of them,' and *kaboom*, the bomb has been dropped."

Austin continued, "And a dialogue with Savannah and Savannah ensues. I really, really like it!"

"And," Dakota added, "by the time you throw your hat into the ring to run for governor, it's yesterday's news."

"And," Gordon had his eye on the future, "the governorship might just be a launching pad back to Washington in another capacity, if you get my drift." Rarely struck dumb, Savannah just looked at him. "Hey, I'd vote for you."

"So would I," Dee added.

*　　*　　*　　*　　*

As the evening wore on, the kids talked Austin into building a fire in the pit so they could roast marshmallows. When the embers were perfect, Dee, Daniel, Daniel's dad, Austin, and Jill all joined the girls, and the roasting commenced. Dee glanced back to the table on the deck where Savannah and Gordon sat closely next to each other deep in conversation. "I've never seen her so happy."

They all glanced over, then Daniel looked at Austin and said, "And I've never been so happy as to see your glare directed toward someone else for a change. You really are a scary guy, you know that?"

"I wasn't glaring."

"Yes, you were," Jill had to agree with Daniel. "I just fear for any boy who sets his sights on one of our daughters." Looking at Dee and Daniel, she added, "We might all have to end up visiting this guy in federal prison where he will be after killing any and all of their suitors."

"Ha ha."

"Aww, he's just protective." Dee reached over and bumped her fist on Austin's knee. "I used to feel very well loved when he went all big brother on me."

"Good idea," Austin rose. "I think I'll just wander over there and go all big brother on Savvy."

"She's the big sister," Shannon told her dad.

"A sister's a sister," he told his daughter.

"Don't be a bully," Jill cautioned as he strode toward the deck.

Much later when the kids were tucked into bed and the embers in the firepit had flickered out and the stars hung low in the heavens, Austin and Savannah started arguing about politics. And everyone knew all was right with the world.

＊　　＊　　＊　　＊　　＊

Savannah awoke in the wee hours to see Gordon sitting up in bed typing on his laptop. A glance at the clock told her it was no time to even be awake, let alone writing. "What are you doing?"

"When inspiration hits, you don't let it escape."

"Oh, yeah, well." She settled back into her comfortable spot and just watched him for a moment. Then on a yawn, she asked, "What inspired you?"

"Your family." His fingers were flying over the keyboard of the laptop. "There are times when I write, it's like the ideas just whip through me."

"When I write my speeches, I feel the same thing. I enter this altered state of consciousness, and the ideas just flow."

"But tonight it's different, the same but different. I think it's your mom."

"What?"

"I mean, I'm writing this article, but it seems like I'm getting an extraordinary boost. I don't know." As before, he was speaking, but his fingers hadn't stopped working; he kept on writing.

"Well then, I can't wait to read what you've written."

"Sure," he spoke absentmindedly as his eyes were focused on the screen. "When I've finished."

Chapter 40

Daniel and his dad, wearing their rented tuxedos, stood in the garage looking at the wall over the workbench. It held the usual particle board full of holes with the hangers holding various tools. But in addition, the wall was also decorated with bumper stickers. They were amusing themselves reading them while the rest of the wedding party finished dressing.

"'Where the heck is Wall Drug?'" Daniel's dad read. But he was also asking as he didn't have a clue.

"When Dakota and I took a trip to the Dakotas the first year we were together, she took me to Wall, South Dakota. The drugstore there is pretty famous. A real fun place. So that's where they got that bumper sticker."

"Here's one right up your alley." His father tapped it with a gnarled forefinger. "'The trouble with practical jokes is they very often get elected.' Will Roger."

"I like this one." Daniel pointed to one that seemed to be placed front and center. "'What can you do to promote world peace? Go home and love your family.' Mother Theresa."

"Certainly words to take to heart." His dad reached out and gripped Daniel's forearm with an affectionate squeeze.

The door leading to the entryway opened, and Savannah said, "Everything's a go here. Why don't you guys go take a position out by the archway? Preacher man is already out here holding his little book."

Daniel's gulp was almost audible, making his dad smile. "I think I'm supposed to have some words of wisdom here. I guess I can rely on Proverbs: 'He who finds a wife finds a good thing, and obtains favor from the Lord.'"

"Well, then." Daniel smiled at his dad. "Let's go out there and get me a wife."

Savannah lined up the flower girl and the maid of honor, checked to see that the groom and the best man, his dad, were in place, then nodded to her Aunt Susi.

Aunt Susi pressed the button, and the music filled the backyard. Chelsea walked down the aisle between the groupings of chairs facing the archway laced with pink tea roses. She scattered daisy petals to the old-fashioned song: *Daisy, Daisy, give me your answer do / I'm half crazy over the love for you / It won't be a stylish marriage / I can't afford a carriage / But you'll look sweet / Upon the seat / Of a bicycle built for two.*

Shannon came next looking like such a young lady that the whole family was stunned at how quickly she was growing up.

When Dakota followed her nieces down the aisle with Austin on one side and Savannah on the other, all eyes were on her. Her eyes, however, we on her husband-to-be; she saw his chin give a slight tremble as if he were on the verge of tears (of happiness, she hoped), then he got a hold of himself and firmed his jaw. When she faced him, his eyes were full of emotion, and he looked as serious as she had ever seen him. Good thing as she was taking the exchange of vows very seriously too.

*   *   *   *   *

At dark they all brought chairs out to the driveway and settled in under the blanket of stars to watch the fireworks light the sky over the football stadium. Every Fourth of July they had always had the best seats in the house. They never had to battle the crowds going in or out of the stadium; they just sat at home and enjoyed the show.

They all took turns oohing and ahhing. Cozy with her new husband, Dakota whispered, "Look over there. Your dad and Mrs.

Rutherford seem to be getting along well. I think that's the first time in nearly twenty years that I've actually seen her smile."

"Hmmm? It makes her look almost pretty."

"I wouldn't go that far." Dakota gave a quiet laugh then focused on the starbursts of light in the sky that seemed a celebration just for her wedding.

Austin leaned toward Savannah and said, "Do you smell it?"

Savannah sniffed and shook her head. "They're too far away to smell them."

"Not the fireworks, Savvy, try again."

She took a deeper breath, then her eyes flew to her brother's. "Daddy's pipe tobacco." Her whisper was full of awe. "I smell it." The wonder in her voice had her brother smiling along with her.

"They're here, Savvy, celebrating with us."

She looked back at the house behind them. "Do you think they are here all the time?"

Shaking his head, he said, "No. As much as Mom liked to travel? No, they don't hang out here. It's not like the house is haunted."

They both gave soft chuckles, keeping their conversation low so as not to disturb the gang who was still oohing and ahhing at the Fourth of July fireworks.

Savannah asked her brother, "Do you think they'd like Gordon?"

He looked over at the man in question, who cuddled a drowsy Chelsea on his lap. "They'd love him."

"But you still have your doubts?"

"I'll clean his clock if he hurts you, Savvy."

"Good to know," she said.

Epilogue

The family

By

Gordon Foxe

(& Grace Quinn)

Being an only child of professional parents who were both only children, I never had the opportunity to be immersed in an extended family unit until recently, and I have discovered for the first time after nearly five decades on this earth what it means to be part of a family. While family is still an unfamiliar territory, a place whose geography I am only just commencing to explore, I am beginning to realize that it is an arena where related people do more than just celebrate, cope, fight, love, and grow as a unit. Family is not just a word depicting a physical blood relationship with others. It is as much a mental and emotional place as well. Words like embraced, acceptance, unconditional all have greater meaning for me now. To have a core group that one can depend upon no matter what is the most comforting feeling there is.

George Santayana proclaimed that "the family is one of nature's masterpieces." And while that hasn't changed, it is true that today the traditional nature of the family, which is as much an ideological concept as it is a reality, is in a state of flux. Change is definitely in the air. Yet the family itself isn't disappearing, it is evolving, and we have to broaden our minds and accept all the variations on the theme of family. Diversity is the watchword of our era, and the complex and changing makeup of the family is one of the arenas where we see this manifesting. There are shifts in age as many people put off marriage and having children until much later than in the past. There are shifts in gender as today we see some households that have two mothers, while others have two fathers.

Different cultures have always defined the concept of family differently. At the same time, almost all of them see certain sanctioned relationships as being the core of the family; kingships, lineages, taboos, and rules are all part of the larger sociological definition of family. For example, we can look to the past and realize that families used to care for their elderly the same way they cared for their infants—perhaps that's something that needs to be readdressed? But rather than dwelling on the various changes we are witnessing in families, it is important to acknowledge that familial relationships are the glue that hold not just the family together but hold all of society together because that larger structure, society, would not exist without the family.

There is no ideal family; in fact, most of them fall far short of the ideal. Family members will fight and argue with one another. Sometimes they will even go as far as to stop speaking to each other. And at the risk of falling into generalizations here, it must be pointed out that there are so many factors in our modern world that are harmful to the family unit. For example, both parents having such busy schedules that, by the time they get home, feed the family, and get them ready for bed, there is no quality time left for the children at the end of the day; or the fact that discipline has seemed to disappear, leaving children without boundaries with far-reaching results; add to that the ubiquitous use of social media and technology that robs nutrients from the family soil when the sprinkling of the reviving water of the one-on-one time the family needs is missing. But even in the face of all the obstacles, far from disintegrating, the family unit is surviving.

In the past it was generally genetics that bound a family together. That is no longer true in a lot of cases. Writer Richard Bach said, "The bond that links your true family is not one of blood, but of respect and joy in each other's life." Bloodline isn't the only qualification to become a family member these days. In addition to adoption, that has been around since the beginning of families, we have sperm banks, in vitro fertilization, and simply people who choose to be each other's family member. "My sister from another mister" or "my brother from another mother" are phrases that are making their way into our idioms. Families share more than just resources or rooms in a house. When all is said and done, it is love that cements a family together. Beyond that, without family, there is nothing.

It all begins and ends with family.

~ Finis ~

Acknowledgments

I am so grateful to the many people who helped this story become a book. For critiquing early drafts of the novel and honestly pointing out where it could be improved: Susan Cade and Anette Rodrigues. For reading a completed draft and doing a final edit prior to publication: Kim Knapp. I am super grateful for Courtney Winder my Publication Coordinator at Page Publishing who guided me from step one to completion in helping to get *Letters from Grace* into print. And especially to my own family: my sons Matt and Anthony Audette and my husband Dave Sluka, it may sound like a cliché but it's true, you are my strength and my life; thank you with all my heart for your love, support, and encouragement in all my writing endeavors as well as all my life endeavors.

About the Author

Priscilla Audette was born and raised in California and received her bachelor's degree from UCLA in 1976 and her master's degree in English from North Dakota State University in 1990. An award-winning author, all three of Priscilla's previous novels have received accolades. *Seismic Influences* won first place in the LuckyCinda Book Contest in 2013. *Court Appointed* was a Beverly Hills Book Award winner in 2016. And *Lost*, released in 2018, was a finalist in the 2018 International Book Awards—Inspirational Category. Priscilla has also been recognized by the Austin Film Festival and the Eugene O'Neill Theater Center for her scripts and stage plays. A gypsy at heart, Priscilla has lived in California, Minnesota, North Dakota, Wyoming, and Maine, where she currently makes her home.

CPSIA information can be obtained
at www.ICGtesting.com
Printed in the USA
BVHW081205030820
585345BV00002B/7